KILL THE
BUTLER!

KILL THE BUTLER!

Michael Kenyon

St. Martin's Press
New York

1279 8045

(B)

Library of Congress Cataloging-in-Publication Data

Kenyon, Michael.
    Kill the butler / Michael Kenyon.
        p.   cm.
    "A Thomas Dunne book."
    ISBN 0-312-08833-7
    I. Title.
    PR6061.E675K54   1993
    823'.914—dc20   92-42572
                                                                    CIP

First published in Great Britain by Macmillan London Limited.

10 9 8 7 6 5 4 3 2

For Victoria

KILL THE BUTLER!

One

'The route to go is surveillance inside the house, undercover, like, say, an English butler. In fact, an English butler is how I see it.'

Having struck a match, the American stopped talking while he applied the flame to his meerschaum. He inhaled, angled his head upward, and blew out smoke.

'If he weighs in at two hundred pounds, that too would be good. He may need to know how to defend himself. Perhaps someone springs to mind.'

This was a question, and the American paused for an answer. He weighed well over two hundred pounds himself and stood six feet six in his polished wingtips, though at this gathering such bulk was not exceptional. Stabbed through tiny hemmed holes in his shirt collar was a gold pin which clamped the knot of his tie so tightly that if a hurricane were to carry him off, or a bomb separate him, swirling his heavy limbs into the air like paper, floating his shredded clothes item by item over the horizon, the knot of his tie and its pin would remain steadfastly in place. According to the card on his lapel he was Gene Rosko, Chief of Police, Dunehampton, New York, USA.

The policeman with the handlebar moustache said, 'You must have coppers in Dunehampton who can play an English butler. All they do is come through the door looking lofty and say, "Madam rang?" and "Dinner is served".'

The physique of the moustached policeman was unremarkable. The card on the lapel of his quiet suit read, Frank Veal, Chief Superintendent, CID, New Scotland Yard, London, UK.

Veal leaned sideways, peering across the crowded hall for the stranger with the urchin haircut who had looked to be unattached, and had stirred his loins mightily, or might do if he could escape

Chief Rosko, get to know her a little, stun her with the Veal charm.

Dammit, he had lost her.

Losing someone here was not hard. Three hundred spruced-up police swarmed at the reception in a shag-carpeted banqueting hall at das Hotel Frankfurt Intercontinental. The noise-level was high and the smoke from those who had not given up hung in shifting swathes of grey and blue. Veal took a swallow of his Mosel, or Riesling, white anyway, though not a Trockenbeerenauslese, which was one of six German words he knew, the others being *Fraülein, Ich liebe dich,* and *Schlafzimmer.* In fact you didn't need to know German to know German, you only needed English. This place was *modern und funktional im Design,* according to the brochure in his room.

The International Police Federation's annual convention was a rare perk. Days off at a fancy foreign hotel, flying the flag for the Yard. Veal had been disappointed that the venue this year, the first year his turn had come round, was Frankfurt, not somewhere steamy and forbidden like Bangkok or Marrakesh, but the hotel was de luxe and ladies were ladies wherever you loved them. The urchin lady, if ever he spotted her again, if Chief Rosko would only keel over in a faint so he could sneak off and hunt her down, didn't necessarily have to be a high-risk proposition, such as the IPF president's wife. If she were German she probably spoke English, which was what mattered. Everyone spoke English except the French.

' "Dinner is served," huh?' The American made it sound like a warning. Anyone hearing dinner announced as Chief Rosko announced it would have chosen not to eat.

Veal looked but failed to spy the urchin lady. All had been going swimmingly until this bloke in his yachtsman's blazer and gold pin had bearded him. He was not going to be easily shaken off. He was serious, almost as if he had flown three thousand miles expressly to chat up a senior Yard officer over the hock and pumpernickel and secure from him the loan of a copper who could double as Jeeves.

'All any of my men would have to say is "Dinner is served" and they'd be blown,' the American was saying. 'Goodbye, butler. This house I'm talking about, this family, they're not stupid. If a phoney butler opens his mouth, they'll know. They'll have the gardener or someone throw him out the door and into the ocean.'

Veal said, 'Any of our lot undercover as a butler might get the accent right but they'd still be a flatfoot phoney and out the door.' Into the ocean? The fellow was talking about the seaside? 'We do undercover builders, decorators, insurance salesmen, pushers and dealers. We could probably do you a shepherd. We don't do royalty or butlers, or we haven't yet.'

'Now's your chance, Frank.'

Frank? Cheeky bugger. There she was, shimmering, shorn – a pageboy coif, the gamine look – glass in hand and bored putrid, Veal was positive of it, by a suave, leering thug from some Latin dictatorship where the technique for coaxing a woman into bed would be to slap her a few times.

Veal said, 'No harm your going through the usual channels. Commander Astle would be the man to get in touch with. I have to tell you, I wouldn't be too optimistic. Would you excuse me?'

'How's Bob?'

'Bob who?'

'Bob Crawford. Your Assistant Commissioner.'

Ah, that Bob. Veal had never heard him called Bob. Sir Robert Crawford ran the CID. Veal winced at his own innocence. Here and now, glugging wine at the convention of coppers, this was the usual channel.

The American said, 'Bob seems to think the Yard might come up with a butler.'

'When was this?'

'Yesterday. Your name was mentioned.'

'As a butler?' Veal's wine, on its way to his mouth, came close to slopping.

'As the one who could pick one. Twenty-seven thousand cops in London, three and a half thousand detectives, right? One of them has to be a butler.'

'If that's what the AC says.'

'Can we find somewhere quieter?'

'Let me get a refill.'

Veal refilled and picked up some pickled herring. In the crush to the left of the bar he saw the urchin lady being pawed, figuratively, so far, by the secret police torturer whose rank would be major or

9

commandant. What was astonishing was she didn't seem to mind. She was smiling at the torturer and picking a hair or something off his sleeve. Probably the fingernail of one of his victims.

A lucky escape. Veal couldn't see what he had seen in her.

The house was Ahoy, an oceanfront summer property with summer staff at Dunehampton on the eastern end of Long Island. The family was Langley. Louis Langley, its patriarch, had died of unnatural causes at three fifteen p.m. on the last Friday of May, three months ago. He had been eighty years old and had come to grief while mowing Ahoy's three acres of grass.

'Death by lawnmower,' Veal said. 'Those big tractor mowers are killers. You've only to go too fast up a bank, or down it, and the brute's over and on top of you.'

'Lou Langley was hit by a truck.'

Make up your mind, thought Veal. He reached for his glass.

They had found a sofa and a coffee table in a lounge area near a wide stairway. Beyond one end of the sofa a spiky potted palm shuddered in the breeze from an air-conditioner. Occasionally a guest appeared on the stairs, and beardless bellboys in uniform who looked as if they should have been in school, but who strode importantly and gave imitations of busyness in the service of the hotel. Veal believed that what they were doing was placing bets for the hall porter and snorting crack in the staff *Herren*. *Herren* was another German word he knew, not that you needed to. All you needed was to be able to tell silhouetted trousers from skirts on the plaques at the ends of corridors.

Out of sight, the police convention throbbed like a faulty refrigerator.

'Lou had six lawnmowers,' Chief Rosko said. 'All sorts, old and new, and two you sit on, but he never used those because they're useless for edges and negotiating round shrubs, and they leave tracks. He used a Toro single-cylinder gasoline mower you start with a string and walk along with.'

'He shouldn't have been cutting the grass at all, his age. Eighty? Couldn't he hire a gardener? What about the one who's going to throw the butler into the ocean?'

'Lou was a lawn fanatic. First sign of spring he'd be out at Ahoy, getting the grass groomed for the summer season. He wouldn't let

10

his gardeners near the lawns. He did them all himself. Mowed, raked, weeded, watered, brushed them with a twig broom, and talked to them.'

'If he was such a fanatic, what was he doing allowing a truck on them?'

'He even did the strip between his hedge and the road.' The Chief had a story to tell and intended telling it his way, each point in its season. 'He didn't have to do the strip because that's Dunehampton property, the town does it, but it borders the front of Ahoy, goes all along Tonic Lane, and he didn't want cowboys with beat-up machines chewing his bit to pieces. So he did it himself. You might say it was his undoing.'

So say it, get on with it, Veal wanted to say. He speared a herring. The American held his pipe in one hand and with the other swirled his glass without allowing the wine to slosh overboard. A deft, pointless exercise.

Rosko said, 'The hedge is fifteen feet high to keep the tourists from ogling in. Either side of the gates it reaches one hundred fifty feet to the next properties. The strip from the hedge to the road is twelve feet, about four paces, which is a lot for a strip, but that's Tonic Lane, where the people who've made it or inherited it have their palaces. The way to mow the verge is lengthwise, like the highways department does it, but Lou mowed it lengthwise one week, the next week crosswise, from hedge to road, road back to hedge, which took him ten times as long because he could only go a few steps before he had to turn and step back into the road, or into the hedge, and haul the mower round.' Chief Rosko was watching the Scotland Yard man for signs that the measurements were sinking in. He had put down his glass, placed his right ankle on his left knee, and stretched his arm along the back of the sofa, like a seducer in the front parlour. 'He had the same criss-cross technique for his lawns. East-west one week, north-south the next. He said this stimulated the cell structure of the root system and generated even growth. Maybe it does and maybe it doesn't. Maybe he got it from the *Astrologer's Lawn Care Almanac*. You don't argue with a lawn fanatic. Not when he's worth a hundred and fifty million bucks. With me so far?'

'I can see what's coming.'

'Lou didn't. We think it was a green Ford pick-up with a dog

in the back, like all trucks in Dunehampton have. No witnesses.'
The Chief retrieved his arm and tested a lump of dripping herring.
'Our reconstruction is, Lou swung the mower round and stepped
back into the road. You have to. If you don't go right back into
the road you're going to have chunks of uncut grass along the
edge. Splat and DOA.'

Splat and DOA? Laconic, the Yanks.

Veal said, 'You think a Ford pick-up with a dog – perhaps. It
didn't stop?'

'Could have been a Rolls. Plenty of those on Tonic Lane.
Except that time of year things are just getting going. Until
the summer people move in from the city at the end of May,
most of those houses are empty. All there is is someone checking
the sprinklers, and our patrol cars. We're pretty vigilant. A
complaint on Pilsudski Street, we'll get there. Anything on
Tonic Lane, we're already there before it happens. Those people
can make waves. When they call their congressman, they get
through.'

'I have the picture.'

'It was a guy from the Highways Department cutting the strip
a quarter-mile on who saw a Ford pick-up around three fifteen.
He noticed it because it was going too fast. Says he'd have been
mashed too if he hadn't been up on the verge.'

'You've questioned everyone on your patch with a Ford pick-up
and half could have been going too fast on Tonic Lane, say two
hundred of them.'

'Thirty-eight.'

'You've ruled out a random hit and run?'

'It's possible, but we have to check every angle. Inviting one
of your people wasn't my idea, it's from way up high, but I'm not
against it. I'm not having murder on my turf and I don't like loose
ends. I'll level with you, Frank. Whether we find a perpetrator
or show it has to have been an accident, either way, it'll be no
bad thing for me. One route or another, I need to satisfy the
Langleys. These rich summer folk, I want their confidence, not
their complaints.'

'If it wasn't an accident, sounds as if it might be someone who
knew the old boy's mowing technique. The family, friends, did
they mourn or did they throw a party?'

'If there was a party it was discreet. Go on, ask the next question.'

'Who stood to gain?'

'The widow, Millicent, gets the lot. On her death it goes to the two daughters, probably. There's a clause in Lou's will recommending that after twelve months the daughters get fifty million each, but it's up to Millicent. Almost like a test for good behaviour.'

'Are the daughters known for bad behaviour?'

'Not that we know of. Gloria's a painter. Romaine rides horses.'

'Married?'

'Several times. The current husbands are something else. One drinks, the other's on Wall Street, except he lost the lot in the crash, Meltdown Monday, including a bunch of money that wasn't his, and he hasn't clawed his way back. Looks like Lou didn't want them getting their fingers in the pot, or not right away.'

'Nothing for a loyal mistress of thirty years? The Langley Foundation for Advanced Lawn Mowing?' Skippit, old son, Veal advised himself. The bloke had flown the broad Atlantic to talk to him. 'Sounds routine.'

'Except there's a codicil.'

Veal swallowed the last of his wine. There'd have to be a codicil or what was the problem? Other than splat and DOA, and evidently no one brought to judgement, not even by a family who could get straight through to their congressman.

'The codicil,' said Chief Rosko, 'gives Ahoy, the house, to Timothy Thwaite, for sale or residence therein, at his choosing, for pursuance of historical researches unfettered by teaching or other requirements for the earning of his daily bread. Words to that effect.'

'Way you describe it, Ahoy should unfetter Mr Thwaite.'

'The valuation is four million.'

'Who's Thwaite and what researches?'

'The resident caretaker and pretty boring ones. The Langley family tree and Pearl Harbor. No connection, far as I know. Pearl Harbor wouldn't have to be boring except it's fifty years ago and everything about it has been researched into the ground, a million times, it's all known, I'm told, or it was known until

13

Tim Thwaite comes up with this document he finds among Lou's wartime papers. Don't ask me, I haven't seen it. No one's seen it except Lou and Tim Thwaite, and maybe Lou never saw it either. It's Roosevelt's Day of Infamy speech and whether he knew Japan was going to attack. The family tree, who cares? The family doesn't, or about Pearl Harbor, not to the point of handing over Ahoy.'

'They want the codicil torn up?'

'The widow, Millicent, she's challenging it.'

'Seventy-nine and feisty. Feisty the word?'

'Sounds good.'

'She and the two daughters and their husbands all live at Ahoy?'

'Most of the summer. The husbands make trips to the city.'

'What city?'

'New York. It's a hundred miles.'

'So any of them might have organised the pick-up to hurry along the inheritance. Thwaite too if he was going to get Ahoy. That the possibility?'

'That's the possibility.'

'One of them might have driven the truck?'

'Not Millicent. She gets chauffeured by the daughters or their husbands.'

'This Highways bloke with the mower, he get a look at the driver?'

'Maybe a baseball cap. Mainly a roar of engine and a rush of air.'

'Are the daughters and husbands short of cash?'

'They won't be once Millicent stops holding up the works and the codicil's sorted out. Like I say, Rudy was wiped out when the market crashed.'

'So you want someone in the house who's part of the furniture but can listen at keyholes.'

'Fine with us if he bugs the place from attic to cellar. If he blows it, at least it will look like we made every effort. The biggest if will be getting him taken on in the first place without preliminaries and interviews. We can fix it for Millicent to know Jarvis is available through the society grapevine.'

'Wait a minute. Jarvis?'

'The butler. Your AC, he'll fix references. Jarvis's previous position is fourteen years as butler to the late Earl of Sowerby. We've looked up *Burke* and *Debrett* and there's no Earl of Sowerby. If the Langley's phone to check, they'll have your home number. You're the new earl. You should know that.'

'Yes, I think I should.' Veal wondered if he was having difficulty with his hearing. 'Anything else I should know?'

'You'll get it all from Bob Crawford. You'll probably be back in London tomorrow morning.'

Veal, stroking his moustache, believed that. The eyes of the unsmiling Chief looked at him in amusement. Scotland Yard was discomfited and Dunehampton-by-the-Sea was finding it funny.

'Sorry,' Veal said. 'Whatever the AC thinks, you don't need us, and I might still have some say in this. Put a cook in the house. One of your own. Or don't you have a cop who can cook?'

'They've got a cook. What they don't have is a butler.'

'I don't either. Who does? Get rid of the cook, pay him off, and give them a cook. What do they want a butler for?'

'They have a large permanent staff in the city. Summers they have a live-in cook and butler to help them entertain at Ahoy. There's also the cleaning ladies who come in every day and the year-round caretaker – Tim Thwaite. They have a raft of gardeners and someone to pick bugs out of the pool and vacuum the tennis courts. The main thing is they've had two butlers in the past three months but they didn't work out.'

'Real butlers or coppers in monkey-suits?'

'Real butlers, American pattern. One was from Arizona and liked tequila. You know, the one with the worm in it? He couldn't walk straight after three in the afternoon. The other kept showing up in the women's bedrooms asking if he could serve them.'

'The daughters?'

'And the mother. Millicent is no spring chicken but he liked ladies. The daughters and their husbands are in their forties. It's in the file, don't worry about it. Worry about the vacancy for a butler. Whoever you send us, give him this, my compliments.'

Like a religious zealot on a street corner, Chief Rosko handed Veal a booklet. On the cover was a Disneyish woodland scene showing a deer, an unidentified rodent, perhaps a rat, and a creature with rings round its tail. Across the deer's antlers was

15

the title, *Lyme Disease*. Veal opened the booklet at unpleasant colour photographs of blotchy, rash-mottled limbs. On the next page were magnified pictures of the adult deer tick. He hoped they were magnified. *Untreated Lyme disease may lead to neurological and cardiac involvement*, he read.

He said, 'Sounds nasty.'

'You've heard of it?'

'Can't say I have.'

'Neither had anyone until a few years back. We've got it in Dunehampton. It's our number one summer topic.'

' "Aseptic meningitis, inflammation of the brain linings," ' Veal read aloud. ' "Bell's Palsy. Irregular heartbeats—" '

'You can stop there. I know about it. My wife has it.' He knocked ash from the meerschaum into an ashtray. 'It's changed her life. Changed everything. You haven't asked about Tim Thwaite.'

'You said there was a codicil leaving him Ahoy.'

'He's the caretaker, meaning he lives there for free in return for answering the phone extension. He keeps a few lights on in the winter when the place is empty and lets in security people when the alarm goes off because it's raining, or it isn't raining, or a crow poops on their satellite dish, or a squirrel sits on the roof. What he does for money is teach history at Dunehampton College. The name mean anything to you – Thwaite?'

Veal shook his head. Chief Rosko had eased himself back into a corner of the sofa and crossed his legs, or more precisely, settled his right ankle on his left knee. The right foot had gone berserk, jiggling as if activated by ants. The Chief was unaware.

He said, 'He's one of yours, lectured at London University, and wrote a book about someone called Chamberlain and a Jameson Raid in South Africa a hundred years ago. He came up with new evidence. Result, scholarly acclaim for the young academic. You heard of it?'

'No.'

'Second, he's a forger. The new evidence was all forgeries. Or maybe not. Or it was but Thwaite didn't know, he was duped. He swore it was authentic, still does, but there were academics who claimed it was counterfeit. They brought in handwriting experts. He resigned.'

16

'I think I do remember. He's in Dunehampton?'

'Teaching on a J-2 exchange visa, which means next year he's supposed to go back to England. He'll be your baby again, maybe someone to keep an eye on. If he discovers an original Magna Carta you'll know to suspend judgement. Or could be he's innocent as the dew' – Chief Rosko pronounced it 'doo' – 'on the rose.'

'Except now he has something new on Pearl Harbor.'

'He's a Brit, Frank, and we're inviting you over.'

Veal plucked at his moustache. That was that then. He was for rejoining the party. Laughter of assorted kinds – neighing, sonorous, metallic – punctuated the refrigerator throb. Veal identified the laughter of the witch and the torturer, no question, swapping stories about electrodes and pain thresholds. The Chief's foot juddered. Veal hoisted an arm but the child bellboy with betting slips stuffed up his tunic, and one in his hand, had turned at the head of the stairs and was striding in the direction of the thrum and laughter. The betting slip in his hand could be the AC's summons.

Veal said, 'You've met Tim Thwaite?'

'Sure.'

'What kind of a bloke?'

'He's your young prof from Central Casting. Twenty-nine, bachelor, skinny, scruffy, and white like he lives underground, comes up a couple of times a day for an apple and a few acorns. Pebble glasses. Talks fast. I don't get half of what he says but that could be because he's from Leeds. You know Leeds?'

'Sure.' I mean yes, thought Veal. 'Does he drive a Ford pick-up?'

'He rides a bicycle. Frank, if you could come up with a short list of butlers like by, say, tonight, cudgel your brains – you say that in England, cudgel your brains?'

'I don't need to cudgel. Will a detective chief inspector do you, about thirteen stone? That'll be what, hundred and eighty pounds? His accent might be a problem. We're talking about a butler?'

'Right.'

'I'm not saying he goes round saying, "Oi, 'ow's abaht a cuppa rosy me ol' china then up the apples and pears and orf wiv the rahnd the 'ouses for a spot of knees up." '

17

'Round the houses is cockney rhyming slang? Trousers?'
'I believe so.'
'Is he a sex fiend?'
'I wouldn't say that.' Veal watched the bellboy who had disappeared now approach, bearing the slip of paper. 'He's a poet, sort of.'

Sort of was unfair, Veal reflected. The verses of Our 'Enry, Bard of the Yard, had appeared in a gallimaufry of public prints, raising the blood pressure of some of the Factory's staider brass who took it as a truth universally acknowledged that poets are fairies.

Some fairy. Our 'Enry had been demoted from inspector to sergeant for breaking a suspect's arm, though this had been many years ago. Before that, in the early flower of his copperdom, his poetic genius had been the last straw leading to his demotion from sergeant to constable, not that the limericks he had chalked on lavatory walls at the Yard hadn't been widely appreciated, bringing under scrutiny as they did the parentage of a certain obnoxious CID commander. But he had climbed back up the ladder, a survivor, a cockney sparrow who had scored successes against bombers, porn merchants, born-again evangelists, coke kings, fitness freaks at a health spa, and a Scotsman who lopped off the private parts of his wife's lovers.

Veal took the slip of paper from the bellboy and opened it. He was to telephone Sir Robert Crawford at the Yard.

He saw two main questions. Could Our 'Enry survive as a butler to these Langley moneybags? And would the Langleys have the mettle to survive Our 'Enry?

TWO

'Dinnah is sarved, modom.'

Sounded all right. Decently modulated, not too much of a tremor, not so foreigners would notice. Might not have fooled Professor Higgins but it seemed to work for this lot. So it should have. He had been practising it for five days before he got here. Four anyway. Since Frank Veal had returned grumpy from his Frankfurt junket for a session with the AC, then steered his chosen recruit to the Feathers for a pint and a proposition.

Frank had made it sound like a holiday at an up-market Club Med, but that was Frank, seducer. Chance of a lifetime it would be for Our 'Enry, old sport. He'd be sitting on the beach surrounded by the oiled flesh of beauties and celebrities out from New York. He should take his autograph book. World famous, Dunehampton was. Glitter, artists, bankers, foreign potentates, only the very classiest criminals, model girls, model boys, Eurotrash, crowned heads – a gossip columnist's fantasy. Lobster, clams, striped bass. Golf and surfing. Parties. Fergie and her prince would probably drop in if they could get away from Balmoral. He must take his typewriter and rhyming dictionary. All he would have to do as a butler would be answer the door and the phone and be obsequious. Keep his eyes and ears open, of course. Find out if someone deliberately killed Lou Langley. He should read up on Dunehampton, it was in all the guide books.

'Thank you, Jarvis,' Millicent Langley said, and rose.

The rest of them, yammering, finishing their drinks, rose with her.

Seven thirty on the dot, Detective Chief Inspector Henry Peckover had opened the high doors which gave from the dining-room into the green drawing-room, stood there like a monument,

19

waiting for madam to meet his eyes, then made the announcement. Now he stood aside while she led the assembly, fairly rowdy from aperitifs, into the dining-room. Jarvis-Peckover inclined his head as she passed, as if she were a funeral, not an animated, even jaunty, silver-haired widow in a red gown and ruby necklace who had been widowed barely three months. He wondered if he should bow to the rest of them, one by one. His two days at the Reginald Butterwick Academy of Domestic Service on Kilburn High Road had told him nothing about bowing, or if they had he had missed it. Not a dicky bird in his notes.

There would be plenty, Peckover feared, he did not have in his notes. The crash course had done its best to give him the nuts and bolts, but as Mr Butterwick had pointed out, sighing, two days were hardly the same as that lifetime in service which was the prerequisite for the making of a butler, he who was irreplaceable, without whom the household would collapse, and who in any case was not made but born, inheritor and guardian of those traditions of flawless service, loyalty, discretion, and anticipation, which were the hallmarks of the world's third oldest profession, after whoring and spying. Peckover had not known that domestic service was the world's third oldest profession. Was there a committee which numbered them? He suspected Mr Butterwick of making it up. The butler, in Mr Butterwick's estimation, was the noblest of all positions in domestic service, surpassing that of cook, chauffeur, valet, footman, groom, housekeeper, and gamekeeper.

'You will simply have to muddle through, old chap,' Mr Butterwick had said. 'Or, as I understand our transatlantic cousins to say, wing it.'

Peckover stood impassively against the door jamb in white jacket, black tie, and buttercup-yellow trousers. On the tie and the jacket's breast pocket was embroidered the word Ahoy. The correct butler's uniform, bought second-hand from Moss Bros, with deep pockets in the tails of the frock coat for secreting bottles of port, was to be worn only on formal occasions. This was obligatory Ahoy summer issue and a size too small. The trousers barely reached to his ankles and the sleeves exposed hairy wrists. He supposed it might have been worse. In California he might have been expected to wear silk leotards or a sarong.

20

The parting blessing of Mr Butterwick had been spoken in a voice hoarse with emotion. 'You'll do it, Mr Partridge,' he had said, having been given to understand that this candidate for intensive training was a Mr Partridge, a cabbie weary of the traffic at Hyde Park Corner, and the mobs at Euston and Paddington with too many suitcases and children, who was about to seek a fuller life in America. 'Just always remember you are superior to them. They are Yanks. You are an Englishman.'

Peckover decided against bowing. He certainly wasn't going to bow to the house guests. They were leaving tomorrow. The problem was that after only seven hours at Ahoy he was not sure in every case who were guests and who family. Madam, fine, she had welcomed him and hoped he would be comfortable, though not a word about his duties. Presumably a professional butler, fourteen years in the service of the late Earl of Sowerby, shouldn't need telling. The bosomy redhead who had shaken his hand and said she was Gloria Benjamin was presumably Gloria Langley, and the thin one with the naked shoulders might be Romaine Pardo, her sister. That made the other two women the guests. But the men? Two were guests, two the daughters' husbands, one of them possibly a murderer.

No time to work on it now. Peckover stood behind Millicent Langley's oak throne at the head of the table. Above the table hung a chandelier, and in the table's centre stood an unlit candelabrum which blocked everyone's view of whoever sat opposite. Would he be expected to light it at some stage? Probably not now, the evening sun flooding through the windows. He hefted madam's chair back, then forward, as she lowered herself. He had no idea whether this was one of his functions but she didn't protest. The bloke in the peach-coloured tie and burgundy jacket was watching him.

Guest or family? A nobody or a killer?

They didn't say grace. Fair enough, he had not supposed they would, though one of them might be in need of grace, and a bench of lawyers. He picked up the platter of cold cuts from the sideboard. Starting with madam, he began to tour.

Serve from the left, clear from the right. That was in his notes. Unless it was the other way round.

He held the platter while they served themselves. Seemed to

21

go all right, so far. The bare-shouldered woman took one sliver of ham, hardly worth dirtying the plate for. Both the ham and the salami went reasonably well but no one chanced the slices of something vividly orange, possibly a galantine of one of those indigenous American mammals like groundhog or possum. Half the company were talking about tennis, the rest whether to chance the new James Bond film in Dunehampton. Two or three, after forking meat on to their plates, said thank you. Mr Butterwick had revealed that saying thank you was an indelible sign of middle-class gentility and supremely vulgar. True blue blood did not thank the waiter or notice him, though of course in America the highest standards would not apply.

Mr Butterwick also had warned that never mind he was being hired as a butler, he might be expected to wait at table, clear it, and stack the dishwasher. He might be asked to polish the cars, fell trees, and babysit. There had been such cases. It depended on the family. The master sometimes required the butler to accompany him on thirty-mile bicycle rides. Former pupils had written to him with tragic tales. His advice was to go along with it as far as humanly possible – he who pays the piper calls the tune, and top English butlers in the USA took back to their pantry a hundred thousand dollars a year – but to try little by little to educate them.

'Rudy Pardo,' said the tubby man in the peach tie, forking awkwardly with his left hand and hoisting his right for shaking. The fellow had a bald spot. 'Good to have you aboard, Jarvis.'

'Most 'appy – happy – to be aboard, sir.'

The platter was half a ton of bone china which, if he were to have a free hand for shaking, he would either have to put on the carpet or pass to the next customer to hold. He turned sideways, lifted a knee, balanced the platter one-handed on the knee, and grabbed Mr Pardo's chubby hand. The galantine slices started to slide.

Peckover retrieved his hand, tilted the platter two-handedly, and carrying it low down and out of sight to the next customer, pushed the slices back from the platter's edge with his thumb, then more or less centred them with a finger. For all he knew the hand he had shaken was the hand of a murderer.

Anyone else wanted to shake his hand, they'd be getting a smear of galantine of chipmunk as a bonus.

He circled with wine. Some would have red, some white, the cook had told him. Mrs Pardo usually had Seltzer, and Mr Benjamin would carry on with martini, but he would go off and get it himself, and might not be seen again. Peckover poured red with his right hand, white with his left, and with concentration, because the left hand lacked the motor control of the right, though the white would become easier as the bottle became lighter, or it would if they drank enough of it. If they drank too much and finished it he would have to fetch a fresh bottle and he'd be back where he started. How he ought to be pouring it, he supposed, was one bottle at a time, red first – 'Hands up the red' – then white, or vice-versa, didn't matter, but all of it right-handed, or red-handed, you might say, if he was pouring red.

Our 'Enry, Bard of the Yard, sommelier pretty damn *manqué* to the nabobs of Dunehampton.

'What is it?' asked a concerned customer, swivelling to stare up at the sommelier.

The sommelier stared back. What was what? Did he look ill? About to swoon? The left hand with the white did not inspire confidence but it hadn't slopped, it wasn't visibly shaking.

'Sir?'

'The red. What is it?'

Peckover looked at the label. A mistake. A sommelier should know what he was pouring. Seven hours at Ahoy and he had blown his cover.

'The Château Cantenac Brown, sir.'

'Brown?'

'The red.'

'I can see it's red. You said brown.'

'A claret, sir. Margaux, *troisième grand cru classé*.' The sommelier appraised the label, holding the bottle a little away from him, lifting his eyebrows. He believed this bugger with the questions was a guest and would be gone tomorrow. Himself, he was a draught bitter man, but he had done the Bordeaux vineyards with Miriam, who knew about the grape, and some of it had stuck. 'We do so concur, sir, a Château Brown does sound improbably French. Yet you will recall that many Bordeaux growths, due to our Anglo-Angevin links dating from the fourteenth century' – Thirteenth? Third? – 'have curiously English

23

names, such as Talbot.' Talbot, yes, but what else? 'Fotheringay. Ribblesdale-Smythe.' Silence had fallen. All eyes were on him. 'Eighty-four, an unfussy vintage, but with a nose, and legs.'
'Huh?'
'Toes?' someone said.
Somebody else said, 'Athlete's foot?' Another voice sniggered. Someone hissed, 'Sssh!'
The sommelier permitted himself the merest quiver of an eyebrow. He said, 'We believe you will find it not unpalatable, sir.'
'You recommend it?'
Bloody 'ell, get on with it. You've no bleedin' choice, chum. That is, if you want the red. No choice with the white either, come to that.
'Without hesitation, sir.'
The cadaverous one in the tartan trousers who refused wine and left the dining-room with his martini glass was presumably Benny Benjamin, husband of Gloria, the redhead. He had his own money, according to the file. He described himself as an art consultant but had managed matters so that no one ever consulted him.
Peckover returned the wine to the sideboard. They had forgotten him, and abandoned Bond for bonds. Not bondage bonds, though he wouldn't have put that past one or two of them, but money bonds. 'This thirty-year issue isn't going to be liquidated until we get our act together in the Middle East,' one of them said.
He gathered up the platter with its untouched chipmunk. The door into the kitchen was narrow and hinged to swing either way. He put a shoulder to it and went through crab-like. The door swung shut.
'You've got leftovers,' he said.
'They know nothing,' said the cook. 'They are nerds.'
In fact they're not, thought Peckover, not if nerd was the same as twirp. He was not about to argue. He hadn't time. 'Just going to check on a couple of things,' he said.
In contrast to the echoing spaces of the rest of Ahoy's interior, the kitchen was poky, little bigger than the galley of a weekend yacht dipping in and out of the coves of Cornwall. Three strides brought Peckover to the door which opened on to stairs leading

up to family floors and down to staff quarters, a laundry area, and acres of undefined space with here a table-tennis table, there a gas boiler, elsewhere storage rooms. Up or down, they were staff stairs, precipitous, with chipped paint and worn carpet.

'Back soon.'

'Very soon, man,' the cook said. 'Hors d'oeuvre is finish quick. The bottom line is, you want a snort, you hang in until the gigot. They stuff in the gigot like for half an hour.'

The cook was a Dutchman, Joop, with a ginger beard, and Peckover's guess was that this was his first job in an English-speaking country. His English was not at all bad – a sight better than the butler's Dutch – but larded with Americanisms which he did not always get quite right, not to Peckover's ear, though he would if he kept at them with the same diligence he showed for smoking French cigarettes and rubbishing his employers. He had worked in the kitchen of the *Noordam*, cruising the Caribbean out of Fort Lauderdale, but he hadn't dug the sea, the sea was for fishes, man, and Dunehampton was Pittsville-sur-Mer, but it was a stepping-stone to the Waldorf, man, and one day the Amstel, in Amsterdam, though he might get out of cooking and hit the manager.

Peckover guessed he meant hit management, as in switch to management, though you never knew, he might have an urge to hit managers. He had the air of a jailbird and brigand, but then so did some clergymen: you couldn't go by appearances. He had been cheffing at Ahoy since the start of the summer, and he'd met Lou Langley then, so he was worth cultivating for what he might know of the family. He was fair-skinned, fleshy, and bushy, in a blue-and-white-striped, grease-spattered butcher's apron. Below he had the largest, glossiest room and bathroom, probably he had taken over the previous butler's suite – the new butler had peeked – but that was okay. His advice that the butler stay put during the speedy cold-cuts course sounded reasonable.

Joop carved the leg of lamb. He positioned slices on a dish, spooned green beans with garlic around, and sprinkled parsley. Pungent tobacco smoke redolent of Paris bistros and old Jean Gabin films mingled with the aroma of roast lamb. On the window ledge above the sink lay a blue packet of Gauloises.

'Start getting with it, man,' Joop said with a Gauloise in the corner of his mouth. 'Potatoes in the oven, sauce on the stove, trays behind you.'

Peckover opened the oven and took a towel to what looked and smelled like spuds in cream and cheese. *Gratin de pommes à la dauphinoise?* Smashing. Except he had no appetite.

'You see much of that young professor, the Brit?' he asked.

'What?'

'The one in the flat over the garage. About your age. Tim Thwaite.'

'That shyster.'

Peckover stepped aside as Joop crossed the kitchen with the dish of lamb and green beans. He had never heard of a shyster professor.

He said, 'You don't dig 'im?'

'Sure, why not?'

'You rap?'

'What?'

'Chew the rap – rag.' How had he got into this? He looked for mint sauce, saw none, but no, there wouldn't be, not from a Dutchman. A little Gouda rind, perhaps. 'You go out with him at all, see a film, Europeans together?'

'When?'

'He's kind of a caretaker. Doesn't he come up here to the kitchen?'

'No way. He is too shy.'

A bell tinkled in the dining-room.

'Hit the road, man,' said Joop.

Peckover picked up an empty tray for clearing. Facing the swing door, he squared his shoulders, touched his fly, and assumed an expression, as far as he could arrange it, of mixed disdain and unctuousness. Jarvis was on his way.

The chatter level dropped as he entered. Benny Benjamin sat in his place with a decent martini. The bare-shouldered woman had eaten a sparrow's bite of her ham. Jarvis cleared from the right.

Life would have been simpler without the tray. Now he thought about it, professionals didn't clear with a tray, did they? They stacked plates on their arm, the pile mounting like a Tower of Pisa towards the chin, the hand at the end of the arm holding a plate of cutlery and scraps. He could imagine no surer road to disaster. But the tray was a desperate encumbrance.

To put a plate aboard he had to lift his knee and balance the tray on it. The tray was made of sounding brass, resonant when madam's plate touched it. Hieroglyphics decorated the rim, and a streak of what looked like congealed egg. A pasha's tray from old Byzantium, sold off to pay for dancing-girls and arrived at Ahoy by way of Sotheby's. He removed the tray with madam's plate and cutlery to the sideboard. The company might suppose this was how it was done in Britain. Madam's plate first, alone and unmolested on the tray. Matter of respect. They had fallen pretty quiet.

Trayless, the new butler developed a technique in which he held the plates left-handed and level with their rim pressed between his hip and ribcage. His right hand placed the next plate on the pile and retained the knife and fork. Come the fourth plate, his hand bulging with cutlery, the system broke down. The hand was not going to fasten on to another plate without releasing a shower of silver which might clatter harmlessly over the table, but which might strike glancing blows to the bald spot now beneath his elbow. Might not be glancing either. The bloke could be scalped. The solution was, all cutlery on to the top plate of the pile, each plate to the bottom.

Still four to go. His arm had developed muscle-wobble. Conversation had lapsed entirely. Talk, you buggers, never seen a waiter before? Cutlery crowded the top plate. A nudge, the merest tilt, the whole load could go overboard. Three to go . . . two.

He tried to avoid thinking about the clearing of the next course. This course was straightforward because such food as had been left was flat, sliced-off fat, circles of salami skin, the nude doxie's ham. Each plate squashed into the next. But what if someone were to leave a load of spuds *dauphinoise*? What, in the future, if someone left eight inches of steakbone? Half a lobster? What then, Mr Butterwick? Do we drop such leavings discreetly on the floor and kick them under the table?

Last plate. He had done it. Oops!

Steady.

Stately and perspiring, Peckover moved with the plates and their glimmering crust of cutlery through the door and into a comforting

27

swirl of lamb and Gauloise fumes. When he laid his burden down on a lemon wedge on a surface by the dishwasher, the cutlery slid, quite slowly at first, then into the air in a shimmering cascade, a sparkling cataract through the gloaming, a silvery shoal of flying fish spraying and playing in the dawn mist. Knives and forks hit the tiled floor with prolonged crashings which must have rattled the Rolexes and necklaces of the company at the table on the other side of the door, and been heard along the length of Tonic Lane and by the shark captains and drugs smugglers out to sea.

'Stay cool, man,' Joop said.

He was sitting on a bar stool reading *Elsevier*, a magazine with a girl in a fur hat on the front. Apart from dressing the salad, if there were salad, and taking a flan from the fridge, the cook appeared to have finished.

Peckover had an impression his own work had hardly begun. He scooped up cutlery from the tiles. One course down, how many to go? He was not a butler, answering the phone, decanting the sherry, intimidating the maids, he was a sodding waiter, and there were nine of them in there, all wanting their grub, apart from the naked one, and expecting it without spillage or clatter. Butling he could have got away with, he believed. This waiter lark was a different kettle. Expertise was needed. Manual dexterity. Three pairs of hands and an assistant. Couldn't be long before they would see through him, if they hadn't already.

He wiped his brow with his white sleeve, picked up a fresh stack of Spode china, and faced the swing door. Courage! Was he not Jarvis, formerly retainer to the Earl of Sowerby, Sowerby Towers, prior to his earlship expiring, or moving to Torremolinos, or whatever he did? He put his knee to the door and slow-marched into action.

No mishap dealing round the plates. Circling with the lamb and beans also went smoothly. When Rudy Pardo in his peach tie asked about the little dark spikes in the meat, he hazarded, 'Rosemary, sir.'

For remembrance. You, was it, murdered your father-in-law?

'We believe you will find it imparts a certain muscular fragility of flavour, sir.'

The spuds casserole out of the oven was on a mat, so they would not burn their delicate fingers, and they passed that themselves.

Peckover opened more wine and toured. He was forgotten again. The conversation was the Dunehampton Classic Horse Show. Evidently the naked woman, Romaine, was competing. Her horse's name was Glad Rags, and temperamental. The amount Romaine ate, he'd have been amazed if she had the strength to climb astride a rocking-horse, let alone flighty Glad Rags.

In the kitchen, Joop had not shifted from his stool. He looked up from his magazine and said, 'You got a half-hour, man. Go for it.'

'I will.' Peckover turned on the cold tap and drank a tumbler of water. Joop seemed to have it in his mind that what he was going for was either dope or grog. 'Back in twenty minutes.'

'Your room is direct underneath. Anything happens, like they want you, I stamp twice. You read me?' He unhooked a foot from a rung and stamped twice on the tiles. 'You hear that, you get the lead out.'

Peckover looked at his watch. He went through the door to the staff stairs, closed it behind him, and started up the stairs, not down. Mealtimes might be the only time the family and guests would be out of the way. He had a murder to investigate.

THREE

The servants' stairs betrayed the age of the house, no work having been done on them since Christopher Columbus, or at any rate Pocohontas.

Peckover's knowledge of American history was patchy, an exuberant panorama with gaps, his information gleaned from random biographies and Hollywood spectaculars, and peopled largely by bandits such as Billy the Kid and Al Capone, and by women he would not have cared to meet, such as Calamity Jane, Lizzie Borden, and Amelia Bloomer. Compensations for these hard cases were manifold. He adored Benjamin Franklin, Judy Garland, Bessie Smith, Muhammad Ali, and Lassie. Lassie didn't send him personally into transports but many the half-hour she had kept the children glued and silent.

The stairs creaked, sloped, and strained. They were speckled with dead bugs and cigarette-ash drippings and smelled of rot and worm. If anyone at Ahoy crashed through stairs to his death, it would be on these stairs, and he or she would be a servant. He had seen the main staircase and it was wide, indestructible mahogany, for family only, with an intricately patterned Persian carpet. On the chipped, bile-green walls of this staff stairway he watched for names, dates, and last words etched with a filed-down spoon. *Annie, beware the Cardinal. I love you. Jack. Friday AD 1674.* The stairs made a left turn and continued upwards past a door.

Further up in garrets and turrets, who knew? There would be a grandmother, mute and cobwebbed, her eye eternally to a telescope aimed at the ocean's horizon, and the chained bones of tweenies and stable lads. Even perhaps a skeleton, powdery to the touch, of a butler.

One floor at a time. Here would be where the family lived, or

30

rather slept, and kept their private skeletons under underwear in cupboards and beneath mattresses. He opened the door.

A carpeted corridor, flowery prints on the walls, and at the corridor's end a landing showing a segment of balustrade. Beyond the landing, more corridors. Rooms everywhere. He would need a week and three men to go through Ahoy.

He closed the servants' door, listened at the first door on his left, opened it, and looked into an office. Metal filing cabinets, Xerox and fax, and unidentifiable technology under dust covers. He went in and tried the filing cabinets. Locked. Not that it would take much.

Across the corridor he opened a door into what he took at first to be a smelly storeroom: crates, a colourful, spattered sink, a chair with mottled overalls dumped on it. Also a skylight, paintings stacked against the walls, and an easel supporting a blotchy canvas. Gloria's studio. Peckover eyed the paintings from a distance. Tachist expressionism? Neo-constructivist baroque? What did her husband, Benny, the drinking art consultant with no consultees, make of them?

The room opposite had twin beds, a Regency flock wallpaper of red and gold stripes, and television. Its far door was probably a bathroom. Ready for occupancy but unoccupied.

Next, another guest room, and occupied, though not at the moment. Suitcases, newspapers, a skirt over the end of the bed, a cup and saucer on the TV, zinnias in a vase. He crossed the room and opened a door. Matching baby-blue carpet, wallpaper, bath, basin, loo. A soggy blue towel on the floor. The guests were slobs.

More guests in the next room. Suitcases and flowers, much jumble, and on the table a pen and the beginning of a letter. A woman's handwriting of lacy loops, as far as it were possible to tell gender from handwriting.

Dear Barb and Emil,
    A quick 'Hi' between beach and the galleries. There's a 60s retrospective you simply have to see – it's coming to Chicago – all those psychedelic soup cans and submarines. Gloria, incidentally, is doing absolutely the most marvellous stuff, her best yet. Weather vile, you know how humid Dunehampton can be.

31

Now, Millicent is bearing up so well we all wonder if she hasn't found the fountain of youth. I mean she'll be 79 next month, the 8th, so do send her a card. (Don't remind her of her age!) Such a shame she had to be stuck with old snake-face Lou all those years!

Tighten your seat-belt! It's Romaine. One, we think she has a man! All the signs are there, and Merv heard her on the phone, only when she saw him she hung up, very flustered, and made it worse – you know Romaine – by saying it was the piano tuner. They still have the Steinway grand they say belonged to Grieg but no one plays so why do they want it tuned? Two

That was all. He would have to return when the letter had progressed a bit if he wanted to read Two. *Two, if Romaine has a man he must like them bony, shoulders like billiard balls. If she falls off Glad Rags in the gymkhana and the nag kicks her it'll cripple itself.*

He reached the landing, a term too humdrum for these furnished bays and alcoves, and tall windows looking at sky and sea. There was much wicker furniture and a grandfather clock. Against a wall stood a vast, rosy vase such as Sinbad the Sailor had hidden in. The air smelled of ozone, mildew, and roast lamb.

Hands on the balustrade, Peckover looked down into the hall, listening to voices from the dining-room and a chink of cutlery. The grandfather clock emitted a grinding sound, then began to chime a tune he could not put a name to, though it was familiar. He swayed back from the balustrade as below, gaunt in plaid pants, glass in one hand, a book in the other, Martini Man walked into the hall.

Benny Benjamin, son-in-law, treading a straight line. Not coming upstairs for a quiet read, was he? The book was a slim hardcover with a drab jacket of drizzle grey. The butler inclined forward and peered down.

Hall and stairway were empty. A door closed sighingly. Benny had gone, walking it off, or perhaps en route to an assignation with his wines and spirits merchant.

Along which passage would be Millicent's room? Peckover was impatient to start with the head of the family. He guessed her room

32

would be facing south to the sea. She presumably enjoyed the sea or she wouldn't be here. Still ten minutes before Joop might start stamping his foot, not that anyone was in the basement to hear him. Peckover aimed for the corridor to his left.

If anyone came upon him, he was routinely supervising, checking that all was satisfactory. True, waiters didn't swan about the family's sleeping quarters, but a butler might. Patrolling the Sowerby bedchambers would have been routine, surely. Putting the warming-pans in the four-posters, picking up dead grouse and bats, shooing away the dogs. The only dog at Ahoy was Prune, an elderly, coughing Dachshund who would not have made it up the stairs.

He listened at doors, opened them. Plush, anonymous bedrooms. The family were tidier than the guests, if these were family. He looked through a window at a striped awning thirty feet below and a board deck with tables and chairs. Then another drop to brambly dunes. Two or three strollers were on the beach. A man was urging a dog into the water, throwing shells for chasing after, but the dog didn't want to go.

Had Millicent slept with Lou or apart? Where did the daughters and sons-in-law locate themselves? He wished he knew what he was looking for. When you didn't know you never found it. A signed confession would be fine. *We drove the truck at Lou because we want his money now, not tomorrow. Sincerely, Benny Benjamin, Rudy Pardo.*

If Tim Thwaite had driven the truck, his confession would not be here anyway. Thwaite lived above the garage, never set foot in the house except in winter. Not a hint of Thwaite would be here.

Perhaps in the filing cabinets, if they hadn't been emptied. The police should know. Lou and Thwaite had had a scholarly relationship so something might be in the filing cabinets. Roosevelt research. The Langley family tree. For Lou, setting Mr Thwaite free to concentrate on research had been worth leaving him Ahoy.

Hastening now, rounding the Sinbad vase, Peckover entered the next passage and without listening opened the first door to his right.

This was better. People, occupancy, an air of summer permanence. He left the door open so he might hear people arrive before they saw him, he hoped. Disciplined elegance, this bedroom, was the summing-up of Peckover, interior designer. Classically co-ordinated with the restraint that bespeaks a discerning, if con-servative, taste. A creamy palette of near-whites and far-blues re-echoing the haze of twilight over Neptune's glassy wilderness.

No letters spread out for his attention. Several paperbacks, a high-heeled shoe poking out from under the bed's counterpane, a bunch of dollar bills and coins on a dressing-table, and beside the loot a fiery red apple of the sort the Queen gave to Snow White. He didn't like to open the drawers in the writing desk because it could be Queen Anne and you never knew with antiques, the handles could come off in your hand. The handles could come off your new car, come to that, but here he was snooping and he hadn't brought glue. The bathroom was bigger than the bedroom and had a gold-plated Jacuzzi and abundant marble. At the gold sinks were toothbrushes with a rubber spike on the end, and Crest, Caresse, Clinique, Brut, Bain de Soleil, and Ysatis de Givenchy.

The bedside book was *Invest and Grow: A Guide to Tax Shelters*, open at chapter seven, 'Market Boldness – Don't Just Sit There! Do It!' Who slept here? Under the pillow a filmy nightgown. Under the adjacent pillow, nothing. Not surprising; it was hot enough to sleep starkers.

He slid open one end of a fitted cupboard and viewed dresses on hangers, blouses and lingerie on shelves, and shoes below. The other end of the cupboard had shirts and men's suits, none, he was sure, with the owner's name stitched inside the neck, as might have been the case had Ahoy been a boarding school. Benjamin Minor, Waterloo House. He looked at a couple of necks, one telling him Bloomingdale's Men's Store, the other Ted Lapidus Boutique Haute Couture Paris. He dipped into pockets and came up with a torn cinema ticket. He felt under a stack of shirts. His fingers touched an unshirt-like item. Moments later he was staring at a gun.

A revolver, six chambers, two-inch stainless-steel barrel, wooden grip, weight about two pounds, might be a .38. Colt? Browning? He had never been a gun enthusiast. His Metropolitan Police pink card, licensing him to carry a gun, had expired eons ago, and he had carefully never got round to retraining. The revolver was not loaded. He put his thumb on the pimply bit on the left, the cylinder release catch, and heard again the command of Sergeant McMaster on the echoing, concrete range. 'With six rounds, load!' He felt deeper under the shirts and brought out a box of shells.

None of it amounted to anything, a gun in a beach palace in the USA. The surprise would have been if Ahoy had no guns. American citizens had the constitutional right to bear arms and shoot each other. The figure he remembered was seventy million American gun owners. Ruling out infants and presumably quite a few old ladies and eccentrics, that meant pretty well everyone. Every year, twenty thousand American citizens killed by bullets. He carefully returned gun and shells to beneath the shirts.

Downstairs they would be sopping up their gravy with bread. The room across the passage was papered not with paper but with linen painted a milky yellow like banana yoghurt. A dozen satiny cushions lay at the head of the bed, geometrically strewn. In the dormer windows were seats where you could rest, gathering your strength before collecting the cushions and putting them somewhere else so you could get into bed.

He must go, play it safe, though he had achieved not very much, and he knew what would happen. He would arrive back in the kitchen and have to dawdle for ever while Romaine continued cutting her meat in quarter-inch cubes and chewing each lump sixty-five times. He rested a knee on the window-seat and looked out.

No ocean. Lawn, flower-beds with trooping blooms, a woodsy patch away to the right, and stone the crows, what was this flying saucer on a rooftop to the left? It was a satellite dish for picking up television programmes from Sumatra, about twenty feet across and weighing in at half a ton at least, the equivalent of several sumo wrestlers. Below him were four parked cars, a fifth in the garage, and a swirl of gravelled, gunmetal-blue driveway which arrived, after a kink or two, from the main gates, out of his view, and departed through junipers and euonymus to a slip-road to the dunes. Bicycling through the gravel at one mile an hour, back bent, shoulders hunched and thrusting – left pedal down, right pedal down – came Timothy Thwaite.

Peckover would have known he was Thwaite even if his photograph had not been in the file. More pink than tanned, with spectacles, sandals with buckles, long khaki shorts, and a military-looking shirt with epaulettes, probably from an army surplus store. The bicycle was a Big Bertha of the bicycle world, built for durability. Even had it been a Tour de France racer, no yellow-jerseyed champion would have streaked through the Ahoy gravel on it. Why, wondered Peckover, didn't the daft Yorkshire tyke get off and push? The bike was dusty black with a loaded basket strapped to the sit-up-and-beg handlebar. It had reflectors and a lamp for night excursions, a bell, and a rear-view mirror which would have been an optional extra and a sensible one had it not been missing a screw. Instead of standing erect where it could be seen into, the mirror swung languorously beneath the handlebar, tapping against the professor's fingers and conceivably immobilising them if ever he needed to brake quickly, which for the present he did not. Man and machine, not braking, ground to a stop and listed. The rider stuck out a sandalled foot. All might have been well but for the two brown, bulging paper bags in the basket.

To prevent them toppling, Thwaite took a hand off the handle-bar's grip and slapped it on the more precarious of the two bags, whereupon their weight swung the basket, handlebar and wheel through a semicircle causing the other bag to fall out. The rear wheel started to skid, the descending bicycle pushed the professor sideways, its crossbar tracked down the inside of his leg from crotch to calf, and the other bag went overboard. Teach himself was now toppling, hopping on one leg while the other fluttered above the sliding rear wheel. It was him or the bike, so he let the bike drop, which did him no good. His balance was lost. He sat with a bump among spilled books and groceries.

Peckover, fascinated in the dress circle, guessed that had he been close enough he would have heard ripe Yorkshire oaths. He did not hear someone call to Thwaite either, but Thwaite did, because he turned his head, gestured and said something, then carried on retrieving sausages, and plums which had rolled quite a distance, gathering gravel. Benny Benjamin with his glass and book strolled into view round a shingled corner of Ahoy.

The two stood talking by the fallen bicycle. They knew each other. No handshakes, straight into talk. They might have been talking about the weather. Benny Benjamin offered his book to

36

Thwaite, who shook his head. Perhaps Thwaite had already read it. Benny put the book in the bag with the sausages.

Looking down, hoping the two below would not look up, Peckover was aware of a need to guard against seeing significance in every detail he came upon. An unfinished letter observing that Romaine had a man. A gun. One of the family giving a book to the caretaker. Might be Benny's vanity-press memoirs, *Aphorisms Under the Influence*, and he was seeking a scholarly opinion.

He also had to guard against being sacked on his first day for absenteeism. So he loped on big, laudably silent feet along the passage, across the landing, then rowdily, crackings and splittings underfoot, down the rotting servants' stairs to the kitchen.

The rowdiness in the dining-room was talk, punctuated now and then by a laugh, but not many of them, and not especially merry. The directors sounded to be ganging up on the chairman.

The butler, with a lightweight tray of something indestructible – he would try again with a tray, he was nothing if not game – stood on the kitchen side of the door, awaiting a lull. Joop was ladling caramel sauce over the flan.

'Mom, we're all agreed, what does it matter?' One of the daughters, had to be. 'Let him stay.'

'I have no intention of doing any such thing.' Millicent. 'We should never have allowed him across the threshold. That two-faced, scheming Brit leaves tomorrow. Really, what a ham, what a creepy— '

Bedlam, everyone talking at once.

Creepy flunkey? Snooper? Eavesdropper? Him, Henry, a ham? Unmasked so soon? The butler, ear to the door, nervously chewed his lip.

'Professor Thwaite will take his bags and bicycle' – Millicent's voice above the hubbub, quelling it somewhat – 'and leave Ahoy.'

Peckover released his lip. The bicyclist, not the butler.

'But, Mom, it's so awkward. If Tim inherits Ahoy— '

'He inherits nothing. We are challenging the codicil and we shall win. Your father was confused. And your Tim, as you insist on calling him, is a hardened criminal.'

'I don't think we can quite say that, Millie.' Rudy? One of the

37

house guests? Mind your own beeswax, house guest. 'Nothing came to court. He was never convicted of anything.'

'He is a forger and Oxford University sent him packing.'

'London University, and he resigned.'

'You are splitting hairs. I have tolerated him up to now purely because of the codicil. Can you imagine the front page of the *Post* if we ordered him out of Ahoy then he bicycled back as its owner?'

'Mom, he's not going to be its owner.'

'Correct. But Mr Tumberley stresses that the codicil needs very careful handling, and his partners agree.'

'You bet they do. They'll be handling it very carefully for the next ten years at three hundred bucks an hour.'

'A possibility we might consider is relocating Mr Thwaite. We might offer him limited access to Lou's papers. To keep the media at bay this might require some small expense on our part— '

'You mean we pay his rent?'

Pandemonium. The butler, ear to the door, beat the tray against his leg and danced a feathery soft-shoe. Here was democracy at work. A Dutch curse sounded behind him, loud and unclear. Joop's Gauloise had dripped a grey worm of ash upon the flan.

Mouthing further Netherlands oaths, Joop licked a finger and drew it along the surface of the flan. From the other side of the door sounded angry argument. 'Rotterdam!' or some such blasphemy, cursed Joop. He took a fistful of confectioner's sugar and sifted it over the smudged ash-track. A bell tinkled in the dining-room.

Jarvis, Peckover told himself, and he tucked in his chin like a Grenadier Guardsman at the Trooping the Colour.

The arguing abated as he entered. Millicent Langley smiled at him and put down the crystal bell. She is a tough and classy lady, judged Peckover, and with this lot she needs to be. But he didn't smile back. Mr Butterwick's golden rule was impassivity at all times. You did not register, share, or notice the moods, sulks and smiles of the master and mistress. He placed madam's plate on the tray.

Immediately he foresaw disaster. He would get nowhere with this tray. Light it was, and of a cheerful floral design in imperishable, non-biodegradable polyurethane, but it was also flexible.

Given more than a couple of plates it was going to bend diagonally, perhaps fold in two. Who dared manufacture such stuff? Unless the load went dead centre, and you kept your arm under the tray, the thing would undulate and its contents slide. He picked up a second plate, put it beside the first, transferred cutlery, and stood without expression, holding the tray steady, waiting for the plates to move.

Everyone else was waiting and watching. A hush had returned.

Millicent Langley said, 'Our trays are a menace, Jarvis. I do apologise. Why don't you forget the tray and do just two plates at a time.'

He did so, silently adoring her.

Dessert was easy because madam served it from her throne. He perambulated with wine, and the conversation flowed again, some of the company thrashing around for an answer to the poser, to see or not to see the Bond film. Romaine intended giving Glad Rags a canter. Benny Benjamin returned with a spirited measure of martini.

In the kitchen Joop said, 'The decaff is finish, man. They want decaff, tell them sure thing. They think the regular is decaff they are hunky-dory, sleep fit to be hog-tied.'

He chuckled. The bell tinkled.

Millicent Langley told the butler, 'We'll take coffee on the veranda. Three decaffeinated.'

'Very good, modom.'

They filed from the dining-room, leaving behind crumpled linen napkins, dirty plates, and disorder. Peckover cleared and decrumbed the table, straightened the thrones, and turned out the lights. Was he expected to do all this? He was sure Joop didn't do it. Someone else, he assumed, came in and vacuumed.

Though not hungry, he realised he had not eaten since the flight over. A day ago? While Joop organised coffee and mints on a silver tray, he found a vegetable knife and ate, standing up, a pound of American gigot, the most succulent to have come his way ever. He included a mouthful of whole garlic cloves for his health's sake and washed it down with Château Cantenac Brown. He rinsed his mouth and fingers and headed with the tray for the veranda, which he found after two wrong turnings.

39

The veranda was a half-mile of white wicker, cushions, and hanging bunches of blue cretonne. Round a television lolled guests, Gloria, and Millicent, who sat fairly regally upright. They were watching a tennis replay, or with their satellite dish it might have been live from Brisbane. Madam declined coffee.

'His late lordship, the Earl Sowerby, was in the habit of partaking of a warming beverage upon retiring,' Jarvis ventured to inform her. 'Should modom enjoy similar, perhaps a Bovril or Ovaltine – we have not yet explored your beverages cupboard – we would be pleased to bring it to your quarters at, say, eleven?'

She wouldn't, but nothing to be lost by asking. Any excuse to rattle around the family area.

She said, 'Jarvis, how thoughtful. I'm sure we must have cocoa. Shall we say eleven thirty? Mr McEnroe is next and I so enjoy seeing him gesture.'

Fine. That gave him a good hour to chat with Timothy Thwaite.

FOUR

To an accompaniment of Stravinsky's Pastorale turned up to unpastoral tumultuousness, Thwaite flexed his finger in the metal ring and pulled with palpitating care so as not to slice in two the fingers of his other hand. Off peeled the lid of the tin of Maine sardines.

One of the happiest breakthroughs in modern technology, in his opinion, was the keyless sardine tin. There had been a time, if you didn't have the slotted key, and often as not it was missing, you didn't open the tin, not without a hammer and chisel, and fish oil squirting over you. He forked sardines into a saucer. Life, after a hiccup·or two, promised well again. He was on course. Like the Japanese pilots that Pearl Harbor morning. *Tora, Tora, Tora!*

'Puddy, Puddy, Puddy,' he called.

He brushed particles of driveway from the carton of orange juice, pushed up its wings, inserted a fingernail between its sealed, plasticised outside and the inner foil, and after much digging drew forth the spout. Usually this worked but not always. Sometimes the spout would not draw forth, even with a knife, so you were reduced to tearing and scissors with the result that the contents poured crookedly and in unexpected directions, including, some of it, if you were lucky, into the glass.

He'd show them, all those rancid academics in their groves of academe where the malice was so bitter because the stakes were so small. Twenty years from now he should have the Chair of Modern History at Oxford. Yale. Dodge Professor at Princeton. Should have but wouldn't. Long memories, academics. Academe would never forget *The Jameson Raid: A Reappraisal* by Timothy Thwaite.

'Puddy Tat,' he called, and poured himself an orange juice.

41

The doorbell rang.

The sole door into the apartment – up the stairs from the garage and along the landing – led directly into the kitchen. He had heard no one and the door had no spyhole. With only a passing qualm about muggings he opened the door.

His visitor was a large man with a genial smile, yellow trousers, a white shirt open at the neck, and something odd about him, but what? No suntan, that was what.

'Evening,' said the visitor. 'I saw the light on. Jarvis, Sydney Jarvis, butler to the Langleys. Started today. Nice music. Got yourself a healthy dollop of volume there.'

The voice was breezily London and already tiresome, threatening non-stop chatter.

'Mr Thwaite, is it? Tim Thwaite? The chef, Joop, he mentioned another Brit being 'ere, kind of a winter caretaker. Thought I'd say 'ello. Bedlam over there, all the dinner stuff, scurry and flurry. Sorry if it's late. Five minutes? Bring you up to date on Merrie Olde.'

Thwaite grudgingly stepped back. Diabolical. It was quarter past ten.

He said, 'Sure, c'mon in.'

They blinked at each other on the threshold, mutually aware that whatever else a Yorkshireman might say, it would not be, 'Sure, c'mon in.'

The kitchen was a kitchen-dining-room which smelled of cat. Peckover looked about him with the impressed air of one about to offer to buy it.

'Been 'ere long?'

'A year.'

'Nice, very nice.' The butler strolled, peered into a corridor, and through a door off the kitchen into a sitting-room with deep sofas, a blood-red rug, outsize TV, books, and one wall which was entirely a mirror. 'Very tasteful. Make a marvellous brothel. Great music. All yours, is it?'

'Yes.'

'Born lucky, you were, Tim. Don't mind if I call you Tim? Put this lot in Knightsbridge, it'd fetch two million quid.'

'It'll fetch that here.'

'Including the house, though.'

42

'No. I don't know. I'm not a realtor.'

'But you've adapted. Realtor, that's an estate agent, right? My goodness, he's a beauty. Come with the flat, did 'e?'

Hunched and munching over the sardines was Puddy Tat, voluminous and tangerine.

'She's a she.'

'Six months quarantine for 'er if you take 'er back home. When d'you go back?'

'Sometime. There's orange juice or a tea-bag. There might be some wine.'

'Wine sounds good.'

The butler sauntered to a ceiling-high refrigerator. Fridges didn't have to have dope stuffed in the grated parmesan to be revealing. He allowed Thwaite time to step in front and open the fridge door.

A bachelor fridge. Eggs, butter, half a tomato, new sausages, a jar of Branston pickle which looked ready for junking, its inside scraped to alternating striations of Vandyke brown and foggy glass. Something he would sooner not know about was twisted up in clingfilm. Why were leftovers in other people's fridges so repellent? Thwaite brought from the back of the fridge a bottle, and said, 'We could finish this.'

Château Blanc Ordinaire. An inch of frigid dregs sloshed in the bottom of the bottle.

'Fantastic!' Peckover said. 'Mind if I 'ave a squint around? Gor, what a pad!'

He headed along the corridor, opening doors. Bathroom. Small bedroom. Big bedroom. A study with more books and a word processor.

'In here,' called Thwaite from the sitting-room.

They sat on opposing sofas, Peckover with his back to the mirrored wall. On the wall above the prof's head was a poster of seated, smiling Josephine Baker, bare-breasted and pearly-toothed. *La Revue des Folies Bergère, 1926–1927.* She wore feathers, mainly behind her, and it was hard to see how they were attached. The record player had fallen silent.

' 'Ow did you find it?'

'Find what?'

'This.'

43

'Advertised.'

'Smashing.' Peckover nodded, soliciting more. Nothing more was forthcoming. 'Joop said you were a teacher.'

'Right.'

'Schoolmaster?'

'There's a college. Good health.'

Thwaite lifted his glass. This Peckover interpreted as: sooner we get it down, sooner this insolent intruder will leave.

' 'Ere's to us expats.' Off-duty Jarvis swirled his tumbler, which did not look very clean, and swallowed with gasping relish a mouthful of the icy, tasteless lees. 'Great to meet a fellow-countryman.' I might be going to put you behind bars, he reflected. 'What d'you teach?'

'History. Politics. Freshman English.'

'Mrs Langley – Millicent is it? – she seems a character. Course, I 'aven't seen much of 'er yet.'

Thwaite watched the cat prowl in through the door.

'Or the rest of the family,' said the butler. 'Gloria's the redhead, is she?'

'I suppose, yes, reddish.'

'Romaine's going in for some 'orse show. See, that's the sort of tidbit you pick up in my profession. Not deep, private stuff, not usually. What about their 'usbands? You get on all right with them?'

'I never see them.'

Short memory, mate. You were talking with one of them an hour ago.

'Too bad about the old boy – Lou. Hit and run, right?'

'So I'm told.'

'You were 'ere?'

'Where?'

Don't push, Peckover warned himself, because if chat becomes interrogation there'll likely be not another peep out of him.

He said, ' 'Ere when it happened.'

'I was at school. My word, hard to believe but term starts soon.' He looked at his watch. 'I've masses of preparing to do.'

'No peace for the weary.' Preparing, this time of night? All right, there were night owls. 'Funny, could have sworn I saw you. I was bringing madam 'er newspaper, and looking out of the window, and you had your bike, nattering away with Mr Benjamin. He gave you a book.'

'What?'

'He gave you a book.'

'Mine.'

'Sorry?'

'A book I've written. He wanted it autographed.'

'What book's that?'

'An early work.' Thwaite loped across the bordello-red carpet and plucked from the bookcase a grey book flanked by identical grey books. He allowed the butler to hold it. *The Jameson Raid: A Reappraisal* by T. Thwaite. He retrieved the tome and replaced it among its brothers. 'You know readers, they like an inscription.' He sat down. 'The personal touch. Though there are cases, of course, where a signature adds to a book's value.'

Tim, you're explaining too much, Peckover thought. Are you going to explain why you're given a book for autographing then you stick it back with the rest of the complimentaries? Why not autograph it and put it on the table ready for handing back?

No, the prof was not going to explain.

Peckover said, 'Lou was quite the historian himself, I gather. You making decent progress with his Pearl 'Arbor stuff?'

Thwaite's head jerked forward. 'Where did you hear that?' He put down his glass, lurched to his feet, and came at Peckover in a crouching run, shouting, 'No!'

Peckover swung himself sideways on the sofa. He could not imagine coming off worst in a scrap but if the bloke were desperate he shouldn't be underestimated. He might have taken karate lessons. Thwaite dived for his feet. Peckover kicked but failed to make contact.

'Don't!' snapped Thwaite from the floor. He surfaced holding the tangerine cat.

'Sorry,' Peckover said.

'Sorry,' said Thwaite, and returned pink and breathing hard to the sofa where he sat with the cat on his lap. 'She likes to bite people's ankles. Just a nip, she's not vicious, but it comes as a surprise. Doesn't it, Puddy Tat?' He nuzzled the beast's head. 'It's her way of saying hello.'

Peckover said, 'I see.'

Cats like that should be permanently sedated. The second and final swallow in the tumbler was now on his trousers, second best place for it to be after the sink.

'What did you say about Pearl Harbor?' Thwaite said.

'December 7th, 1941. I 'eard Mrs Langley saying Lou had papers which showed Roosevelt allowed the Japanese attack. Someone named Thwaite was working on them but I didn't know' – lies, all lies – 'he was you, not till Joop mentioned you. She didn't sound ecstatic about Roosevelt.'

'She's a Republican.' Thwaite studied the butler from behind pebble lenses. 'You're interested in history?'

'Just the two world wars, military strategy, that sort of thing. Pearl 'Arbor was a right disaster, eh?'

'Depends.' Thwaite pushed the cat off his lap, took a tissue from his khaki shorts, and mopped rising damp from his brow. 'Roosevelt knew he was going to have to fight Hitler but America was ninety per cent isolationist, it wouldn't have allowed it. Pearl Harbor solved his problem. All it took. One Sunday morning of bombs from out of the Rising Sun. *Tora, Tora, Tora!* The German ultimatum followed and America was at war.'

The cat jumped back on Thwaite's lap. He tossed it to the floor, stood up, and set off across the rug, a resolute hiker with bristly legs.

'If the end justifies the means, Roosevelt was justified.' He paced. 'War against the Nazis was the end. The means and the sacrifice were the Pacific fleet.' He sidetracked to a window where he vigorously unfolded and closed shutters. 'Nineteen ships wiped out, a hundred and thirty aircraft, two thousand soldiers and sailors dead, twelve hundred civilians.' Striding, stumbling over the cat, he threw his visitor a combative look as if to say, I've done my homework. 'Roosevelt and his inner circle knew Japan was going to attack. They could have stopped them, they only had to make it public. If Tojo and Hirohito and the top brass had known America knew that *Kido Butai* was on its way – that was the carrier force – they'd have recalled it, no question. But Roosevelt kept quiet. He chose to let it happen. It may have been for the best, that's not the issue. It is an issue but a different one. What we're talking about is deception, a fraud on the people, which wouldn't matter in most countries; fraud and deception are the daily fare, they're how things get done, but when you get a nation born as – dedicated to – as' – he came to an emergency stop, brow furrowed – 'to an *idea*, to majority rule of, by, and for the people, then you can't deceive, not on the scale of Pearl Harbor, because it just doesn't work, not in the long run. In this case it's been half a century.'

'Is it a question— '

'There's nothing new about the question. The question is, did Roosevelt deliberately allow Japan to attack Pearl Harbor? What's new is that now we know.'

'We do?'

'I do.'

'You?' The butler, rapt, let his mouth hang open in admiration. 'Sounds like your reputation's made. Thing is, if there's to be money in it, would your average book club middlebrow like me understand what you're on about?'

'Would you understand if I said that Roosevelt wrote his Day of Infamy speech *before* the Japanese attack?'

'Blimey,' breathed Peckover, not understanding.

'Exactly! Roosevelt gave not a hint of the attack to the top military in Pearl Harbor – Kimmel, Short, those people. They were made scapegoats.' Thwaite was on the march again, back and forth in sandalled feet across the rug, head lunging like a hen's, stooped from the waist as if battling a gale in the Yorkshire Dales. 'After the attack, the cover-up. Investigations, hearings, trial by newspaper, trial by politicians, on and on through the war and after, and succeeding. Why? Because the evidence for Roosevelt knowing of the attack in advance wasn't there, it was all destroyed. The log of the Royal Netherlands Navy ship. All the "winds" execute messages, the intercepted despatches, the records tracking *Kido Butai* – aagh!'

He had trodden on the cat, which squawked, then lay in the blood-red carpet's dead centre, but Thwaite wasn't to be interrupted in mid-flow. 'I'm not saying there's still a cover-up. There isn't. All the Pearl Harbor records – army, navy, FBI – they've been available for thirty years. Can you imagine that happening in Britain? *Brrph!*' He emitted a wet, rubbery raspberry, or as Peckover believed it was called here, a Bronx cheer. 'We're an elected dictatorship, a totalitarian bureaucracy. If Pearl Harbor

47

had been our problem we'd have had D-notices slapped on every scrap of paper from top secret to Mars Bar wrappings.' He had arrived at more shutters and was having difficulty closing them, swollen as they were with humidity. He dealt hearty, futile thumps, abandoned them, and resumed pacing. 'So if new evidence were going to turn up it would be by luck, accident. Like transcripts of phone calls between FDR and Harry Hopkins which escaped filing or burning because they got put in the wrong box with the grocery receipts, or a memo from Marshall that the President marked his place in his stamp collection with. But there's been nothing. Not until Lou.'

'The Day of Infamy speech,' whispered alert Peckover.

The bloke didn't need interrogating or even prompting. He was a non-stop lecturer.

'Not the final draft to Congress, naturally. The speechwriters had to have their say. Roosevelt had more speechwriters than any President until Nixon, but he wrote most of this one himself, he was making changes up to the last minute, twelve thirty the next day, Monday, in the House of Representatives.' The prof paced and his lecture accelerated. 'But the first version, the bones of it – no mention of "infamy", not yet – Roosevelt wrote that on Sunday morning, Day of Infamy day, probably before breakfast, before he got involved with Hopkins and Hull and Marshall and Stimson and Knox, not that they probably weren't in on it, Hopkins anyway. They'd all spent most of the night at the White House. He had breakfast on a tray in his study.' Thwaite halted in front of Peckover and blinked and breathed at him. 'That first draft starts, "Yesterday, December 7th, 1941, a date which will live in world history, the fleet of the United States of America was simultaneously and without warning"' – Thwaite knew it by heart – '"attacked at Pearl Harbor by" et cetera. See, an attack was expected but not at Pearl Harbor. Nobody guessed Pearl Harbor. But Roosevelt knew. He wrote that hours before the first bombs fell.'

'Stone the crows!'

Thwaite blinked and beamed. 'Still,' he said, and looked at his watch. 'Really must do some preparing, if you don't mind, Mr – um – Mr – '

'Reg Jarvis.'

48

Bugger. Was he Reg or Syd? Didn't matter, this prof wouldn't remember.

'Fantastic,' Peckover said. 'This is the making of you, Tim, I can see it.'

He led the way into the kitchen and put his glass in the sink. Now, on your way out, was when you might get a nugget, if you played your exit with proper casualness. The customer was so happy to see the back of you that his guard was down. Put a question when you were halfway out of the door, he might drop something he'd never have said when you had your notebook and tape recorder at the ready. Newspaper reporters knew that.

Not that Thwaite was about to reveal how he had beguiled Lou into leaving him Ahoy then killed him with a Ford truck, because perhaps he hadn't.

'Can't wait to read the book, Tim. Course, I'm not a scholar but' – Go on, 'Enry, chance your arm – 'I'll still want convincing this Infamy draft is genuine.'

'It's genuine.' Thwaite sounded not in the least put out. He sounded delighted with himself. 'Handwriting, ink, the lined legal paper Roosevelt always used. Don't worry, I've made comparisons with the papers in his library at Hyde Park – New York's Hyde Park. You're right, it'll need authenticating, but it's genuine, the whole boxful.'

'Boxful of what?'

'Waste paper. Memos, duplicates of reports, surveys, Pentagon stuff, the week's Oval Office junk, December 1st to 7th.'

'The Infamy draft doesn't sound like junk.'

'It was junk until someone spotted it.'

'You?'

The tyke, the white rose from the county of broad acres, the Yorkshire pudding, could not help but crack a smile. Peckover reached for the handle of the door to the outside, indicating that he was on his way. Not that Thwaite wasn't enjoying himself as tutor and peerless historian.

Peckover said, 'This was a load of waste paper that escaped shredding?'

'Incinerating. No shredders in those days.'

' 'Ow did it escape? Furnace on the blink?'

'The messenger who collected it every Sunday at noon, regular as clockwork, he had a lunch date. A typist on Eleanor's staff. He put off the burning, then the bombs fell. He thought he'd hang on to the box as a souvenir of his days in the White House. Next day he enlisted.'

Grinning, endlessly admiring, keeping the prof chatty, Peckover said, 'Do I get a prize for guessing the messenger?'

'That's who. He stored the box with his belongings and never got round to opening it until last year. Wasn't as if the papers were exciting, like share prices. Then his caretaker turns out to be a historian and he remembers them.'

'Serendipity's what I call it, Tim. Only problem is, Lou's dead. Don't we need 'im to swear he collected the box when he said, December 7th, before the bombs came down?'

Thwaite's cheerfulness left him. He looked annoyed. 'There's the internal evidence, the rest of the papers. That's what I'm working on. All the Congressional stuff and memos pertain to that one week. I can make it cast-iron.'

'Marvellous. Where d'you keep this Infamy draft?' In for a penny. Thwaite was now glowering. 'Mean to say, prize document like that, rewriting 'istory, putting you up there with Toynbee, and the French Revolution bloke, Carlyle, was it? What I'm saying is it's under lock and key, I 'ope.'

'Are you the press?'

'Press?' Peckover laughed merrily. 'That's rich! Look, sorry, got to be off. Brew milady's bedtime beverage. G'night.'

He clattered down the stairs. Thwaite restrained the cat and locked the door.

'What do you think, Puddy Tat?'

If his visitor wasn't the press, some Fleet Street rag hounding him – they didn't let you rest – who was he? Even a butler should have known whether his name was Syd or Reg.

He turned off the kitchen light and looked down through the window at his visitor striding across the driveway to the house.

Peckover, on duty again, strode with the purposeful pace of heavyweight butlerdom. Lightweight butlers might shimmer and sidle but the heavies trod like the approach of doom. Who knew if someone in one of the high, lit windows ahead might not be looking down prior to closing damask curtains? Behind him, from the windows over the garage, music started up.

Weakest bit of Thwaite's tale had been Lou doing nothing with his souvenir box of White House waste paper for fifty years until, lo, Ahoy's new caretaker turns out to be a historian.

Possible, though. On his road to riches Lou might have riffled through the box a couple of times and been sent instantly to sleep. He hadn't been so desperate for cash as to need to flog the stuff to a dealer. The one paper which might have caught his eye, the alleged Infamy draft, might not have been there anyway. Might have been a later insertion, courtesy of Thwaite.

In which case Thwaite's worry could be that the box of junk had not sent Lou to sleep, Lou was familiar with every paper, and he would reject the Infamy draft as an intruder and a fake. To prevent which, run the buzzard down with a truck. What was his name, the American who forged the Howard Hughes autobiography?

Clifford Irving. Brilliant bloke. Fooled everyone except Hughes. Irving's mistake had been not to have been a killer. Hughes alive and well said he'd never written any autobiography. Clang went the cell door on Irving.

The provenance was all. If the Infamy draft were a fake, best for Thwaite if Lou were not around to cast doubts on it.

If it were genuine, Thwaite still wasn't out of the wood. He had that little episode in his past. If Lou found out about it he might take exception and tear up the codicil. He could give the Infamy job and Ahoy to some other historian.

The prof didn't look like a killer but neither had Dr Crippen.

Immediate question was, was there cocoa?

Sleep-groggy Jarvis walked through the staff basement area. A light shone under the door to Joop's room, and from within burbled TV noises. He climbed creaking stairs to the kitchen.

Here at the back of the cupboard it was. Hershey's Cocoa, Great for Baking. Lid a bit rusty. Probably been here since the Roosevelt administration. He hoped it wasn't going to poison the old girl.

FIVE

'You must stop this nonsense. You must break it off immediately. It's worse than outrageous, it's futile. You'll bring nothing but grief on yourself. It's not as if he were one of us.'

'Mom, you're such a snob.'

'I prefer to regard it as a matter of standards. I can't imagine what's made you go off the rails like this. Think of your husband.'

'Must I?'

Pause.

'I suppose not.'

Millicent and a daughter. Peckover, outside the door, knuckles poised for knuckling, was torn between waiting, hearing more, and fear of being discovered listening. He held a silver tray bearing cocoa in what he judged to be a cup of the Ming dynasty. Next to it he had placed a few Joop coconut confections in an unusual high-walled bowl. This was Prune's bowl but the butler was not to have known that. The cocoa had been smoking hot when he had left the kitchen. That had been a while ago. He had made false stops at bedroom doors behind which sounded gunfire, laughter, and weather forecasts. Any of the rooms might have held Millicent, languishing for her drink. They hadn't, though, because here she was, disciplining Gloria, or Romaine, over a liaison of some kind. If he had his bearings correct her room looked over the ocean.

'Anyway, I'm hardly going to be seeing much of him when we're back in the city.'

'You're going to be seeing nothing of him anywhere. You will telephone him in the morning. If you don't, I will.'

'You don't understand. He's not like you think.'

'He is precisely as I think. What you should understand, my

girl, is that your position is weak. I've no wish to sound dramatic but unless you end this ridiculous business you may find yourself disinherited. I have that small power.'

'Mom, you wouldn't.'

'The subject is closed.'

No, no, it isn't. More, keep going, which daughter is the fallen woman? The liaison sounded like sex. Romaine and her boyfriend?

Ear to the door, Peckover heard nothing more. They would be glaring at each other, or avoiding doing so, and trying to decide if the subject really were closed. He stole back along the passage, then advanced heavily in an attempt to make public his arrival. The floor being firm, its carpet thick, he arrived without a sound. Short of dropping the tray, he could think of nothing to indicate that now was his arrival time, that he was not given to listening at keyholes. He knocked.

'Who is it?'

'Jarvis, modom. Your beverage.'

'Perhaps you would leave it outside. Thank you, Jarvis. Goodnight.'

'Goodnight, modom.'

He slept under a single sheet which was round his ankles when he awoke and opened his eyes to the blackness of the bottomless pit. He had not the haziest idea where he was. Miriam was not here. Had Sam or Mary woken up and she had gone to their room? But here was not home. Home had the luminous clock and dim light from the landing filtering through the door left ajar. Here was hot and smelled of salty damp.

Ah, yes.

He tried to recall on which side of the bed was the lamp, and groped delicately, because the lamp might be Sèvres, once at the bedside of Madame de Pompadour, and would take unkindly to being nudged to the floor and into a thousand shards.

Not Madame de Pompadour, she would have had candles, wouldn't she? Tim Thwaite would have known. He had been dreaming of Thwaite. Clad in white, as if for croquet, he had been at the Ahoy dining table with Thwaite, also in white, who had been tutoring him about Christopher Columbus, 1492.

Thwaite had held in both hands a letter in Latin on a parchment with a red blob of a seal hanging from it. Columbus had written the letter to President Roosevelt. Thwaite was demonstrating that the letter was probably a forgery. He wore handcuffs. Crouched in a crystal chandelier above their heads had been a tangerine cat.

The noise that had awakened him was not the ocean, though it rustled in his ears like dry leaves. He might have hazarded a single cry of a seagull, except when was anyone awakened by a seagull? The house was filled with people and down here there was no telling what was going on up there, what crying and clamouring they might be making. All was silence though, apart from the ocean. He decided he had been awakened by silence, jetlag, and loss of weight.

He switched on the bedside lamp. Its base was a misshapen lump of turquoise glass with a clock in it. The shade was a piece of sackcloth. Not Sèvres but not Woolworth's. Time: two fifty a.m. He reckoned he would be lucky if he were asleep again by dawn.

His room was light, fairly airy, apart from a smell of damp, and had a Japanese motif and en suite bathroom. The walls were hung with watery Japanese prints of people in kimonos walking or simply standing about. The wallpaper and matching sofa and armchairs had a chrysanthemum design. A blown-up photograph of smoke billowing from the American fleet in Pearl Harbor there was not, perhaps in deference to Japanese staff who might come and go. He had a telephone for assignations with the housekeeper, if there was one, a television, and more space than he knew what to do with.

He put his still-packed suitcase on the bed and took from it the locked briefcase containing items which he preferred not to leave lying around: the Langley file, handcuffs, his passport, not in the name of Jarvis. He sorted his few clothes into drawers, returned the briefcase to the suitcase, and put the suitcase on the floor at the back of the cupboard. On the chest of drawers he set a framed snapshot of the butler's wife and bantlings in the back garden at Collins Cross. Miriam had been caught bending with a trowel and was laughing. Sam's tongue was stuck out at the camera. Mary was tasting soil.

'Something tells me this could be a very dodgy business,' he told them.

He dressed in the shorts and short-sleeved shirt he had brought for his day off from butling, or in this case, for the sleepless small hours. Then he walked through the staff quarters, past slumbering washing machines and a ping-pong table and out of the house for his first look at the ocean.

There was no moon. He bumped against a chair on the deck. He counted four stars. Others may have been lurking but all were useless as far as lighting up planet earth went. He descended wooden steps to the dunes, holding the rails, feeling for each step with big feet shod in running shoes which he had never run in.

The dunes were lumpy hillocks, swollen here, valleyed there, like an arty photographer's shot of a Rubens nude. They were heavy with chiaroscuro, and scratchy. Clumps of umbrageous vegetation with thorns and spikes stabbed his legs. Skirting an area where the reeds and bushes were chest high, he cracked his shin against a log of driftwood.

He should have worn long sleeves and long pants but he wasn't turning back to change. Calamities like this Lyme disease were what happened to other people, not to blameless visitors on a visitor's visa.

The public health booklet Frank Veal had given him about Lyme disease warned against going bare-legged and bare-armed near water or in wooded areas. These dunes weren't wooded but they were decidedly scrubby, and out there the sea was water, though perhaps not the sort of water the booklet had in mind. He hadn't smeared himself with tick-repellent either, because he didn't have any, but he would do as the booklet said and inspect himself when he arrived back in his room, take a shower, and wash his clothes. Actually, he'd be damned if he'd wash his clothes, they were fresh on. The ticks apparently waited on leaves and in long grass and latched on to you as you brushed past. After they'd bitten and drunk they inflated to what looked to Peckover, in the gaudy photo, like a filled, rubber hot-water bottle, though admittedly a small one. A right blight, if anyone were to ask him. Here in suffering Dunehampton and environs, according to the booklet, victims were plentiful, increasing, and numbered around half of

55

all reported cases anywhere. It'd be raining now in dirty, littered London, but London didn't have these pestiferous ticks.

The going was slow, not that he was pressed for time. His feet sank in the soft sand. Great air. Would a swim help him sleep and how cold was the water? A naked plunge might wash away any adhering ticks. He could not yet see the ocean but he could smell it and hear it, its melancholy, long, withdrawing roar, retreating, to the breath of the night-wind, down the vast edges drear and naked shingles of the world, and such and so forth.

He was not alone, he was sure of that. The rustle he had heard from not far ahead, and now could not hear, had come and gone, less a rustle than a momentary scrunch, and certainly not the sea's rustling. He stood still, listening.

Didn't have to have been a human scrunch. Might have been a native dune beastie, something singularly American like a bandicoot or a turkey.

He tracked onward and for the most part upward, though soon the dunes were going to have to drop to the beach. If whatever had awakened him had been a human cry, others should have heard it too. Not Benny Benjamin, Martini Man, sleeping the sleep of the stewed, but others whose rooms faced the ocean, such as Millicent. But no commotion had followed that he was aware of: slamming doors, telephoning, seeking help from the butler. He looked behind him. The two lights in the towering silhouette of Ahoy with its absurd satellite dish would probably be on a landing and stairs.

Onward. Where was the bleedin' beach?

Scrunch.

Peckover stood motionless, weight on his front foot, sinking millimetre by millimetre into the sand.

Boll weevils? Lovers?

He doubted lovers. For lovers there were scores of public dunes. In front of some of the palaces, such as here, Joop had told him, the beaches were private. The riff-raff were permitted to cross them, doffing their tennis visors, but not to dally. If the scrunch sound were lovers he hoped that they had their clothes on. If they hadn't they would fetch up raw from thorns, weevils, and the dreaded tick.

The scruncher did not need to hide to be invisible in this shroud of night, only to sit and be quiet. Himself, on the other hand, quiet as a mouse, was surely monumentally visible against the sky. He seemed to be on the dunes' summit. He could see the sea. From here the dunes sloped bumpily to the beach. The tide's fringe glimmered. Far out was a spark of light from a boat. There was no horizon, no seeing where the sea met the sky.

Ah, the sea, the sea, the wine-dark, seal-barking sea!

He said loudly in his Jarvis voice, 'Beg pardon, I hope I do not intrude, whoever you are, sir.'

Or madam. If he were being watched, he preferred that whoever was watching knew he knew he knew he was being watched.

He took an exploratory downhill step. As far as he could see, the dune was fairly sheer, but bare of bushes, and only ten or fifteen feet before it became the beach. He might not swim but he would test the water. He would take off his shoes and paddle like a day-tripper at Brighton.

Scrunch.

From behind him. To his right.

Peckover went down the dune on his heels, hands, and rump, his shoes filling with sand, then climbed on hands and knees. Where the dune began to level out he lay flat, one ear in the sand, the other to the sky.

Something tiny alighted on his skyward ear and stayed there. When it started to walk he swatted it.

He crawled over the parapet of the dune and peered into the dark. Nothing, or very little. Fuzzy outlines of bushes, the nearest not far from his nose. A little further off, one bush moved behind another. The bush which had moved left behind a dim space where previously there had been blackness. Peckover lay with his chin in the sand.

That bush that had moved was no bandicoot, nor a cuddly, tick-laden deer either.

He squirmed sideways, watching ahead, then on elbows and knees towards the bush closest to him. Before he reached it he saw the bush further away divide in two. The mobile part ran and was engulfed immediately in night and silence.

Peckover watched, hearing and seeing nothing. He elbowed to his bush. He knelt and peered round it, observing dark spaces and darker vegetation. Nothing moved. If he could see no one, chances were fair that no one could see him.

He's still there, he sensed. He hadn't cleared off. Even with the grinding of the sea in his ears, anyone clearing off through this jungle, he'd have heard him.

Why hadn't the bloke cleared off? What did he want, fooling with a butler? Who was stalking whom? Which of them had more patience if this were to be a waiting game? Waiting for what?

Bugger this for a lark, Peckover decided. Taking a semicircular route he ran in a crouch for the bush which had divided in two, where the bloke no longer was, unless he were the phantom of the dunes, nowhere and everywhere.

Phantom or flesh, the prowler had disappeared. Peckover, squatting, gazed about, listened, and heard only his own breathing. The bush had flowers of a light colour he could only guess at. He guessed a strong pink. They smelled like the cosmetics counters at Selfridges. Passion des Dunes.

Scrunch.

Too late, Peckover spun round, or tried to. Spinning from his squatting posture called for greater agility than he had known for some years. Merely by trying to spin, he lost his balance, which was fortunate. Falling sideways, he presented a moving target. The blow struck his shoulder, though he could not have said whether from a fist, foot, or perhaps a golf club. Dunehampton was golfing country. A blur of bony anatomy crashed into him with a momentum which carried them both into the bush.

Peckover flailed, kneed, and punched one-handedly. His other hand was pinned somewhere, as was one leg. His assailant punched and kicked too, but with little better success, or not until a lucky thump landed in the kidney region, eliciting a gasp. They were street fighters plucked from the street and dropped amid thorns and roses. The bloke's clothes were slimy as if he had walked out of the ocean, though it might have been sweat. When an ankle, or wrist, or the bleeder's nose tracked across his mouth, Peckover grabbed whatever it was – it was not a nose, it had a wet sock on it – and bit hard into it. Then a bang on the head stunned him.

Oh, Miriam, goodnight.

The next moments were foggy. He lay curled, face in the sand,

58

hands over his head, while the winner punched and kicked. Go, harder, get it over, Peckover voicelessly urged. He heard receding grunting and scrunching as the winner departed.

Then he heard only his own moans, and the ocean. He began to worry about sand in his mouth, and Miriam's reaction to whatever lumps the tussle had left on him, whether she would scold him, or fuss with witch hazel and pinch fleshy leaves from the aloe to daub him with.

Of course, by the time he had finished helping to make sense of the Langley business – or made so little headway the Yard would have recalled him – the wounds would have healed.

By then there might be new wounds. Something was rotten in the Ahoy homestead. He needed help.

Might have nothing to do with the Langleys, his phantom of the dunes. Might have been a stray dunes vagabond who liked to fight.

Had he been left for dead, or dying, or merely warned off? Warned off what? Nobody could be warned off if he didn't know who was warning him and why. The attack was point-less.

The sand was a soft, snug bed. He did not want to get up, not yet, for fear he would be unable to.

He needed a fellow-fool to cover his rear and confer with. Someone like DC Twitty if he weren't on leave and undiscoverable among the King's Road boutiques and the cast-off clothes stalls of Brixton Market and Camden Lock, buying costumes and hats further to swell his mad wardrobe.

He would phone Frank Veal. Frank could put it to the local lot in Dunehampton. Easing Twitty into Ahoy as staff would be the problem. What more staff did they need? Second butler? One butler could hold the tray while the other stacked the dishes on it. A groom for Romaine's Glad Rags?

Meanwhile the sand was cosy. If he closed his eyes for five minutes he might begin to feel better.

He opened his eyes to gaudy sunshine. A policeman in a blue short-sleeved shirt with badges was dragging back the curtains. The clock in the lump of turquoise glass said nine ten a.m.

Gawd! Breakfast! He should have been up and about being

59

busy with tea and kidneys and kedgeree and telling everyone good morning, sir, we trust you slept well, modom.

The presence of the boyo in blue told him that all was perhaps well, he was not being missed upstairs. Or he was not being missed upstairs because all was not well.

He should have felt worse, all things considered. He recalled taking a long hot bath. He certainly might have looked worse, from what he remembered observing in the bathroom mirrors. Apart from a pinkish blemish below the right eye, nothing else would show once he had his clothes on. The nastiest knock had been on top of his head. It had bled but his hair covered the spot.

'Vito De Voto,' said the policeman.

'Jarvis,' said Peckover.

'Whatever you say. Going to be another hot one.'

'What's 'appening?'

'Everything. Get up. This your wife and kids?'

'Yes.'

So now you can put it down. What did he say his name was? Feet of the Photo?

'Good tits,' the policeman said. 'She got teeth?'

Peckover hesitated before getting out of bed. Not because he was naked under the sheet but because once up he believed he might recover the photo with one hand and thump the bloke with the other.

The policeman said, 'She smiles nice but she don't show her teeth.' He put the photograph back. 'I thought English broads had big horse teeth.'

'Just the upper classes.'

Peckover headed for the chrysanthemum chair where clothes lay draped. They turned out to be beach gear. His butler's costume hung in the closet.

'What's the marks on your ass, English? Love bites?'

Peckover sat in the chair and pulled on his socks. Never had he put socks on first or so slowly. He said, 'You fancy me? Lock the door. How long do we 'ave?'

The policeman swore and turned away. Mid-thirties, Peckover judged, and a pain in the neck, unless this were some sort of test. He had a wispy, untrimmed moustache which would get egg and ketchup and muck on it, bound to, when he ate. His belt was festooned with equipment. Gun, handcuffs, radio, truncheon, or nightstick or whatever it was called, and pouches and boxes of who knew what. Probably towelettes for swabbing eggburger from his moustache. His tanned face had the beginning of wrinkles. Skin cancer, Peckover hoped.

He buttoned a clean white shirt. Several pairs of feet clumped along the deck outside. Voices talked indistinctly. Other footsteps clattered on the servants' stairs.

'What time you went to bed, English?'

'English' might have worked in a Hemingway story about the Spanish Civil War but from this bloke it didn't.

'Midnight,' Peckover said.

'Hear anything in the night?'

'The sea. Seagulls.'

He hadn't heard seagulls, not if whatever had awakened him had not been a seagull, and it hadn't. Seagulls slept at night same as everybody else. He supposed they did. He climbed into buttercup trousers.

'The breeze in the bushes,' he said. ' 'Eartbeats and 'eavy breathing.'

'What're you talking about?'

'Had a set-to with someone on the beach.' He hunted for his black tie. 'Not the beach if we're being exact. The dunes. So what's going on?'

'You better tell me. Who was the someone?'

'Never saw 'im,' He tied the tie. 'Likely he'll 'ave teeth marks, though. Second and first bicuspids, cuspids, and lateral and central incisors, upper and lower. I don't think the molars came into it but I'd not take an oath.' He took his white jacket from its hanger. A faint, fawn smear of lamb or flan across the left pocket would have to be dealt with. 'You're looking for someone with two rosy sickle-moons on his ankle, though I'd not swear to ankle either.'

'I'm to believe this garbage?'

'Frankly I don't give a monkey's.'

'Hold it!' The policeman had his hand on his gun. 'Where you think you're going, English?'

'Bathroom.' Peckover opened the door to his bathroom. 'Then

upstairs. If you won't tell me what's going on, p'raps Millicent Langley will.'

'She won't find it easy. She's dead.'

Peckover stood with his hand on the doorhandle.

The policeman said, 'And you may not find this easy, Peckover, but you are off limits. You may be one big panjandrum in your Scotland Yard. Here you're nothing. You're not wanted.'

'You mean I can go?' Peckover grinned an ape-grin. 'Pack? Next plane out? We'll never see each other again?'

'We'll see each other. This is my ball park. I am owner and manager. I bat, I pitch, I run the popcorn concession, I sing the anthem. Every move you make, you tell me.'

'Mr Feet of the Photo.'

'What?'

'Old cock, you've got it wrong. I report to whosit.' Damn, what was his name, and why in twenty-four hours hadn't he got in touch? Not the red carpet and cocktail reception, didn't have to be that, but a telephone call to say hello, one miserable buzz on the blower. 'Chief Rosko.'

He was untutored in American police ranks. They probably differed from state to state. They had lootenants and captains, which London didn't have, unless you were in the army. But a chief had to outrank a sergeant. Maybe Chief Rosko looked after all Long Island, or half of it, meaning he'd never know what was happening in any one place at any given time. This berk, Feet, with his belt of accessories and unweeded moustache, might be Führer in Dunehampton.

' 'Ow did she die?' Peckover said.

'Drowned, could be. Couple of early surfers found her an hour ago. Could be you know something about it. You were out there wrestling with someone you never saw, is that what you're saying?'

'Where do I find Mr Rosko?'

'He'll be here.'

'Anyone else know Jarvis is Peckover?'

'Not unless you've told them.' He had taken his hand from his gun to scratch an armpit. 'Just stay in line.'

'Permission to go the bathroom, sir?'

Sergeant De Voto swore at him.

62

Peckover went into the bathroom, unhappy but not totally downcast. Millicent Langley hadn't seemed suicidal. On the contrary. Had all her faculties, too much sense for midnight swimming on her own. Grim. Shocking. Peckover gulped when he paused to consider that he could have been arm-wrestling with a murderer.

SIX

The sisters Eve and Hannabelle O'Kaplan, cleaning ladies to the Langleys, drove from Ahoy in glee. Their services would not be needed today, because of the tragedy, but they had been paid anyway. Peckover believed it was best they were leaving. Their battered car was vast and not a great deal of space remained in the forecourt. He was tempted to call from the window, 'Let 'em all come! Bring caravans, bring petrol tankers!' Most homes round the world would have been hard put to play host to the present ambulance, five police cars, four plain cars, a stretch limousine so stretched he could not see how it did not sag in the middle, a pick-up truck (Dunehampton Landscaping), and a delivery van (Clothespin Laundry). Ahoy's driveway accommodated them with space over, so far, for three-point turns. He guessed more might be parked on Tonic Lane but he could not see beyond the hedge. Neither could he see Joop's rust-mottled eyesore of a semi-wreck with its cracked windshield and caved-in hood, kept, at Millicent's request, on the lee side of the garden shed.

He came to attention inside the door into the green drawing-room and coughed delicately.

He did not seem to be interrupting anything momentous, and he had nothing to announce, but being here to surveil, he was not going to surveil much by sitting in the kitchen polishing the silver. They weren't eager for breakfast, or not yet. Just as well with Joop gone. Mr Butterwick had worked with him on the delicate yet carrying cough.

The assembly looked his way, then away, as they might from some trifling irritant, such as someone handing out pamphlets on the street. All except Gloria, who offered him a wan smile, and

64

even stood, as if prepared to come over to him, perhaps to take his hand and comfort him.

Anorexic Romaine was absent, no doubt calming Glad Rags, or sobbing on the shoulder of the lover who was not one of us, if it were she who had the lover. Benny was also missing, possibly face down somewhere in a dish of martini.

Rudy Pardo, Romaine's tubby hubby, the failed financier with the bald spot and peach tie who had been glad to have him aboard, was present without the tie. Unlikely, at summertime Ahoy, he possessed a black tie for mourning, but he would know enough to know that this morning, peach, plum and nectarine hues were unsuitable. Is it you the cuckold? silently enquired Peckover. Rudy was in discussion with a wavy-haired male model with silvery threads.

The daughters were now orphans worth a hundred and fifty million dollars between them.

If they wanted to keep Ahoy, they could surely do that too. They needed only a couple of killer lawyers who would prove the worthlessness of the codicil to their father's will.

The guests, aching to hotfoot out of it, stood nodding and being of assistance to another of Feet's troops, this one wearing acid-washed denim and a boyish grin: the kind who would squeeze your testicles until they squeaked. Wishing they had never heard of Ahoy, the guests had hand baggage at their feet. They would have given their names, addresses, where they were last night, watched it all written down, and now strained to be released into the limo. One was hung with a Leica primed to record the goodbye to a memorable visit. Another would be the letter-writing guest. Peckover wondered if she, he, had ever finished the letter.

He approached Gloria Benjamin.

'Perhaps, modom, a pot of tea would not come amiss?' The cup that cheers but doth not inebriate, he was on the point of adding, but perhaps this was not the moment. No telling what state her husband might be in. 'A little toast?'

'Who to – the Queen?' Gloria Benjamin tried to smile but failed. 'I'm sorry, Jarvis. We're a little distraught. Tea, yes, why not.'

Was this the voice of the one behind the bedroom door, the floosie who was carrying on and stood to be disinherited unless she ended it? He might have suspected yes but for the letter

65

mentioning Romaine. For all he knew both daughters might have a man on the side. This older one had a certain blowsy adulterous ripeness. Forget the silver spoon, twice-a-week hairdo, dietician on call, and the neospatial objectivism on the canvases upstairs, and you could picture her glisteningly lipsticked and welcoming on a bar stool at the Dog and Duck on Whitechapel Road, eager for a gin and a sing-along. Well, almost.

As for the affair, she, or her sister, no longer had to worry about ending it.

'May we offer our deepest condolences,' he told her in a vibrant baritone, 'on your grievous loss.'

'Thank you, Jarvis.' She was peering at his left cheekbone. 'What happened to you?'

'A door, modom, in the night. We are not yet wholly familiar with the geography of Ahoy.'

'You must look after yourself. I'm afraid I must also ask you to look after the kitchen today. It's most inconsiderate of Joop. Are we going to see him again?'

'We understand he has taken his passport, modom.'

'He might always have it on him.'

'This is true, though with respect, we deem unlikely.'

'He's left his car and clothes and everything.'

'Indeed, it is a puzzle. We have been given to believe that the car is devoid of petrol.'

'It is? How do you know?'

'Our duty to whom we, in our profession, serve, modom, is to be apprised, as far as possible, of multifarious phenomena, because one never knows.'

Gloria Langley's eyes glazed over. She said, 'Perhaps you would pick up some frozen dinners at the store. You can microwave them. The Crunchy Clam Platter is good. My husband is fond of the Oriental Beef.'

'Lean Cuisine or regular?'

'I really couldn't say. Some of both.' She sounded momentarily testy. 'Use my father's car, it's still in the garage, a white Cadillac. The keys should be under the driver's seat.'

'Very good, modom. The tea – Darjeeling or Lapsang?'

'You decide, Jarvis.'

He did not know if the kitchen had either. He had seen Lipton's tea-bags, but doubted if anyone was going to be alert enough this morning to notice the difference.

The empty kitchen reeked of bread and Gauloises. Joop had baked enough currant loaves to feed the entire burgher population of Rijswijk. They were still warm, just. How many hours did currant bread take to cool? Two, three? Miriam would have known. The floury work surface, seasoned with little mounds of dripped ash, resembled an aerial photograph of a bombing raid. He would have given a tenner for a look at Joop's ankles.

He found sliced white bread but no toaster. How could a kitchen not have a toaster? Had Joop taken it? He had taken little enough of his own stuff. The microwave would produce toast but he was chary. The only time he had put bread in a microwave he had turned his back and the bread had burst into flames. He studied the controls.

The drawing-room was deserted when he returned with tea, toast, and slices of burgher's currant bread. He put the tray down and through a window watched a departing limousine, the guests air-conditioned behind smoked glass. Gloria, Rudy and Romaine – with neither a lover nor Glad Rags – dutifully waved goodbye. The male-model copper in silvery threads stood apart, not waving.

Craning, Peckover could see the corner of the garage and the flat above. Had he been running things he would have had two men up there questioning Thwaite.

Perhaps Feet did have someone up there. How was a butler to know? Being in the thick of all this but without authority was frustrating. No information, no one to shuffle ideas with. He wanted to organise and give orders, to throw open the window and yell at the wavy-haired copper to stop standing there and find Joop. Amid all the milling and police activity he felt irrelevant.

What police activity? Judging from the number of cars there ought to have been twenty police here and he had seen only two. Three with Feet. The house pulsed with emptiness. The driveway accounted for a single copper, hands patting his flourishing hair.

The boyish testicle-squeezer came into the room and said, 'So what's the peep-show?'

'Sir?'

'You're Jarvis?'

67

'That is correct, sir.'

'We get a statement from you?'

'Certainly, sir, though we failed to catch the officer's name. A Mr Feet or Fit? Fit O'Folio? An Irish-American, no doubt. He wears a distinctive, if skimpy moustache.'

'Vito De Voto. Sergeant to you. Don't leave the house, Jarvis.'

'We had considered visiting our friend across the way, Mr Thwaite, for quotidian discourse, should that be permissible.'

'The professor?'

'The same.'

'He's giving his statement. He's with the Chief. Quit spying out of windows and get on with your work.'

'Might we interject that the family expressed a wish for sustenance but would now appear to be missing. The toast and the currant bread are cooling.'

'Maybe they're on the beach with the Sergeant and everyone else.'

'Shrimping?'

'What?'

'Quite so. A synonym for investigating, sir.' Had he gone too far? 'From the Old World.'

'Watch it, Jarvis.' The policeman approached the tray. 'This the currant bread?'

'It has the semblance of currant bread, sir.'

'Don't be wise with me. I'm going to tell you something else. I know what quotidian means. Get out before I break your ass.'

Jarvis moved to the door at a seemly pace. His spirits were lifted because he had got up the nostrils of this specimen from the Dunehampton Police Department. Chief Inspector H. Peckover existed after all. Two flowers of the DPD he'd now met and he had succeeded in irking them both.

'But you said that when you can't sleep you walk on the beach,' Chief Rosko said, coming back into the kitchen in the apartment over the garage, zipping his fly. 'You sleep badly, Tim?'

'No,' said Thwaite. 'Sometimes. I said perhaps a couple of times.'

'Personal problems, is it? Hardly be money if you're going to inherit Ahoy. College must be a worry, all that grading and kids who don't know anything.'

68

'They know stuff we don't.'

'This morning you walked to the beach, in the dark, and you found you weren't alone.'

'I didn't walk anywhere. I was asleep.'

'You go barefoot when you walk on the beach, Tim? Like Sally Henny-penny?'

'Who?'

'"I go barefoot, barefoot, barefoot." *The Tale of Mrs Tiggy-winkle*. You take your socks and sandals off?'

'No. I suppose I might. I don't go on the beach.'

'When were you last on the beach at night, Tim?'

'Months ago. I said I've only done it twice.'

'When were you last on the beach, period?'

'Weeks. I don't keep records. Ages.'

'In this weather?'

'I don't like the beach.'

'You have a busy social life?'

'Watch your ankle. Hey, pssst, Puddy Tat!'

Puddy Tat prowled from the kitchen.

'You have friends visit you here?'

'Some.'

'When was the last time?'

'I don't remember. Week or two.'

'How about last night? Jarvis, the butler.'

'Oh, yes. He's not a friend. I've never seen him before.'

'You've seen me before, right? We're still looking for a hit-and-runner, Tim. Between you and me, we know who he is. What you don't seem to know is co-operation gets rewards. How often you clean this place?'

'When it needs it.'

'You take a shower this morning?'

'Yes. Why?'

'Anyone else take one – here?'

'Who else?'

Chief Rosko, peering down, walked towards the kitchen door. He stopped and slid his foot lightly backwards and forwards over the tiles. There came a faint grating sound.

'There's sand in the shower too, Tim. Someone's been on the beach.'

69

Thwaite said nothing.

'Make it easy for yourself. Who're you protecting? Rudy Pardo?'

'This is absurd.'

'He's not worth it. Do yourself a favour. Was he carrying any-thing?'

'Like what?'

'You tell me.'

'I've told you, for God's sake! I wasn't there!'

'Was he alone?'

'It was too dark— '

Thwaite's mouth stayed open but nothing further sounded from it. From behind the pebble lenses his eyes stared unblinking at Chief Rosko.

'Yes?' prompted Rosko.

No reply.

'Was there a moon, Tim?'

'I don't know.'

'You didn't take a flashlight?'

'I didn't go anywhere!'

'Were you thinking of going anywhere today?'

'College.'

'Term hasn't started.'

'I use the library.'

'A library's a proper place to think in, Tim. I'd like you to think carefully. Will you do that for me? I can help you but you'll have to co-operate.'

Between Ahoy and the foamy ridge of the ocean were two score humans, not all of them police. There were too many cameras for police. Television crews and the press abounded. And tourists.

Detained by constant telephone ringings, the foraging for at least the beginnings of lunch, clearing away cold tea, toast, and currant bread, plumping of cushions, and feeding the hound, Prune – was Jarvis not now the entire staff of this caliph's castle by the sea? – the butler walked at last down the wooden steps he had negotiated not so long ago in darkness, and into the salty outdoors.

He had correct reasons for entering the action. Having ignored the tea, might not the family be ready for coffee? Not that he could see any family other than Benny Benjamin, not a noted coffee-drinker. He might also propose refreshment for Dunehampton's boys in blue. He thought he wouldn't, though, and not on your nellie for the press. They would only accept.

Benny Benjamin, adequately upright in white slacks and a lemon V-neck, stood on the dunes in a conclave of four, one of them Sergeant Feet. Another was an elderly fellow with hand baggage, and the fourth a big bloke puffing a pipe.

Beyond them an area of beach had been cordoned off with yellow ribbon. Inside the ribbon, police, as casual in short-sleeved blue as Benny in his summer duds, kept the public outside and answered, with meticulous inaccuracies, questions as to who lay under the sheet and what went on. Many of those outside the ribbon wore swimsuits. Dogs chased each other, rock music thudded from a radio. A police jeep was getting nowhere trying to extricate itself from the sand.

Beyond the beach, breakers surged and crashed. *A wave breaks at the point where the depth of water is one and a third times the height of the wave.* Amazing, thought Peckover, the schoolroom trivia that stuck. *Hic haec hoc* and the square on the hypotenuse. He wondered if he could remember half of Thwaite's lecture on Roosevelt and Pearl Harbor. Away from this semi-private parcel of ocean-front, surfers rode the waves, hundreds of sun-worshippers smeared themselves with oil, toddlers spat out sand and teenage girls daring the breakers squealed, were knocked off their feet, and yearned for the lifeguard to rescue them. The lifeguard, a bronzed Adonis, stayed put on his high platform, impatient for evening discos, and pulling down the knickers of these same or similar girls. Walking, squinting in the sunlight, the butler would have conceded he had never seen such beaches. They beat even Blackpool. Yellow sand as far as he could see and knockout weather.

You had to look for them but far out to sea were several boats. Or ships. Beyond the horizon would be what, eventually? He was unsure of his compass points, he would have to look at an atlas, but he believed that if he struck out with his steady, splashy trudgen

71

he would reach, in time, Cornwall. If an undertow took him, perhaps Nigeria. First of course he would have to get beyond the breakers.

He had no need for his carrying cough. The foursome, watching him, had fallen silent.

'Good morning, sir.' He addressed Mr Benjamin. 'Might we be regaled with a demitasse?'

Sergeant Feet in sunglasses scowled. The gent with hand baggage dabbed a tissue across his brow. The bottoms of his trousers were furled into his socks. Peckover, lowering his eyes, waited to be told that under the sheet was Mrs Langley, these were police, now was no time for demitasses, and would he get the hell out. Benny Benjamin might have teeth marks on an ankle but it seemed unlikely. Unless he hiked up his pants legs and pushed down his socks there was no way of knowing.

'I'll fix my own,' Benny Benjamin said. 'You're doing a fine job, Jenkins.'

'Jarvis, sir.'

'Good. Hope you've settled in, got everything you need.' For the benefit of the others he clenched his fist at waist level and punched the air, a short jab to its midriff. 'Hang in there, men. Up oars and steady as you go.'

As Benny started back across the dunes to Ahoy, Peckover intercepted a look between the Sergeant and the big fellow in a seersucker suit with a pipe in one hand, a box of matches in the other. The look indicated that Benny was barmy. Once upon a time, in the schoolyard, he and his mates had registered such an opinion by twiddling a forefinger against the temple.

'Gene Rosko,' said the man with the pipe.

He too had tucked his pants cuffs into his socks. Protection, Peckover supposed, against the dreaded Lyme tick.

'You've met Vito,' Rosko said. 'This is Dr Webb, our medical examiner.' He settled a hairy paw, like a Shetland sheepdog's, on the doctor's shoulder. 'Everything you can give us, Morrie, fast as you like, and you don't have to set it to music.'

That sounded to Peckover like a dismissal, and to the medical examiner too, who mopped his face and trekked away through the dunes.

Rosko said, 'He doubts she drowned. There's seawater in the gullet and windpipe but he says it proves nothing, it would've got there anyway. Practically every bone in her body's broken. Up in Maine she could've drowned then got mashed on the rocks but we've no rocks here. Be warned, Henry, Morrie's report, when we get it, may not be like you're used to at the Yard.'

'As long as 'e gets it right.'

'He gets it right but it takes some decoding. He turns it into this deathless prose like he can't wait for the book to come out. *Collected Autopsies*, by M. Webb, MD. He's writing an opera. It's what happens to people who come to Dunehampton. They get creative. If they're not writing an opera, or putting paint on canvas, or they're sculptors— '

'Or fag poets,' De Voto said, sunglasses trained on Peckover.

' —they feel they shouldn't be here, they should be selling insurance back in New Jersey.' The Chief surveyed the beach and dunes. 'Vito, you blew it. If she was killed in the house then carried to the ocean we've got problems with tracks.'

They watched the mob of police and press trooping and milling. One man stood on one foot while stabbing the sand with the other, as if hopeful he might uncover evidence, or destroy it.

'Forget tracks,' Peckover concurred.

'No one asked you,' said the Sergeant. 'Surfers and early risers were trampling everywhere, time we got here. We cleared them back.'

'Henry,' Rosko said, 'I'm not excited about being seen talking to you. Why would I talk with a butler? Okay, I would. Butlers see all, hear all, say nothing, right? All the same, show us where you were mugged, then we'll split.'

Peckover could only guess at the relish with which the Sergeant had told the Chief how the nosey-parker from Scotland Yard, on his first night, had been ambushed and blitzed. He led them towards a crushed beach-rose bush and halted ten paces from it.

'Get your specialists 'ere. Any little gold coins with 'er Majesty on them, they're mine. They're one quid apiece. Anything else you can keep.'

'You're pretty flip, Peckover,' said the Sergeant. 'There's an old lady been murdered.'

'Oh, go play with some jellyfish,' Peckover said.

'Shut it, both of you,' said the Chief. 'So all this we sift. Anything particular we're looking for?'

'Blood. I chewed 'im. He bumped my head.'

'When can you get away?' Chief Rosko was watching two policemen coming towards him from Ahoy. 'It'd be nice to say hello.'

'Two thirty? I'll advance their lunch.'

'How do you figure Benny?'

'No idea, not yet. He drinks.'

'Drinks?' echoed the Sergeant. 'He sits down with the *Dunehampton Blade* and goes through the police blotter, the drunk drivers, to see if his name's there, because he's not going to remember.'

'Could be that boozing's what it suits him people should think,' Rosko said.

'Nah,' said the Sergeant.

The Chief said, 'Henry, there's a place on Lot's Lane, the Passenger's Seat. I'll wait till three. You can tell us nothing about this guy who mugged you except you chewed him, you don't know where, and he's male?'

'Male, wet, and I'd guess an ankle.'

'Wet like he'd been in the ocean?'

'It's possible.'

'Thwaite isn't admitting it but he was on the beach last night, or the dunes, or close enough to see you. He saw someone. I've talked with him and he was there, I'm sure of it.'

'See his ankles?'

'Not yet.'

'I'd be happier with help in the house, I can tell you. I'd like to phone the Yard and requisition a cook.'

'Okay with me. You'll have to fix it with the Langleys. Go on, off you go.'

Going, Peckover heard one of the coppers arriving say, 'Chief, the flower-bed directly under the old lady's window, we may have got something. The flowers and shrubs and stuff, they're all broken and mashed to hell.'

Dead simple then, thought Peckover, trudging through sand. Millicent Langley is dropped or thrown from her bedroom window, whereupon, if she's not dead before being dropped, now she is. In a half-baked attempt to make the death appear to be either suicide or an accident, the killer carries the corpse into the ocean. Alas, returning soddenly from Poseidon's empire, the briny deep, he spies the butler. Unless he's one of the Ahoy household he might not know the fellow is the butler, but whoever he is, for fear of being spotted he stalks and beats him senseless before he can be seen and perhaps recognised.

So all that was required was to identify the bloke and apprehend him.

Of course, the fellow would have been better off lying low, hiding among the beach-rose bushes until the butler had gone away. Four or five more little flaws in his reconstruction came to Peckover before he had even started up the wooden steps to the house.

SEVEN

Starting from the blue veranda, Peckover wound through downstairs Ahoy, establishing his presence, or he might have established it had anyone been there to notice him. Sun-room, a sitting-room with hanging greenery, a conservatory with a backgammon table, bookcases, and books with mildewed spines. Portly, think portly, he told himself, because you never knew, someone might be watching. Giving an impression of portliness was less of a problem than he would have wished.

He was the family retainer, strength and comfort to generations of Langleys as his father before him. He quite enjoyed the fantasy. He must surely have the soul of a butler as well as the stature. He would have gathered up filled ashtrays but the ashtrays he saw were empty. He had seen Benny with a cheroot but there didn't seem to be any other smokers, not now Joop had disappeared. Ha, a martini glass! The butler collected it and sniffed the puddle in the bottom. *Rien de rien.* Melted ice.

In the green drawing-room Rudy and Romaine Pardo sat in hot discussion on a sofa. The plump and the skeletal. Jarvis uttered not the cough which carries but the milder cough prefatory. Needlessly. They had shut up and were looking at him. Would they suppose he often worked with a martini in his hand?

'Coffee, modom? A little Perrier with lemon?'

Given milord and milady together, so ran the Butterwick rule of thumb, address her ladyship. Come the crunch, she it was who brought joy or suffering.

'Thanks, no,' said Romaine. She had on a sleeveless blouse which showed gravy-coloured arms. Would he ever see her in jodhpurs and the round black riding cap with the long peak and the pimple on top?

76

'A cup of bouillon?'

Like on the old transatlantic liners, when they existed. He didn't know what he would do if they said yes.

'Nothing,' Rudy said. 'We're busy.'

Well, excuse me.

Rudy, who had welcomed him aboard, was still tieless, and wearing a silky, sickly and custard-bright collarless jacket which would have looked better on his wife, but not much better, being beyond looking anything other than absurd on anyone except perhaps a juggler in a circus. He also wore a harassed expression and was biting at a wart on the knuckle of his thumb.

Not yourself today, sir, are we, and in need of a shave, mused benign Jarvis. The bloke was suntanned daft. They all were. In a world suntan contest these people would carry off every prize.

Portly with a martini glass, Jarvis flowed from the room.

Gloria requested that lunch be served on the sundeck, inappropriately in the butler's opinion, the sundeck having a panoramic view over the dunes, beach and ocean. The body and cordon were gone, the police presence had diminished to desultory searchers at the rose bush. All the same. The family at lunch, those of the family who remained, kept looking towards the distant spot where a sheet had covered Millicent Langley.

Peckover had whipped up a jaunty, for the most part cold lunch out of cans and the challenging odds and ends he found in the fridge. Into the blender had gone canned kidney beans, fava beans, chick peas, tomato paste, and for a more liquid consistency, vinegar, cranberry honey, and the watery remains of a tub of vanilla yoghurt. He had spread slices of frozen white bread with the honey and exposed cream cheese from the neglected back of the fridge, carefully incorporating the greenish parts for colour and interest, and microwaved them. He had cut them in triangles, arranged them round a hill of leftover lamb, criss-crossed the lamb with a lattice of anchovy fillets, and sprinkled the lot with raisins and chopped walnuts. Canned blueberries and burgher's currant bread for dessert.

Now, on the sundeck, they ate their lunch. He had little to do except hover. The talk lacked animation. He heard no revelations.

'So much for the show,' Romaine said, tackling her third

77

honeyed cheese triangle. 'This could have been Glad Rags's year. Everything's so pointless now.'

'Romaine, you ride Glad Rags, you hear? That's what Mom would have wanted.'

Not all she wanted, though, reflected the butler, setting forth with iced, minty tea. She wanted you shot of he who is not one of us, correct? That was yesterday. Today you may sleep easy and with whoever you please. You can inherit *and* keep your lover man. So all's well that perishin' ends well.

Circling, topping up glasses, he observed from the corner of one eye Romaine reaching for another triangle. If she kept this up she'd become the fat lady of the gymkhana circuit.

He sat dialling in a chrysanthemum chair in his butler's room wearing the Marks and Sparks boxer shorts with the London Underground motif. *Zero-one-one* – slow, slow, or something would trip in the machinery and he'd fetch up with the Battersea Dogs' Home – *four-four* – pause – *one* – pause – he didn't have Frank Veal's office number, not without the palaver of unlocking his briefcase – *two-three-zero* – pause – *one-two-one-two*.

Brr-brr.

Crikey! Technology!

It was the Factory too, a saucebox on the switchboard hoping he was having a lovely holiday, and putting you through, Mr Peckover, sir. Five hours difference? The *Standard* would be selling well with the close of play cricket scores.

Frank Veal was rapturously pessimistic on the chances of any Met copper – forget lowly Twitty – flying off to join Our 'Enry sunning himself among the rich and pampered of the Hamptons, no matter Chief Rosko having said it was fine with him. He'd already phoned, endorsing help for the butler. But was he, demanded Veal, to be trusted? Chief Rosko called you by your first name before you'd been introduced. He jiggled his leg like a metronome gone berserk.

'Money well spent,' argued Peckover. 'I've got wounds. It happens again I'll be an 'ospital case and who says it won't? You know what an 'ospital will cost you over here? We'll be wiped out. Questions in Parliament.'

'Aieee!' wept Veal, though whether for Henry in hospital or for the bill Peckover was uncertain. 'You're insured, aren't you?'

'Mrs Coulter should 'ave fixed up something. Ask her.'

'She's not in. She's got a virus.'

'Tell 'er from me she's lucky to 'ave a virus where she is, not 'ere. She 'ad a virus 'ere, she'd 'ave to go on the streets. Listen, just let me 'ave one foot-soldier. This is a messy business and it's not finished. It may only be beginning. After we've sorted it out for them' – best to sound confident – 'they'll be so grateful they'll award us a holiday home on the beach, exclusive for Yard personnel.'

'Ta-ra, Henry. I'll see what I can do.'

He phoned Miriam. She wanted to know about the food, weather, and when he was coming home. She had started cutting out a dress for Mary.

He talked to Sam and Mary. Sam was silent and grudging, having been hauled away from the television. Mary would not stop talking. He understood little of what she was saying but it had to do with Celeste, her best friend, also aged four.

He stood in front of the mirror and combed his hair with his fingers, refraining from examining the wound. Crunchy Clam Platter? Oriental Beef? If he stepped on the Cadillac's gas, and found a shop with frozen food, he could get it done before the Passenger's Seat pow-wow with the big chief.

Could be a lark, the Cadillac. He'd never driven one before.

The driver's seat in cracked whitish leather sighed as Peckover lowered his bulk into it. The Cadillac might not have qualified for a vintage car rally but it wasn't recent. A hundred and seven thousand on the clock. Uncomputerised, no underwater voice barking at him to fasten his seat-belt, but comfy, classy, cared-for, smelling of horse harness, and its engine burping into life first go. He adjusted the rear-view mirror and backed cautiously into the forecourt. They don't make 'em like this any more, he mused. Perhaps they didn't, perhaps they did. He had no idea, but the observation was one he could imagine car freaks making.

A hand was flapping against his driver's window. Behind the hand appeared a contorted, spectacled face, mouthing.

Peckover braked. Instead of troops of electric buttons the door had a handle for winding down the window.

Breathless, Thwaite said, 'Give me a lift? You're going my way?'

'Which way's your way?'

'Which way are you going?'

'The village, a grocery, if I can find one.'

'I'll show you. Great.'

Thwaite scampered round the front of the car and in beside Peckover. He carried a canvas satchel, probably from the same army surplus shop as his shirt.

He said, 'Left through the gates then first right on Sandy Neck.'

Peckover coaxed the car purringly through the gates and on to Tonic Lane.

'Where do I drop you off?'

'Not yet. Take the next right.'

Sandy Neck. So long and straight the end was not to be seen. High hedges, colossal houses, occasional cars, bicyclists in shorts, a scuttling rabbit, stop signs. Thwaite kept looking at his watch.

He said, 'Could you hurry it up?'

'Thirty mile an hour limit, chum. And these signs say Stop.'

'Please.'

'Got a train to catch?'

'How did you know?'

'I didn't. Just an expression, isn't it? 'Ow long 'ave we got?'

'Six minutes. Turn right at the end then on to the lights.'

Peckover wondered if he might be aiding and abetting the escape of a felon. He could hardly have said no to the lift, not if butler and caretaker were to stay best friends and enjoy revealing conversations. If he'd known how far the railway station was he could have tried to time their arrival for the moment the train was pulling out. Bell clanging, whistle throatily whistling, whatever Long Island trains did when departing.

'New York, is it, Tim? Fun and games in the Big A?'

'Possibly.'

Possibly? What kind of an answer was that? Waiting for a gap in the traffic at the end of Sandy Neck cost a minute. To Thwaite, mumbling and gulping, it clearly seemed like half a day. In the traffic flow into the village there was no choice but to belt along at thirty.

80

The light ahead was green and stayed green. Thwaite, on the edge of his seat, gave directions which seemed to avoid a cluttered business street.

'Next right.'

Shops, houses, a restaurant, a spruce white church with a steeple which pierced the blue, a railway bridge. Peckover was enjoying the Cadillac.

'You're a cagey one, Tim. In a pig's eye it's fun and games. I bet it's the Infamy draft. You've got an appointment with a documents expert.'

Thwaite, urging his driver on with bent, pointing arms, palms facing each other as if measuring a trout he had caught, gave a shake of his head, and a nod.

Peckover said, 'In the satchel, is it?'

Thwaite switched on a sickly grin and patted the satchel.

'Gor, let's 'ave a look,' Peckover said.

'Isn't time. Turn right there – no, there! *Here!*'

Peckover swung the car up a slope into the rail station. Here was a one-storey shed, a dozen customers with bags and backpacks, and desultory cars snoozing in the sun. A train, mighty and grimy, was pulling in. A guard in blue hung from a doorway like a circus act.

'Show me when you get back? I like 'istory.'

'All right.'

Peckover parked by the platform.

'You'll be back tonight?'

'Yes. Imagine so. Thanks.'

Thwaite slammed the door and bolted for the train.

Cheeky bugger never had the least intention of showing me where I get the Chunky Clam Whatsit, Peckover reflected.

Alone with coffee and remnants of salad in a booth for two, Gene Rosko lit his pipe and watched the door. The place was not ideal. Two acquaintances had already asked him how he was doing, how the wife and kids were. Another would have left the bar to join him had he been invited. A police chief was going to be known to someone wherever he sat and waited. The plus for this place was that the limey shouldn't have any problem finding it.

81

Here he was now with his London fog complexion, out of the sun and into the gloom, peering and squinting. Frank Veal's choice for butler may have been shrewd but there was no certainty of it so far. A butler who was hardly off the plane before he was letting himself be slapped around on the dunes didn't promise well.

The fellow's face was practically phosphorescent. No tie, but a hat, for pity's sake, and a jacket. A lightweight jacket, but all the same. Was he expecting frost? No one was going to confuse him with the vacation hordes parading outside along Lot's Lane in their shades and bracelets and knee-length shorts and doeskin moccasins. He looked like a London cop masquerading as a butler on his afternoon off.

Chief Rosko offered, 'Beer? Coffee?'

'Tea. And a glass of water. A jug of it.' Peckover set his hat down beside the ketchup. 'It's Dante's inferno out there. Abandon hope all ye. Dunno where I've parked the Cadillac but there's a fire plug in case it goes up in flames.'

'We'd better move it.'

'I jest. Anyway, the Langleys get a ticket, Sergeant De Voto can fix it for them.'

'Vito's a good cop. Forgive him his trespasses, Henry. You want him on your side.'

'I want nothing to do with him. I'm an intruder and a bleedin' foreigner, that's Vito's opinion. Sooner I'm gone 'ome, happier he'll be.'

'Like I feel about the FBI. If you see me with the FBI and I'm coming to the boil, help me out, cause a diversion. Announce drinks on the patio.'

'The FBI are here?'

'On their way.'

'Thought they were kidnapping and bank robbery. 'Igh treason. Federal stuff.'

'Fraud against the government is federal stuff. Faking a document showing Roosevelt allowed the Japs to hit Pearl Harbor is federal.' Rosko put down his pipe and selected a tomato segment from his salad bowl. 'So what've we got?'

One, Peckover said, one of them kept a gun under his shirts in his bedroom. He didn't know which one but someone who read guides to tax shelters, so perhaps Rudy, the financier, except as a bankrupt financier he'd hardly be excited by tax shelters. Perhaps he was a dreamer.

Two, Rudy's missus, Romaine, she was having an affair with someone unsuitable her mother had insisted she finish with, else not a penny.

Three, could be it wasn't Romaine, might be Gloria. Siblings' voices could sound similar and he'd heard it through a door. But one of the guests had written a letter saying it was Romaine. The guest should be found and questioned.

Four, he had talked with Thwaite. Also had just dropped him off to catch a train for New York City. Thwaite was in an almighty hurry and had a satchel with the Infamy draft in it.

'You saw it?'

'No. I don't believe the document was in his satchel. I suggested it was and he agreed. Ask me, what's in his satchel is his lunch.'

'Thwaite is unreliable. He told me he'd be in his apartment or at the college. And he saw you on the dunes, or saw someone.'

'Five,' Peckover said. 'Back to Vito. I just thought of this one. Did you see the cartoon somewhere where a librarian is recommending a book, 'olding it up and saying, "This is the one with the surprise ending where the policeman did it."?'

The Chief laughed. 'If you want to stick Vito with this, go ahead. We're overdue for some infighting and amusement at headquarters.'

The waitress had brought water, which Peckover gulped, and hot water with a tea-bag in it. He lifted, lowered and swung the tea-bag's string.

'That's about it,' he said. 'Serve from the left, clear from the right. Got myself assaulted on the dunes. I could try you on 'ow President Roosevelt let Pearl 'Arbor be attacked but the truth is I 'aven't really grasped it. What would be nice would be to see this draft speech about the day which will live in infamy. It's going to rewrite history, so Thwaite says. Nice to 'ave it authenticated or thrown out, one or the other. Once we know, we might be a step closer to a motive for two murders. What've you got for me?'

'Millicent Langley may have been poisoned or she could have died from a broken neck. She didn't drown. We'll know soon. We probably know already, or the doc does. You brought her cocoa last night?'

'Blimey.'

'Yes?'

'I killed 'er with cocoa?'

A man in a denim shirt with a row of pens in the breast pocket slowed as he passed the booth and said, 'How's it going, Chief?'

Rosko said, 'Good. How're you?'

The man said over his shoulder, 'Bring on winter. This summer crowd's the worst yet.'

Rosko told Peckover, 'This summer crowd gives that bozo his living. He spends the winter in Florida at the racetrack. Drink your tea. Let's go.' He leaned from the booth, seeking the waitress.

'Wouldn't be surprised if the cocoa killed 'er,' Peckover said. 'Instant ptomaine. Looked to me to 'ave been in the cupboard since before Pearl 'Arbor. But I didn't break 'er neck. Tell you the truth, er – Gene' – he was sooner or later going to have to call the bloke by his name, or Chief, and Gene was easier than Chief, which made him think of Sitting Bull – 'you have me at a disadvantage. I'm not suggesting your medical man isn't up to his chin in qualifications but it shouldn't take much to know if someone's dead from cocoa or if it was a broken neck.'

'She had a broken neck, broken back, two broken legs, and a broken skull, and none of it has to be how she died. You put the cocoa down outside her room?'

'Who told you?'

'Romaine. It was Romaine you heard talking with her mother. Then you left?'

'Then I left. All this is hypothesis and a bit of a waste of time until we get the report. D'you have the cuppa cocoa, what's left of it?'

'No.'

'Someone could have sneaked rat poison in after I'd gone. Romaine might have. Spoonful of weedkiller. What I've seen, the lawns, and that bit of a copse beyond the swimming pool, the garden shed must be stacked to the roof with that sort of stuff.'

'It's padlocked.'

'But everyone will know where the key is. There'll likely be a murderous anti-tick spray against whatsit – Lyme disease. Did Lou and Millicent spray?'

'Easy to find out. I spray, Jesus, do I, my place, and we've no woods in a mile. Spent a fortune on the muck. But I'm paranoid.'

'Frank Veal told me about your wife. I'm sorry.'

'One of those things. It comes and goes. But it's been three years.'

Rosko fell silent. He gazed at a patch on the table where there was nothing to gaze at. His head nodded mildly and rhythmically as if he were not forty but eighty.

Peckover said, 'We've searched for this cup?'

'It wasn't in Millicent's room, and there's one missing from the set, and a saucer. We're searching.'

'Keep searching. Outside, the garbage, the roadside ten miles away, Thwaite's place. We're looking for Crown Derby with silver filigree from a matching set of twelve.'

'Romaine told us. Was the cocoa in a jar, can, or what?'

'Can.'

'What did you do with it?'

'Put it back.' Peckover considered. 'Unless I left it by the stove. But I wouldn't, probably. What else would I do with it?'

'I don't know, Henry. It's not in the kitchen. Vito's had every can and packet out and opened and inventoried.'

'We're not shining, are we?'

'Before I say anything else, let me say this.' Dunehampton's Chief of Police regarded his London colleague with a degree of intensity, as if about to tell him interest rates had risen and his mortgage payment was overdue. 'It's good to have you here, Henry. Say hello to Frank Veal for me next time you check in.' A bill alighted and Rosko scooped it up. He leaned forward across the table, eyes which had been cloudy on the subject of ticks now glitteringly lustful. 'While you're here, try the clams. And scallops. And swordfish, oh boy. You're doing good, Henry. Loosen up. Trust Vito. Enjoy Dunehampton. It's summer. People pay an arm and a leg to be out here in the summer. Fridays they suffer for ever on the expressway, the world's longest parking lot. Don't forget your hat.'

EIGHT

Walking, weaving, separating from Peckover, rejoining him on the other side of gaudy, sidewalk-hogging clumps of summer people in shorts and lurid tank-tops who were going nowhere, were simply there, licking ice-cream cones and staring in shop windows, Rosko said, 'This is calm.'

'I can see it is.'

'They're all at the beach. You should be here on a grey day. They walk up and down Lot's Lane and Main Street hoping something will happen but it never does. They might go into a gallery but they come right out again. If there's a Stephen Spielberg matinée, that's the Promised Land. Otherwise there's nothing to do here except walk up and down and look and buy things.'

'I'm looking. There's nothing to buy.'

'What's wrong with butterflies?'

They stopped at a window displaying dead, bright butterflies with a six-inch wingspan trapped in slabs of something transparent. The window and the walls and counters behind it held nothing except framed butterflies.

Peckover said, 'What do they do when the shops shut?'

'Screw around, have barbecues. Who knows? The literati – your kind' – Chief Rosko glanced at the Bard of the Yard for a reaction but there was none – 'they read *Moby-Dick* aloud, non-stop round the clock, a chapter each. Takes them about a day and a half. If you need to read *Moby-Dick* it's as good a way as any.'

Peckover cringed from the fluorescent pinks and marsh-gas greens of the shirts and slacks worn by some of the older men idling with their wives along Lot's Lane. If they were strays from the golf course, their object there would be not so much to strike a little white ball into a hole as to cause a fit in the opposition, thereby winning by default. He looked in a window selling ethnic baskets. The most exclusive windows had very little to sell and ventured no prices. In one window were two women's shoes, when you spotted them, positioned among decks and sawn-off stairways resembling a set for the Ziegfeld Follies. Kool Kitchen had a veined marble table and on it, labelled, or Peckover would not have known what they were, a corn teaser, a meat stomper, and a mushroom brush. He wondered if Dunehampton had anywhere you could buy something you might want, like aspirin.

'The life span of some of these stores is about the same as one of those butterflies,' Rosko said. 'Come back next year, there'll be new ones with identical stuff. Same difference.'

What had Rosko meant, telling him to loosen up? Peckover believed himself to be fairly relaxed. He may not have been relaxed when they had met on the beach but he'd been Jarvis then. Being Jarvis was quite taxing.

'Police station,' said tour-guide Rosko, pointing through traffic to a columned acropolis wedged between boutiques. 'Where no visiting butler would be expected to visit, okay? Unless the phone's knocked out by a hurricane, you don't visit.'

'There's going to be a hurricane?'

'A big one named Doris left the Gulf and is coming north but it'll probably blow itself out over the Atlantic. You never know, though. That's the museum, part of it.' He pointed to a shack. 'It was built as a goldsmith's in 1650, thirty years after the *Mayflower*. I know that's not old by your standards.'

Fifty years was old by Peckover's standards. Every Yank he had ever met abased himself for not being able to offer Hadrian's Wall or Reims Cathedral. He steered Rosko along an alley and into a parking lot the size of Wembley Stadium, with trees. Every city in Europe would have swapped its cathedral for free parking such as this, or any parking. The sooner the better too. Most of the cathedrals were crumbling into a fine powder.

He had failed to find a space beneath a tree. If the hurricane didn't blow itself out over the Atlantic he would have to remember to stay clear of trees. He wouldn't want to return Lou's Cadillac with a maple log stuck through its roof. The policemen heaved

87

themselves on to scorching leather, closed the doors, and wound down the windows.

Peckover said, 'Tim Thwaite killed Lou to keep him from changing his mind about the codicil. Our prof was afraid sooner or later Lou would hear about his previous forgery, if forgery is what it was, and his brush with the law. Stop me any time. I'm trying to get my bearings.'

'Go on.'

'When I say he killed him, he may have hired someone. So anyway, Lou's dead. Thwaite may have forged a Roosevelt paper which could make his reputation, bring him a bundle on the bestseller list, and he's got rid of the one big risk – Lou. Flushed with success – you 'ave to admit he's not doing badly – he kills Millicent.'

A truck with an apricot-coloured retriever panting in the back crawled by in search of a slot.

'I was 'oping you might have a thought on that.'

'He was fed up with her holding up the will. He wants Ahoy and he wants it now.'

'Money's in this, doesn't take genius to see that, but is it all? Is it even in first place? You 'aven't mentioned the 'uman heart. What about passion?'

'Whose passion?'

'We're creating?'

'What's to lose?'

'Millicent Langley tells Romaine to finish her nonsense with a person unknown. Unknown to us, that's to say. Suppose the person is Thwaite. He qualifies as not being one of them. He's their caretaker, sort of equivalent to Lady Chatterley's gamekeeper but with brains in place of brawn. I wouldn't imagine brains impress the Langleys too much, not Thwaite's sort of brains. He reads books and he doesn't play the stock market or ride horses. He has enough of a problem riding a bike. Why wouldn't he want money? Everybody wants money. If he 'ad money he could get shot of the bike and buy a Rolls. No reason he wouldn't be a fortune hunter. You don't 'ave to ride an 'orse and wear a tricorn to score as a fortune hunter. My guess is there could be quite a few in a fancy place like Dunehampton. Thwaite started wooing Romaine before 'e knew 'e would inherit Ahoy. Perhaps he fell in love, and she with him.

'Worst about Thwaite, though, far as Millicent Langley was concerned, he's a foreigner. There may be foreigners less suitable than Brits but it's not as if 'e talks like the Queen or could get them tickets to 'er garden parties. He's one of the pointless Brits. Thwaite knows all this. He also knows that what counts is Romaine's passion for him and 'ow it's going to stand up under family pressure, meaning Mummy's pressure. If you're thinking this is fairyland, that a sophisticated riding-school lady like Romaine wouldn't look twice at a sweaty twit like Thwaite, how would we know? She's at a tricky age, got a useless 'usband, and Thwaite's there, available, other side of the driveway, in a flat with mirrors and a red rug. She might 'ave the notion that being English and a scholar are exotic. All we know, he's a snarling Yorkshire terrier in bed, and her Rudy's a flop. Bleedin' financier and 'e's lost his finances. Easy to believe she's 'ad it up to the eyeballs with him. Perhaps Romaine and Thwaite were talking marriage. You're not happy.'

'I'm listening.'

'I 'aven't a glimmer if his passion for money is more or less than his passion for Romaine. Doesn't matter. When she phones 'im last night with the bad news, Mummy's ultimatum, what he sees is that she stands to lose her money if she stays with him.'

'He's going to inherit Ahoy. What's he want Romaine's money for?'

'He's greedy. And he can't be sure he'll get Ahoy. Mummy's against it and Mummy has heavyweight lawyers. All he's sure of is if Romaine caves in to Mummy he loses her and her money, both. Not to be theatrical about it but Mummy's ultimatum is Mummy's death warrant. Thwaite sneaks into Ahoy—'

'The alarm being conveniently inoperative.'

'The alarm, mate, is raring to go and Thwaite is the caretaker. He has keys to the house and when he gets through the door he has ten seconds to punch the code on the buttons on the wall and keep the thing from wailing. He's done it a hundred times, all winter, every time he goes in to water the spiderwort. He goes upstairs, spikes the old girl's cocoa with concentrate of drain-opener, and skulks around while she takes it to bed and gets dead, or groggy.

The rest of the household are asleep. He's chancing his arm but if anyone challenges 'im he saw someone round the side of the house, thought he did, and came to investigate like a dutiful caretaker. He didn't rouse the 'ousehold because he might've been mistaken and didn't want to spread anxiety. He goes in to Millicent, who's finished 'er cocoa, thoroughly enjoyed it, and is comatose, and drops 'er out of the window. If she wasn't dead before, she is now. He can't carry 'er out of the house because now that would be embarrassing if he met anyone, and what's more, Thwaite isn't your Mr Anabolic Steroid Man of the Year. Lifting the two-volume *Oxford English Dictionary* is his limit. On the other hand, desperation giving him the strength of two, he manages to drag 'er across the dunes and beach and into the ocean. Questions?'

Rosko grinned. 'I wouldn't know where to start.'

Peckover said, 'It gets better. Why, you are about to ask, into the ocean? Thwaite is scholarly but he has gaps, such as medical matters. Everyone else knows the simplest thing in the world is to tell if drowning is the cause of death. Not our Tim. Too bad he's ignorant and doesn't know it but he wants Millicent's death to look like suicide, and drowning is how. Not an overdose, or jumping from 'er window, but striding like a bride into the embrace of the sempiternal deep, Neptune's kingdom. You can see why it made sense to him. Millicent Langley lived by the sea— '

'Like Puff the Magic Dragon.'

'Who?'

'Go on.'

'The sea was 'er passion. It wasn't Lou's, 'e was a green grass man, which was his undoing, but Millicent breathed the sea, she still swam in it at nearly eighty – Joop said she did – and if ever a time came she'd had enough of this mortal coil, the sea's where she'd choose to shuffle it off. So surmised Thwaite. She was old, Lou was gone, Romaine was a pest, who knew what else – does anyone really *enjoy* Gloria's paintings? – so it's plausible she may 'ave wanted to bow out. He couldn't strangle 'er, cut 'er throat, let it be thought she'd been murdered, because apart from the police and questions, what about Romaine? If her mother had been murdered and she thought her exotic lover knew anything

90

about it, it'd be finished between them. You don't kill your girl-friend's mother. Inventive enough for you?'

'I didn't say that.'

'Thought I'd detected a note of scepticism. Who's Puff?'

'You were getting carried away.'

'It's the nature of we of the literati. Let the earthbound dust for prints and make their door-to-door enquiries. What we should be doing right now rather than sitting 'ere.'

'Vito has seventeen men on this and he's getting more from the county. I may be about to surprise you, Henry, but I like the passion and money motivation.'

'You do?'

'It's the nuts and bolts of it that don't work. I don't have to tell you. Thwaite skulks around waiting for the drain-opener to take effect? In Ahoy, the caretaker, at midnight? Damn right he's taking a chance. The cocoa was outside Mrs Langley's door, where you put it, but Romaine, when she leaves to call Thwaite about her mother's ultimatum, she steps over it? She doesn't take it in to her? Mrs Langley doesn't collect it either, not yet. She waits, what, maybe an hour later, until Romaine's talked to Thwaite, and he's come in and topped it up, and it's cold, but she brings it to bed and drinks it anyway? Thwaite finds the cocoa outside her room and just happens to have poison in his pocket? Or has Romaine told him the butler's brought cocoa? Why would she say that? It's hard to know where to begin. I could buy Thwaite. But I can tell you everyone's not going to.'

'Sergeant De Voto?'

'He's going to look first at the people living and sleeping in Ahoy, people who can go up and down the stairs without being noticed. Wouldn't you? He won't look too closely at Gloria and Romaine. Matricide's a tough one. That leaves four men. The two husbands, the cook, and you. Six if we include the departed guests.'

'And a dog. Prune barks at strangers.'

'That's okay. Thwaite is no stranger. Prune? What kind of dog?'

'Dachshund. Stay out of 'er way.'

'I'm out of everyone's way for the next couple of days. The Vice-President's going to be at Beachport. What I'm saying, four

91

men in Ahoy, six with the guests, and the circumstantial evidence points one way.'

'That had crossed my mind.'

'Vito is going to want to know more about that cocoa. Don't get rattled if he wants to search your room. He'll certainly want to hear more about your phantom assailant – that's what he's calling him, the phantom of the dunes. My advice would be not to be adamant he was Thwaite. You said it yourself, Thwaite's limit is lifting a dictionary.'

'I said desperation might give 'im the strength of two.'

'You believe it was Thwaite?'

'Gawd, I dunno. Yes, might've been. Feet – Vito – he's amazing. I'm a London bobby. Never 'eard of these Langleys before last week. I get here yesterday. Does he believe I killed Mrs Langley?'

'He'd like to,' Rosko said, and he laughed, a triplet down the scale, two crotchets and a minim – d, c, b-flat – an octave higher than his speaking baritone, and to Peckover's ear quite melodious, though he could not see what was funny. 'Listen,' Rosko said, 'ask him about the Yankees. He's a Yankee fanatic. Only problem, he could insist on taking you to Yankee Stadium.'

'Football?'

'Don't play innocent, Henry. The New York Yankees. "One, two, three strikes you're out, at the old ball game."'

'Until we get to the ball game he's not going to listen to me, so before you go off to take care of your Vice-President you might suggest to 'im it'd be nice to have that Pearl 'Arbor document, if he and his lads get a moment, and to line up an 'andwriting expert. Line up a few because I've known some and they don't always agree, same as doctors. My opinion, what it's worth, the forgery angle is the key. If these White House papers are the real thing we're probably going to have to forget Thwaite.'

'Henry, take it easy. Believe me, Vito's a pro. How's the butling? Think you'll get an ode out of all this? What rhymes with butling?'

'Scuttling. What we butlers never do. We step, we tread, we sail like galleons on the boundless main, but scuttle, never.'

'Drop me off at the top of Lot's Lane, will you? Hang a left past the ice-cream parlour – see it?'

'You want to watch if I drive on the right, right?'

* * *

Alone, driving on the right at between nought and ten miles an hour, there being no choice in the stop-start August traffic, Peckover passed banks which bore as much resemblance to the jailhouse Barclays and NatWests on any British High Street as a dollar bill to a baron of beef. These banks stood on enchanted lawns, their architecture varying from classical Greece to log cabin. He would not have guessed they were banks had they not said so. Bank of Dunehampton. Rogue Harbour Savings and Loan. Indeed, the Marine Maritime was perhaps not a bank but a fish restaurant.

The Cadillac hummed along sweetly. Sam and Mary could have driven it, given a few cushions. Miriam would have remarked on the faintly fruity, horsey smell, as if apples had been bought, forgotten, and lay rotting under the seat, but the smell being less potent now Rosko had left, he supposed it was the fellow's cologne. At a delay at a crossing he looked under the seat for apples, found a dime, and confiscated it. On the crossing a teenage traffic warden in a brown uniform beckoned and halted the traffic, as though the crossing in itself were not enough, and these pedestrians were not adult members of the summer zoo, but helpless children.

If he carried on through the lights at the end of the street he would be out of the shopping area and back in *House and Garden* country. In a few minutes he would be at Ahoy. He saw little profit and no pleasure in that. He doubted he was being missed, unless by Feet. Snooping was out. Too chancy at this time of day.

The best hope was that tonight Thwaite would be back, feeding Puddy Tat, and available for conversation. At least at Ahoy there was cold water to drink. A cooling bath.

He would compromise. Tool around for half an hour getting the gestalt of Dunehampton. Perhaps he would spot a celebrity. He still had to pick up the frozen dinners. Then to Ahoy for a bath, the black tie and butling costume, and his matchless services made visible and available to all. 'Would sir require a further slug of Beefeater in his vermouth or are we happy to wait sixty seconds?' He slowed behind a car signalling left and followed it into a leafy side-street lined with alternating maple trees and No Parking signs. A dog's heaven. The car in front swung into a parking lot.

The street was short, residential, its lawns emerald where there

93

were sprinklers, tawny elsewhere. Compared with Tonic Lane the houses were for the failed and exploited. Four bedrooms at most. The house he was passing was barely visible behind maples and a barrage of rhododendrons. Gloria Langley was walking along its path towards a front door of frosted-glass ugliness. On the shingling beside the door were a bell and what looked like – had looked like, he had passed it – a plaque.

A funeral director? Priest? Hairdresser?

He pulled over on to the verge and was hooted at by a car behind. 'Piss off,' Peckover said, and the car behind did so, hooting again as it accelerated past him.

If the plaque said merely Beware of the Dog, what was Gloria doing slumming on this side of the tracks?

His job was to know such things. From such trivia sprouteth yet greater trivia, trivial beyond understanding. He waited for a gap in the cars behind, reversed, and drove into the parking lot.

NINE

The plaque beside the frosted-glass door was not brass but it was a formidable semblance in some form of poly-plastic which echoed hollowly when Peckover tapped it with a knuckle.

Helga d'Albanese Prettyman, BA. Polarity. Shiatsu. Crystals. Channelling. Mon–Fri 3–5 p.m. By appointment: 282–6772.

She was not a workhorse. What did she do mornings, evenings, and weekends, Ms Prettyman? Perhaps her services so exhausted her she had to lie down a great deal. Channelling he had read about somewhere, in *Time* perhaps, in the waiting-room during the weeks he'd had four molars crowned. In California, where channelling had started, where everything started, it was long out of date, superseded by electro-magnetic hats which pumped psychic force into the brain. Your hat was connected to a generator which cost roughly the same as a missile system, or the fee for receiving psychic force through your electro-magnetic hat.

No sign of Gloria. She was inside having her polarity attended to. Peckover had decided he would retreat, leave her to it, when the frosted glass flew open.

'Are you for channelling?'

A zealot. Her springy white hair stood upright as if shocked. Her eyeglasses had blindingly orange rims. She was orange, white, intense, and sixtyish, in a Madras cotton gown and jogging shoes. A eurhythmic channeller? An astrologist with bad feet? She would fairly certainly be a vegetarian, nuclear disarmer, and pro-choice. He had not known the breed existed outside certain pockets of Devon, Saffron Walden, and York but evidently it knew no frontiers. In England her husband would be an educationist in sandals. Their six children would be loonier than the parents. They would all eat raw vegetables off wobbly pottery they had

95

hand-thrown in their own kiln, play unusual stringed instruments, and recycle everything they could lay their hands on.

'You're new, aren't you? Hurry, we're just starting.' She pulled him by the sleeve into a cramped hallway and closed the door. 'Give me your hat.'

She took his hat. He would need to remember it when the moment came to flee.

'Sign in here.'

She steered him to a pen and a ledger on a table. Beside the ledger were a credit card machine and an open cigar box holding cheques and dollars. The hall was gloomy in spite of the frosted glass. Where was his hat? She had already put it somewhere for recycling.

'It's thirty dollars.'

'Ah, sorry, a misunderstanding,' Peckover explained. 'You see, truth is, I wasn't— '

'Twenty. You're entitled to our special introductory offer. Since you've missed the beginning.'

The previous entry in the ledger was Gloria Benjamin, Dunehampton. Underneath, Peckover wrote H. Peck before he remembered who he was. He felt flustered and harried. He had no wish to be channelled and he doubted it would be to his advantage if he were spotted by Gloria peeping out from behind the curtain of the shiatsu parlour, prone on a stretcher, clad in a white gown, her face caked with mud and shiatsu. After H. Peck he hastily added, Dunehampton, then in a different hand, holding the pen in a fist as some left-handers do, entered, Sydney Jarvis, Dunehampton. He brought out his wallet and tossed into the kitty forty dollars from the pristine assortment presented to him by Frank Veal, like Monopoly money from an unused game. The orange and white vegetarian towed him along a corridor. She put her ear to a door, a finger to her lips, and said, 'It's the overture. You've only missed the breathing. Vivaldi, wouldn't you say?' She opened the door and propelled him into a densely inhabited living-room.

A sixties scent of smouldering joss-stick hung in the air. Furniture had been pushed back against the walls to make space for a score of channellers, if that was what they were. They sat cross-legged on the floor in two circles. Most had their eyes shut.

Those with their eyes open turned their heads to observe him. He hadn't missed the breathing, or not all of it, because someone was chanting, 'Breathe, breathe.' A Mata Hari brunette with glistening lipstick and glossy hair cut in a fringe a mere millimetre above her eyebrows stood between the circles, her arms raised as if in surrender. Her feet were bare. She wore slacks, a white blouse, and multiple bangles.

'I am that, that I am, I am,' she intoned. 'Breathe, breathe. The I is a swinging door which moves when we inhale, when we exhale.'

'Sit,' hissed the vegetarian woman who had taken his hat and his money. 'Do you have your question ready?'

Gloria was sitting with closed eyes in the nearer circle. Peckover tiptoed to the further circle. Not wanting to wake anyone up, he halted between two women who had their eyes open, though he could not be absolutely sure about the one in the sunglasses. Most of the customers were women. These two looked up at him, the one in sunglasses smiling, the other not. They made room and he sat and crossed his legs. Everyone was going to have to hold hands at some point, he was sure of it.

The music was Vivaldi by an orchestra of massed strings.

'Kufu, it is I, thy channel,' the woman with bangles intoned through the violins. 'We are swinging doors and I am ready for thy light. Dost thou hear me, O little one, at play on thy Tibetan hillside thirty-five thousand years ago?'

'I shall ask about citrus fruit juice futures, and maybe interest rates,' whispered the friendly woman on his left, her mouth to his ear.

She was plump, her fingers were weighted with rings, and the tortoiseshell rims of her sunglasses swept upwards to a point. Peckover had never understood why people wore sunglasses indoors, unless their eyes were bloodshot or in some way repellent. She smelled of peppermint. Would he have to hold her hand? He would do it.

'She hates my questions,' the woman whispered. 'She likes questions about peace and light and dead husbands but I've paid my money and she knows it. Last session I asked about Unicorp and she was furious, she'd have liked to have stuffed her crystals up my you-know-where, but she communicated with Kufu and

97

he said go ahead with Unicorp. D'you know next day they were up one-and-a-quarter?'

Peckover tried to look genial while saying 'Sssh.' The only question he could think of was what was he doing here? Not here on planet earth but here in this room, being a swinging door, and waiting for Kufu. Gloria in the other circle had her back to him. If she hadn't seen him already she would when it was over and they got up to thank Kufu, hold hands, and sing the channelling song.

If he were still here. He could tiptoe out anytime. He could trample out like a water buffalo, though he would haul his jacket up to hide his face. He couldn't see he was committing an offence which might get him sacked from Ahoy, not here, a classless society. Still, Gloria would be Queen of Ahoy now, with power of dismissal, and he knew nothing about her. She might take umbrage at sharing a channelling session with the butler.

The woman calling on Kufu he assumed to be Helga d'Albanese Prettyman. Her vegetarian doorkeeper, the orange and white lady, was stalking about, lighting more incense, lowering the volume on the tape recorder, then raising it. She was a distraction, Peckover considered, in what surely ought to have an atmosphere of reverential quiet. He thought of Catholic cathedrals in France and Italy where families would eat and chatter and mill about and bring their dogs to weddings.

'Kufu is ready,' announced Ms Prettyman. She lowered her arms to her sides, whereupon the bangles clattered to her wrists and glittered there. Keeping her eyes shut, she pointed at Gloria's circle. 'Here is our eastern vortex. In the east all things begin and have begun and the light is a living radiance. First question?'

'Where's my cat?' A scrubbed Rotarian, perhaps the president of Coca-Cola on his Dunehampton holidays, had raised his hand. 'He's been gone three weeks.'

'Gone where, sir?'

'Dammit, that's the question.'

'From where? Gone whence? Kufu hears. He requires your address and a full description of the cat.'

'Neutered male, tabby, six years old. Felix. I'm across from the helicopter pad on Wyandanch, the house with the spires.' He kept his hand aloft as if voting for a salary increase. 'Greatest little fella in the world.' He began to weep.

Ms Prettyman started to tremble. Her eyelids fluttered then sealed shut. 'Felix is at an address on West Ocean Drive,' she said in a throttled tremolo. 'One of the even numbers past the golf course. He is rejecting Miaou Seafood Delight. Next?'

Peckover thought Ms Prettyman should rest before taking on another question. The tremors had barely subsided.

'Does Kufu recommend I keep on with the Tucson Acid Diet,' asked a woman in a silk headscarf, 'or can I switch to the one in *Good Housekeeping* where you eat like banquets one day but the next two you fast, nothing, only water?'

Ms Prettyman began to shake again. The bangles jangled. Her face was becoming shiny from effort.

'Stay with Tucson. Next?'

The next two questions were about departed relatives, though not from Gloria. They received answers which may have given comfort but in Peckover's opinion were barely adequate. One of the departed had attained ultra-consciousness on another plane but was maintaining an active interest in life on this plane. The departed brother of the other questioner was reincarnated as a squirrel in a wood in Tasmania and living off beech nuts.

A man asked, 'Where can I find a parking place, say within three blocks of West Eighty-Second Street and Seventh, weekdays?'

'She's not going to like that,' Peckover's neighbour whispered in his ear. 'Parking questions unsettle Kufu's aura.'

'Sssh,' said Peckover.

His neighbour was right, though. This time Ms Prettyman was not suffering convulsions. Her trance was contemplative.

Peckover's neighbour whispered, 'It's always New Yorkers who ask about parking. She told us. She's going back to California where she gets real why questions. Why are we put on this earth? Why did my husband leave me? She's been asked plain Why?'

'Kufu says,' said Ms Prettyman 'Seventy-Ninth Street.'

'She made it up,' whispered Peckover's neighbour. 'She makes up answers to parking questions.'

'Sssh.'

'Next?'

'My mother, Millicent Langley' – Gloria speaking – 'do you – is she – can you give me news?'

'She is on another plane?'

'Yes.'

Peckover had an image of Millicent Langley travelling not on a Pan Am plane, as anticipated, but by KLM. The tremors had started, a shaking first of the head, fringe flapping, then the shoulders, then arms, causing a clanking of bangles, and finally hips and legs. Voodoo, thought Peckover. A good question, though, the best to date.

'Millicent regrets she did not say goodbye,' Ms Prettyman shudderingly intoned. 'She leaves behind unfinished business. She wishes you to continue channelling and stay in touch. Mistrust one who is close to you. Your mother's harmonious integration is not yet but will be in time on the plane where there is no time. Next?'

Mischievous gibberish, Peckover thought. Demand your money back, Gloria. Damn right she wants you to carry on channelling. She needs the fare for California.

The channel was answering a question about weather prospects. Yes, there would be precipitation. No, there would be no hurricane.

'Are interest rates going to rise in the fourth quarter and what about the New Year?'

It was his neighbour. Question-time from the western vortex. What had happened to citrus fruit juice futures? Ms Prettyman began to shake but not violently. Peckover could not believe that Kufu, little Cro-Magnon boy on his Tibetan hillside, would be any more excited by interest rates than by parking places. On the other hand, Ms Prettyman was rabbiting on about deficits and balances as if she had been boning up from the business pages, as perhaps she had. She would have come to expect Wall Street questions from her Dunehampton customers.

'Next?'

'Where is the cook?'

Why not? He had paid his money. All the same, his voice alarmed him. He had not intended this. Equally astonished, Gloria Langley had turned her head and was staring at him.

'The cook,' echoed Ms Prettyman.

'He's on this plane,' Peckover said helpfully. 'Far as anyone knows.'

'Perhaps yes, perhaps no.' The convulsions had begun. 'Kufu requires the name.'

'Joop. A good cook, as cooks go, and as cooks go' – Why didn't he belt up? Gloria was not the only one watching him – 'he went.'

'He is on a journey. You will not find him at his domicile.'

He knew that. The convulsions were less acute than for questions on the departed but more violent than for parking spaces.

'The first stage of the journey is a great city,' intoned Ms Prettyman, clanking. 'I see New York. The second stage will take him beyond. Far beyond. Kufu is disturbed.' She was subsiding. 'Next?'

Pretty damn thin. She had done better with the cat than she had with Joop. Someone was asking about her husband's gambling problem. The wife's problem was that her husband lost, Kufu observed through trembling Ms Prettyman. If he won there would be no problem. The answer lay in polarity and calming of the spirit. Next? More questions and convulsions followed. Then everyone held hands and did nothing for a while except breathe, allowing 'blank knowingness', as Ms Prettyman termed it, to permeate. The beringed fingers of the neighbour who had wanted to know about interest rates squeezed his hand. Mounted topazes and lapis lazuli bored into his flesh. Did she know she was causing him pain? He would have liked to have delivered a karate chop to her wrist – '*Haagh!*' – but to have done so would have required extracting his other hand from the hand of his blameless neighbour on his right, which would have been ungallant. The orange and white doorperson came back into the room and switched off the music. Everyone stood up and milled and chattered.

'I'm going to buy you a drink,' the neighbour with the rings and cruel sunglasses told him. 'I'm Crescent Rump.'

Peckover was not surprised. Her immigrant grandfather would have been Rumplemeyer and he had shortened it. Rump was possibly preferable to Rumple. Peckover would have stayed with Rumplemeyer. He pleaded a pressing engagement, touched her arm to show how much he had enjoyed channelling with her, and dodged from the room.

101

He remembered his hat. Outside he raised it to Gloria Langley. Evading her would not have been difficult but to what purpose?

'A most agreeable surprise, modom.'

'Dumbfounding.'

'We were not apprised that you are of the channelling persuasion.'

She was a moment taking this in. She said, 'You channel in England?'

'You will be familiar with the English Channel?' He smiled inanely. 'We channel and we tunnel, regardless of cost. Jesting apart, while the nomenclature differs, the substance is similar, or should we say, hardly the substance' – Peckover gave a light laugh – 'more the ectoplasm.' He believed he was losing her. 'We have an aunt who is a medium. In Shropshire.' He had three aunts, in their seventies, all living in Bethnal Green. They attended bingo but not, as far as he knew, seances. 'We are pleased your mother's harmonious integration is not in question, rest her soul, yet confess to disappointment with what we can only regard as vagueness on Kufu's part. Unfinished business? Mistrust one who is close to you? Whomever can he be thinking of?'

Of who can he be thinking? Of whomever can he or it thinking be? The Jarvis butlerbabble was a hell of a strain.

Escorting Gloria across the street, Peckover took her arm, and immediately released it. Mr Butterwick had said nothing about escorting your employer across the road but chances were you didn't hold her, not if she were able-bodied with her capacities intact and she had sturdy gams.

If she were going to sack him, now seemed as good a time as any.

She said, 'What on earth possessed you to come channelling to find Joop? Surely you'll manage. He's not that great a loss.'

'That is so, modom, and we had not intended the question. We had thought to enquire after your late, sorely missed mother. As your question pre-empted us, we were left considering what else we might usefully ask.'

'Jarvis, I'm touched. Thank you.' She had halted in the entrance to the parking lot. 'Tonight I will help you in the kitchen. The Reverend Roberts and his wife will be with us. Mrs Roberts is extremely keen on omelettes. We'll still need some frozen dinners so be sure to pick up enough.'

She glided away into the parking lot. Peckover walked briskly along the street. He would give her a couple of minutes to clear off then scurry back and clear off himself. The parking lot had looked filled and active and nothing was to be won by butler and milady reversing into each other.

'Mr Jarvis, can I give you a ride?' Crescent Rump drew alongside in a Mercedes. 'It is Jarvis, is it – Sydney Jarvis, Dunehampton?'

'Jarvis, correct.' She had done her research. He raised his hat an inch and resettled it. 'Thanks anyway. I have a car.'

'You're British, aren't you?'

'Ha, you guessed.' He beamed and raised his hat in farewell. 'Have to be toddling along.' Pip-pip, old girl. 'Charmed to 'ave met you.'

'On vacation?'

'Sort of. Passing through.'

She had not yet switched off the engine but her head was out of the window and she had taken off her sunglasses, either the better to see him or to seduce him with her melting orbs.

She said, 'You know Gloria?'

'Gloria?'

'Gloria Benjamin. How many Glorias are there? I noticed you chatting.'

'Yes, well. That's to say, not well. Acquaintances. Ships that pass. You know her?'

'I introduced her to the channelling, after her father. You understand. She showed at my place.'

'Showed what?'

'Her paintings, silly boy. What do you think she showed – her birthmarks? I have a gallery on Lot's Lane. Mid-June it was, quite a success, you should have been there. She sold fourteen.'

'Good heavens!'

'She'd wanted to cancel.' Ms Rump had become conspiratorial, dropping her voice and emphasising her points with flickings of the sunglasses. 'Her father had just met with his accident but Millicent insisted she go ahead. Oh my, and now Millicent, isn't it too ghastly?'

103

'Yes, grim.'

'I've got it! You're a friend of Tim Thwaite!' She switched off the engine, leaned further through the window, and brandished the sunglasses. 'From Britain. You're visiting with Tim.'

'Can't keep anything from you, can I? You know Tim?'

'He helped Gloria with her exhibition, brought her paintings to the gallery. Helped pack the ones we didn't sell. Took them back to Ahoy.'

'What in?'

'Cardboard. In the trunk. How d'you mean, what in?'

'Doesn't drive, does 'e?'

'Course he drives.'

'He does? Didn't used to, not in the old days. Must've learned. He doesn't have a car though.'

'Gloria's car then. How do I know? Really I don't supervise every loading and unloading.'

'Not a truck?'

'What truck?'

'Who knows? Green pick-up? Dog in the back?'

'You mean?'

Peckover shrugged, indicating that he meant nothing. All he meant was that she keep talking. She might know something. Somewhere somebody had to know something. This one with designs on his body, unless it was his accent, knew Gloria and Thwaite. She might know the rest of the family, maybe their friends and foes. She might be the subject for a respectable, sit-down grilling.

'Something's fishy about you,' she said, and switched on the engine.

'Don't say that. Once you know me— '

The Mercedes erupted away. She had to brake immediately because of cars and dogs and people but she had made her point.

Peckover walked to the parking lot. He had blown that one. He climbed aboard the Cadillac, manoeuvred out of the parking lot, and aimed for Main Street, composing.

> Bejewelled and plump, Crescent Rump,
> Whom 'Enery thought 'e might pump,

Set out with illusions
Then came to conclusions
That 'Enery gave 'er the 'ump.

At a supermarket he filled a basket with frozen stuff, almost entirely side dishes such as lima beans and french fries, because his mind was not on what he was doing. And, as an afterthought, en route for the checkout, he tossed in a box of cocoa.

TEN

Peckover showered and put on his butling uniform. He didn't want this uniform, he wanted an apron. Come back, Joop, all is forgiven. Drip your ash in the vinaigrette and blend well. He walked from his room and into Benny Benjamin.

'Hi there! Settling in, are you? Everything ship-shape?'

'Most comfortable, sir.'

Wet from the pool, towelling himself, wearing a knee-length psychedelic swimsuit fashionable among teenagers, Benny was taking a short cut to the servants' stairs. He paused by the ping-pong table.

'Apologies about all this. Not exactly what you're accustomed to, am I right?'

'Sir?'

'You know. Everything. Place crawling with *carabinieri*. We've got the OGPU here, so I gather. Our Federal Bureau of Incrimination. We're all in it, Jessop. I don't mind telling you, nothing's what it was or ever will be again. You're not going to tell me it's anchors aweigh for you too.'

'Beg pardon?'

'You're not leaving the sinking ship?'

An affronted expression lighted on the sun-kissed, pinkening features of Jarvis or Jessop.

'The cook – gone.' Benny did not sound distressed. His manner verged on the breezy. His swimsuit stuck to his groin in an assemblage of panchromatic lumps and hollows. 'If you ask me, he should have been given the yo-heave-ho long ago. A loose cannon, that one. Sailed too close to the wind from the start. Do you cook, Jessop?'

'We have been informed we do a presentable suet pudding, sir.'

106

'A what?'

'Variously termed baby's bottom, spotted dick, or leper's leg.'

'Jesus!'

'Boarding-school terminology, sir. A suet pudding coated with treacle or custard is not unpalatable.'

'Ten days of suet pudding with treacle or custard. Maybe we'll close the place down after the funeral. We were thinking of it. No way we'll find a cook this stage of the season.'

'If I might put my oar in, Captain – er, sir – a colleague of our acquaintance, a chef of cordon bleu attainments, lately with her eminence, the Duchess of Mincinghampton, may conceivably be available, should we have your permission.'

'No kidding? Jessop, get that colleague's ass aboard and into the galley. There could be a head-hunter's fee for you.'

Probably not if you taste his cooking, thought Peckover. The Factory was never going to send him Twitty and just as well. For all he knew the lad might be cordon bleu with rosettes but more likely his level was toast. He watched Benny mount the stairs, humming a chantey and wrapping his towel round his head like a sultan.

At the top of the garage's solid board stairs the door into Thwaite's kitchen was open. If Thwaite is back, Peckover thought, I can tell him I've met his friend Crescent Rump. He stepped into the kitchen. Sergeant De Voto withdrew his head from the refrigerator and said, 'Where's that cocoa, English?'

'You don't think you're going to find it in there, do you?'

'You're the last one saw it.'

'You're never going to find it, or the cup, and you know it. If you're seriously looking, start by digging up the beach.'

'You're the last one saw Thwaite too.'

'Marvellous. I've done away with Thwaite because 'e saw me killing Millicent with cocoa. That what you're saying?'

After several expletives the Sergeant said, 'I'm saying you shouldn't have driven him away from Ahoy without our knowing it. We should have had him followed.'

'I'm just the butler, I could hardly have refused. Still, you 'ave a point. You'll have alerted your airport police, naturally.'

'We have. Naturally.'

'Hello, it's Puddy Tat. Watch your ankles, Feet.'

'Huh?'

The tangerine ankle-biter prowled through the kitchen, sur-
veying the scene, and took up a sedentary position in the open
doorway, looking out at the stairs. Behind the cat came the
wavy-haired model in the silver suit. He nodded to Peckover and
told him, 'Hi.' He was carrying a shoebox of papers which he put
on the table.

'Two things may be of interest,' the model said. 'One passport
and a bunch of money.'

He picked out of the shoebox a blue hardback booklet and
a white envelope and handed them to the Sergeant. Peckover
watched the Sergeant for a sign that might tell him if he were
Peckover or Jarvis. Jessop was finished with, at least until he
bumped into Benny again.

Sergeant De Voto turned the pages of the passport. 'If he's
headed for the airport he's not going abroad.'

Jarvis said, 'Perhaps if we might peruse Mr Thwaite's passport
in confirmation of its authenticity or otherwise, being as we are a
fellow national and familiar with this particular document of Her
Britannic Majesty's Secretary of State for Foreign Affairs.'

'Flush the act, Peckover, it gives me a rash.' The Sergeant
handed him the passport. 'This is Detective Davy Pugh,
Dunehampton Police.'

'You might 'ave told me.' Peckover leafed through the passport.
'Gene Rosko told me you, me and him were the grand total in on
the act.'

'Okay, now there's Davy, and there may have to be more. The
Chief's looking after the Veep at Beachport and no way I'm
looking after you, not on my owny-o, so I'm sharing the pleasure
with Davy. Davy, this is Chief Inspector Henry Peckover, here
to tell us our business.'

Peckover and Pugh shook hands. 'What's our business Henry?'
He was grinning. The question was not nastily meant.

'For a start, 'ave you fed the cat?'

The Sergeant's hands being filled with money, Peckover dropped the passport back in the box, and said, 'J-2 exchange-teacher,
legal and valid for another year. So 'ow much have you got
there?'

'One grand,' the Sergeant said. 'Tasty sum for a young

108

exchange-teacher to have sitting around. Is he a secret playboy? Is he selling crack? What's his salary, Davy?'

Davy Pugh shook his head. 'Skimpy, college like Dunehampton. He's passing through, he doesn't have tenure. Ten? Fifteen?'

'So has he just withdrawn it and if he has what's it for? Or is he about to pay it in and if that's the case where'd he get it?'

'He was given it last night and he doesn't quite know what to do with it,' Peckover said.

'Yeah?'

'Theorising. Don't take notes. Benny Benjamin gave him a book, the one Thwaite wrote about Jameson and Chamberlain and Rhodes and the Boers. I saw them from a window. The money was in the book. If you're delivering surreptitious money you don't flaunt it, not even in an envelope. Especially in an envelope. Envelopes are suspicious. But you could stick it in a book.'

'You saw the money?'

'I saw the book. Thwaite didn't want it so Benny put it in his shopping bag. Saw it again on 'is bookshelf. It'll be there now. He said Benny wanted it autographed. I think he was lying. Question is, what's Benny give 'im a thousand dollars for?'

'If he did.'

'Yes, mate, thanks. Thought I'd said that already. A bribe? Something on account for something to be done? A pay-off for something already done?'

'Like murder Millicent Langley?' said Davy Pugh. 'Benny?'

'Never mind Benny,' said the Sergeant. 'One gee for murder? Come on.'

'Thwaite didn't want it because it wasn't enough,' grumbled Davy.

'He didn't want it because it was a tip for biking to the store for booze and it was too much,' the Sergeant said, and he put the envelope of hundred-dollar bills on the passport. 'If it's okay with you two, that's enough theorising. We'll take this box. What else is in it?'

'Letters, receipts. Nothing. I haven't had time.'

Peckover said, 'Welsh, are you, Davy? I mean a generation or so ago. Daffyd Pugh, a fine Welsh name. You've not come across a paper which is a speech Roosevelt made about Pearl 'Arbor?'

109

'The Day of Infamy speech which doesn't mention the Day of Infamy. When I find it, you'll know.'

'When we find it you could be the last to know,' the Sergeant told Peckover. 'You've been here a coupla days. What have you achieved except theories? Anything you're keeping to yourself?'

'I've fed the cat,' Peckover said. 'See? Watch.'

Peckover took from the fridge a partly demolished can of sardines. Puddy Tat had not eaten today. Unless he was a successful mouser. Taking his time, he shook the sardines into a saucer and set it on the floor. He poured water into a bowl and put the bowl beside the saucer.

'Fed the cat, got myself beaten up, taken Thwaite to the train, and that's about it,' said Peckover. 'True, doesn't amount to much when you think about it. Fact is, I'm a full-time butler, a fill-in cook, and I 'aven't the opportunity you blokes 'ave to go looking for stuff. So what I 'ope you're looking for, now we're co-operating so nicely, is that Pearl Harbor paper. Can we sit down? I've a heavy programme ahead dishing out the frozen dinners. It's a guess but it all comes back to Thwaite. Want to hear about it?'

'We've heard about it,' said the Sergeant, fluffing up his wispy moustache with a forefinger. 'We've heard guesses you wouldn't believe, like Thwaite spiking the old lady's cocoa after you left it for her, if that's what you did. Thwaite the champion heavyweight beating you senseless on the dunes.'

'These you 'eard from Mr Rosko?'

'We're in touch.' The Sergeant stood at the sink drinking water. 'Put it this way. We're not heading off with our tennis rackets in the expectation you'll have this business sorted out by suppertime.'

Peckover watched Puddy Tat leave his sentry duty in the doorway and sniff the sardines. His guesswork had been passed on by the Chief and the Sergeant didn't think much of it, any more than the Chief had. He wasn't overwhelmed by it himself. If ever he and Vito de Voto were going to work civilly, now might be the moment to play the Yankees card.

'Sergeant, we're not getting on brilliantly. What if we took an hour off together. If there's baseball on the box, like the New York Yankees— '

'Don't waste my time. I know where you got that line.'

'Well, I tried.'

110

'Stop trying. Go be a waiter.'

Peckover, smiling, pushing back his cuffs, stepped towards the sink. He said, 'Move aside, would you mind? I don't want to be felled by halitosis.'

'What? What did you say?'

Peckover turned on the tap. He sensed Davy Pugh, somewhere behind him, retreating a pace or two.

'Sarge, old matey, has it occurred to you that if I am totally unloved and unsupported I just might start dropping my aitches all over the Langleys out of frustration and plain misery? It could 'appen. I could blow it. Jarvis could be unmasked.' He washed sardine oil from his fingers. 'If he is, it'll be at least in part from lack of encouragement which can give rise, unfortunately, to a sod-everything attitude that often as not leads to doom. If the Langleys find out Jarvis is a copper, you and your Chief Rosko and Davy here and the whole Dunehampton fuzz are going to look fantastic. I'm not in Ahoy for any reason except you put me here.' He dabbed his hands on a cloth stiff with filth. 'Can you see the 'eadlines, the letters to the editor? They'll 'ave to put out a special supplement. Now, this may cause you grief but I ought to be going. Any chance you 'ave a spare copy of the autopsy report for my bedtime reading? Lie to me, tell me you 'aven't, and you'll be down in my report as the most bolshevik bloody-minded apology for a thick, idle, obstructionist flatfoot I've met anywhere, ever. You couldn't investigate a five-year-old's birthday party and you can't grow a moustache.'

Sergeant De Voto, glowering, had turned an autumnal russet. Peckover took a step back. He would not have been too surprised if the Sergeant now pulled out his gun and shot off a British ear. Instead the Sergeant grinned.

He said, 'Sounds like some report. You've got a way with words, Henry. Davy, fetch our colleague the autopsy.'

The soup was the butler-cook's own invention: Campbell's clam chowder into which he had sprinkled ginger, squirted a dozen cloves of garlic, and swirled a bowl of leftover fruit cup. The powdered but sluggish ginger came out of the container hardly at all, then it came with a rush, much of it into the atmosphere, causing Peckover to sneeze copiously.

111

'Potage Gauguin, a Tahitian speciality,' he told the inquisitive biddy with lips like a peeled chestnut whom he took to be the Reverend Roberts's wife or mistress.

The Reverend seemed a jolly enough cove, though a mite sixties and laid back with his open-neck shirt and gold chain. Where had he parked his sitar? Would he tip the cook?

They were not six for dinner, as Gloria had forecast, but five. Gloria, Romaine, Rudy, the Robertses. Mr Benjamin had been called to the city.

A likely story.

Now, aproned in the kitchen, Gloria made omelettes. Peckover manned the microwave. With his other hand he dashed off a vinaigrette for the salad. His frozen food selections having turned out to be side dishes, except for lasagne, Gloria added substance to her omelettes by packing them with canned palm hearts. She had looked at the packets of lasagne and said, 'Those won't do at all, Jarvis,' without explaining why.

'Such a sadness that Mr Benjamin is not present to enjoy your omelettes, modom.'

No answer. 'Sadness' was a bit much. He would have had no answer either.

Measuring vinegar, back to back with Gloria at the stove, their bottoms so close they might have touched had either of them chosen that they should, Peckover wondered what it was about a kitchen that could bring two people closer than anywhere else. The shared purpose, sweat, and deadline of cooking were capable of fomenting true love, raw lust, rage, and assault. Was Gloria aware, as he was, that the merest shuffle and twitch and their bums would engage like men-o'-war at Trafalgar?

He said, 'But you will be accustomed to such summonings away.'

No reply, and his bum a whisker away. He believed he felt the brush of a string of her butcher's apron.

'If we may permit ourselves, Mr Benjamin is clearly deeply distressed by the demise of your dear mother.'

No answer. How the hell did an undercover copper uncover anything if his questions were ignored? Was she concentrating so hard on her omelettes that she was incapable of speech. He had not yet heard the sizzle of egg into hot fat. He looked round.

The fat was not hot. He wondered if it were even warm. Had she

112

let the light go out? Over Gloria's chiffony shoulder he observed egg strewn with palm hearts congealing in a pan. Either she was using the slow method or she had never cooked an omelette before. She had already finished two. They lay on a plate like items of harness for Glad Rags in the horse show, eye-blinkers perhaps, or kneepads for softening collisions with fences. Was this how the Langleys liked their omelettes?

'Mr Benjamin, modom, will doubtless have informed you that we are acquainted with a most sought-after chef who, should fortune smile on us, may be free to replace Joop. Mr Benjamin evinced considerable keenness.'

'You don't say.'

Ah. Not an immediately encouraging response but none the less.

He said, 'We understand that his *croquembouche* won the Prix Napoléon.'

'Why didn't you tell us you knew Tim Thwaite before you came here? Is it a secret?'

'Modom?'

'And pretend you were just visiting Dunehampton? I was under the impression you were employed here.'

'Might I enquire, is the lady Crescent Rump conceivably the source of these misconceptions?'

'It's extremely fishy, Jarvis.'

Peckover heard what he believed to be the slap of a horse's kneepad on to the serving plate. Vigorously he stirred mustard into the vinaigrette.

'We regret the misunderstanding, modom, but we did not say we knew Mr Thwaite, merely that we wished we had. After all, such intellect, such cerebral majesty. Ms Rump's auditory faculty may have been impaired by traffic noises.'

Slap went a kneepad. Gloria was speeding up.

'However, we admit to misleading the lady by refraining from giving Ahoy as the address of our present employ, not wishing to be tracked down. We trust this will go no further, milady, but we believe Ms Rump may have hoped for, shall we say, a liaison.'

'Crescent? With you?'

'Indeed, it is most absurd.'

'I didn't mean that. But after five minutes, one channelling session, Crescent, a liaison?'

113

'We understand five seconds may be ample, given the correct chemistry.'

'Oh, Jarvis, you dashed her hopes.'

Gloria sounded to be stifling merriment.

'We gave her, I trust, the bum's rush,' the butler said.

Slap went another kneepad. Jarvis tossed the salad.

Gloria said, 'It did seem just a little fishy. I don't feel I'm in control.' Now she sounded beset, dispirited. 'It's all so unsettling. We'll probably be returning to the city in a few days. I don't know, perhaps we can use your Napoleon person there.'

She took off her apron, rinsed her hands, and carried the kneepads into the dining-room. Jarvis followed with microwaved side dishes of french fries and lima beans, salad, a block of New York cheddar, and sliced Wonderbread in a Chinese porcelain basket of the early eighteenth century. He opened wine. The Reverend Roberts's consort was prattling about a store which had sent her the wrong curtains. Peckover could not see why serving was as straightforward as much the same performance, yesterday, had been a descent into the inferno. Practice makes perfect. Millicent Langley's vacant throne seemed to fill the room. Ought he to have removed it from the table to a remote corner? A butler couldn't think of everything, no matter Mr Butterwick would have said that thinking of everything was precisely a butler's job. Then again, moving the throne from the table might have been an act of egregious insensitivity. Hard to know.

Back in the kitchen, his ear to the swing door, he heard Rudy say, 'If the cops come out of their stupor they're going to ask themselves who benefits moneywise, apart from Thwaite, if he ever does. Who went from riches to rags on Meltdown Monday? So go on, who? Say it. Who hasn't ten bucks to his name but might expect to be shored up by his wife's inheritance when her mother gets gathered to the golden shore?'

Either Romaine or Gloria – probably Romaine – said, 'Asshole.'

Chink and mumblings. Peckover wanted to rap on the door and call out, 'Speak up!'

The next audible topic was funeral arrangements. The Reverend was proposing as a requiem the Beatles' 'Let It Be'. Peckover decided he would not offer bedtime cocoa.

Eating currant bread and sipping Château Cantenac Brown, in his pyjama bottoms in an armchair with a chrysanthemum motif, a zigzag of sweat trekking downwards through the hairs and crumbs on his chest, Peckover read Dr Webb's interim report on Millicent Constantia Langley.

The good doctor had become carried away by a murder trial in England, in 1699, in which the question was whether Sarah Stout had been strangled and was dead before her body entered the water or whether she had drowned. Comparing seventeenth-century forensic medicine favourably with today's, he waxed lyrical over the unreliability of modern attempts to prove drowning by analysing blood for variations in electrolytes, and cautiously pooh-poohed microscopic examination of bone marrow for diatoms which entered a victim's circulation from the water. All of this was beside the point. Dr Webb, windbag, went on to list fractured femurs, fibulas, tibias, ribs, radiuses, ulnas, skull, and every other bone in the human anatomy, and arrived at the conclusion that Mrs Langley had died from a fall of between thirty and fifty feet. Until something better and preferably briefer came along – more was threatened following hydrolosis and further laboratory analysis – Peckover was happy to go along with this. He was surprised that the doctor offered no opinion on why anyone should go to the trouble of hauling Millicent into the ocean when she was already dead. He had opinions on everything else.

He checked that he had locked the door and went to bed. When he awoke at five o'clock it was from dreams of troops of uniformed menials, an unending procession of the servant class winding in and out of doorways and up and down stairways. Sam and Mary in gold braid were bootblacks. Miriam, suspended from a string like Peter Pan, orchestrated the performance with a baton. He sat in the armchair and in his notebook wrote:

Song of the Domestic Servants

Which group would you say is the greater
    Of civilisation's adults:
Those who insult the waiter
    Or those whom the waiter insults?

Butler, buttons, busboy, bonne,
Slavey, flunkey, scullion,
  A new dawn breaks – rise up, march on!

Shoeshine, maître d', away!
Femme de chambre, cook, valet,
  Maid and footman – greet the day!

Major-domo, page, au pair,
Groom, tweenie, gamekeeper –
  Your hour is come! To arms! Prepare!

Bring salvers, mops, the pantry key,
Dusters, floor wax, cutlery,
  Bring every prop of butlery!

Upstairs, downstairs, hand in hand –
  To your posts, the minion band!
You also serve who only stand!
  Rejoice to do your lord's command!

A divide like a barbed-wire equator
Splits civilisation's adults
Between people who insult the waiter
And those whom the waiter insults.

Needed work. Needed something. He returned to bed and to
sleep, to be awakened by sizzling sunshine, knocking, and Gloria's
voice through the door requesting breakfast for three on the west
deck. Nothing elaborate. Scrambled eggs, bacon, muffins, juice,
coffee. Romaine would have tea. As soon as possible, Jarvis,
please. Thank you.

He sat up.

'And Jarvis?'

He thought she had gone. He had been about to tilt back his
head and give forth his Pavarotti waking-up call, a bugling groan
as from a water-buffalo alerting the herd to a scent of lion. Nothing
like it for revivifying the blood.

'Mr Thwaite didn't come back last night. That police officer said
to tell you. The Sergeant. Why would he want to talk to you?'

'Police routine, modom.'

'We'll have breakfast first, if you don't mind.'

116

ELEVEN

Saturday. By noon the temperature was ninety-three degrees Fahrenheit and the air saturated. Doors and drawers would neither open nor shut. Matches would not strike. Those who sat down to lunch in shorts, bare moist thighs on vinyl, rose from their chairs with a sound like tearing calico.

Couples, singles, families, and carloads of weekenders from up-island mobbed the beaches, these being largely the point of summertime in Dunehampton, except for people with ocean-front castles and pools who never set foot on them. At the A&P a shopper might stand eternally in line with his chariot of groceries. Every parking slot on Main Street and Lot's Lane was taken. Cars seeking a space honked in ill-temper at the car waiting in front at a stop light. The locals blamed such rudeness on the out-of-towners. Day trippers from Queens and Brooklyn were unaware they were thought to be rude, regarding the year-round residents as rustics who would wait all day at a stop light – red, green or yellow – if they were not honked at or bumped from behind. As the day advanced, police would arrest half a dozen youths drinking beer outside the museum, and others for possession of a controlled substance. They would try not to arrest the three topless sunbathers on the beach but such an incident might drag on to a point where reinforcements would arrive, though not summoned, until eight or ten policemen stood over the topless ones, who would be French or German socialites pretending, in protest against American prudery, not to understand 'Please cover your boobs, lady.' At twilight police would arrest a man who lay full length in the middle of Quahog Road singing 'Soldier, soldier, won't you marry me?' Later, squad cars with flashing lights would attend a fire in a potato barn, a burglary, and sundry road

117

accidents. Fourteen people – male and female, young and elderly – would be arrested for driving while intoxicated.

The peaceful majority of the summer population showered, adored their suntan, and headed for restaurants, outdoor concerts, gallery openings, discos, parties, the Dunehampton Theatre, a sexplex which in three years, by stages, had advanced from one decent-sized screen to six tablecloth-sized screens, and events. An event might be an exhibition of seventy birdbaths designed by America's leading architects, or a masked ball for charity at a thousand dollars a ticket on the Throttle Neck Lane estate of the Marchioness Posy Poussin, hostess of Huguenot extraction, she claimed, though in the Mosholu Parkway neighbourhood of the Bronx remembered as Myrna 'Hot Pants' Czysczoniwicz. Others of the law-abiding majority went nowhere in particular, merely meandering, looking in the boutiques' lit windows. The dull and contented stayed at home.

Peckover, at noon snooping in the missing Thwaite's apartment, was too tired from being both cook and butler to be aware of these toings and froings or to concern himself with them. He had talked with Feet. The Sergeant's news, apart from Thwaite being absent, was that Thwaite's bike had been recovered. Peckover had not known it was missing and he suspected the Sergeant hadn't known either.

Where, Peckover asked himself, would he hide a single sheet of paper?

More to the point, where would Thwaite hide it? Unless, not being in his right mind, he really did have it in that repellent satchel, prey to hurricanes, footpads, and the satchel-louse.

Did a draft speech by Roosevelt on the subject of Pearl Harbor need to be hidden? In this case, yes, being valuable to Thwaite, like his whole life, whether the real thing or a forgery. If he kept it in his pocket, or the satchel, each time he fell off his bicycle, or got himself mugged on the sidewalks of New York, it would become increasingly wrecked.

The Sergeant had found Thwaite's bike, or rather two boys had found it, three miles away in a gravel pit off the highway. Thwaite hadn't taken it, he'd taken a train, so who? The Sergeant was taking the credit for its recovery, that was clear, and who could blame him? To date he had dug up nothing else.

But that wasn't to say the Pearl Harbor paper might not be here somewhere among the books and sardines.

Sergeant De Voto in a white wicker chair on the blue veranda chatted with Rudy Pardo informally and fruitlessly, not for the first time. Mr Pardo had seen and heard nothing on Thursday night. He had been reading in bed when his wife came in around a quarter of midnight and a few minutes later he had fallen asleep. Yes, he believed his wife had been with her mother but he hadn't asked why or what they'd talked about. They were often together, being mother and daughter and under the same roof. Yes, he'd lost everything in the stock exchange crash, and yes, he hoped Romaine's cut of the inheritance would put him back in business. The Sergeant postponed the question 'Who is your wife diddling around with?' because he was not sure how to phrase it, not in this peaceable first innings of the game.

Some game. But these were people who knew people could pick up the phone and suddenly your promotion might be out the window.

He had sent two men to sift through Thwaite's desk at the college and they had come up with a boxful of White House waste paper, early December 1941. No Day of Infamy speech. Others were searching the gravel pit where the bike had showed up. No sighting of Thwaite at JFK, La Guardia, or Newark. He had called the NYPD to say their best pitch for Joop den Beets could be restaurants and hotels, and he'd been told, thanks, bub, for that gem of intelligence. The beauty from Scotland Yard, who might be a poet but wasn't an idiot, had suggested he might do worse than find out why Benny Benjamin had gone to Manhattan, if that was where he was, because the answer to Millicent and Lou was going to be within the family, and if he and his troops could keep an eye on family ankles, or any ankles, discreetly, for teeth marks, that might be no bad thing either. The nerve of the guy.

'If that's it, Sergeant, I've some phone calls to make.'

'That's it, Mr Pardo, for the moment. Grateful for your co-operation.

Sergeant De Voto watched Rudy waddle away. He could sit five minutes. He could sit the rest of the day for all he would be missed now the top guns had moved in. The white wicker,

119

the festooning blue drapes, the grinding of the ocean, they were something he could grow accustomed to.

Fifty men on the case now, lieutenants, captains, specialists with college degrees. Half the time he didn't know who was the law and who the media. The more the out-of-town hotshots with their assistants and technology swarmed in, the punier his own role, like he was a rookie again. Like a rookie pitcher anchored in the bullpen with nothing to do only watch the boss and sigh and cheer when you saw the boss sigh and cheer.

If the guy from the Yard came up with anything, and of course shared with his favourite sergeant, there could be hope. One case-cracking deduction from the butler with his eye at keyholes, the nugget passed his way, the perp in the slammer and the file closed, and he'd be on chat shows. Move over, Chief Rosko. Peckover might come up with something. Crazier things had happened.

Detective Davy Pugh, lost in Ahoy, stepped in error into an airy chamber with bamboo screens, rattan chairs, fans, and palms, like a set for one of Channel Thirteen's bygone British series about rioting and rape in colonial India, all bristling moustaches and twirling parasols. The space had been commandeered by the FBI, two of them in seersucker suits at a table with coffee cups and briefcases, observing him, waiting for him to introduce himself. He assumed they were the FBI. They were not family or tourists or ragamuffin reporters or any cops he knew. They had that blank look that was no look. Eyes in aspic. If he backed off they would summon him. He advanced to be recognised.

They went so far as to shake hands and tell him what they wanted. They wanted a draft speech about Pearl Harbor, Professor Timothy Thwaite, and a cook, Joop den Beets. Didn't we all, thought Davy Pugh. The FBI was on absolutely the right track. They didn't sound excited about Joop, but neither was the Sergeant, so Joop was either marginal or they were all making a cardinal blunder. They made no mention of Langleys, dead or alive, or the butler being thumped on the dunes. Once they had the speech and Thwaite all would be resolved.

'We're about to take Thwaite's place apart, Davy,' said Agent Carson Eisner, the one with the shorter hair, so short as to be mere stubble through which glowed a burnished scalp.

120

'We'd be grateful for the corroborating presence of one of your boys.'

'You, for instance,' said his partner, whose hair was a millimetre longer. 'You look spare.'

'I don't know,' Davy said. He really didn't. 'I'd have to clear it with my sergeant.'

'Do that,' Carson Eisner said. 'We'll wait here.'

Crimping with both hands his gorgeous hair, Davy went in search of the Sergeant and in the kitchen found Peckover unloading the dishwasher. He said, 'Butlers do dishes?'

'Dishes, haute cuisine, you name it, mate. It's not actually discussed, what you do. You just find yourself doing it.'

'You sound cheerful.'

'I've had a modicum of progress,' said Peckover, sorting cutlery. 'I found the Pearl 'Arbor paper.'

'Where?'

'Most obvious place.' Big spoons here, little spoons there. Egg on that one, hard as rock. 'You've read Poe?'

'The letter was hidden in the letter rack. Load of garbage, I always thought. So the Pearl Harbor paper was in the file labelled Pearl Harbor.'

'It was with his green card stuff in an Immigration and Naturalisation Service envelope.'

'No it wasn't. I looked there.' Detective Pugh was now looking in the fridge. He brought out a jar of peanut butter. 'Bottom left drawer of the desk, under a pile of eyeglass cases.'

'You didn't look inside the instructions on how to file the form, pages of it, questions like 'ave you ever been found guilty of moral turpitude? I'd thought that was what Gloria cleaned 'er paintbrushes with. Never mind. Possibly the world's most boring reading after tax stuff. Unless, of course, you're a foreigner and want a green card.'

'What's the green card got to do with Pearl Harbor?'

'For Thwaite, everything. We'll 'ave to ask him. He wants to live 'ere in America and be legal. Here's where all the Roosevelt stuff is, and Roosevelt scholars, and where he's going to write his Day of Infamy book and make it big as an 'istorian, be in demand, blink at us like a traffic light out of magazine covers. No future for 'im in England, not with 'istory, he's persona non grata. He

121

wants resident immigrant status, a legal alien – the green card. The Infamy draft is with a photocopy of Lou's codicil giving him this house. It all ties together. Roosevelt's speech, Ahoy, a green card, our Tim's got it made. If he doesn't get charged with murder.'

'I still say it's a crummy hiding place. What's wrong with up in the roof or under the floorboards?' Davy talked with his mouth full of peanut butter. 'That Poe theory was always junk.'

'Fooled you, Daffyd bach.'

'We'll see if it fools the FBI. They're waiting for me. They're about to gut Thwaite's apartment. They'll probably start with the cat.'

'The cat will have to take its chances. I'm handing nothing over to the FBI. "Name's Jarvis. I happened to light on this while nosing through Professor Thwaite's abode." They'd have to be told and I'm still supposed to be incognito.'

'We're talking about the FBI.'

'Today the FBI, tomorrow the traffic wardens, the gardeners, and the geezer who lifts bugs out of the pool. Your Sergeant can be a right blister but he can 'ave it.' Peckover picked wine glasses from sudsy water in the sink and rinsed them. 'Tell the FBI it's been found. No sense them reducing Thwaite's place to rubble. Tell 'em you found it.'

'I just told them no one's found it.'

'Now you just have. You had an inspiration it could be in with Thwaite's green card application.'

'I say I found it, you get no credit.'

'Credit schmedit. That how you say it?'

'So where's the speech? You don't have it on you so I have to guess, right?'

'Right.'

'The most obvious place. Under your pillow.'

'That's your first guess.' It was like a game with Sam and Mary. He placed glasses upside down on a paper towel. 'Two more.'

'In the freezer in a waffles box.'

'One to go.'

'You left it in the green card instructions.'

'You'll make a detective yet. Save the cat, Dafydd. Get up there before the vandals start sawing the place in pieces.'

'First thing I'm doing is taking photocopies.'

'As you like. Whether the paper is genuine or a fake only the technicians are going to know and only the original will tell them. They've got to date the paper itself, not a photocopy. Check it's not been artificially aged. You do that by sending an electric spark through it in a controlled environment like, say, an ozone-filled aquarium. They'll measure the diffusion of ink. They'll track the movement of the ions with scanning auger microscopy dating.'

'No kidding.'

'I'm not just a pretty face. And I've made photocopies. Get your skates on. Stop. Is anyone upstairs?'

'Where upstairs?'

'The bedrooms.'

Davy shook his head, indicating either no, or he didn't know. He put his hands to his hair and moulded it.

'I've had enough scullery work,' Peckover said. 'Time for dusting. If I go missing, last words you 'eard me say were I'm going aloft.'

'Take care.'

Snoozing Prune opened one eye and gave a single, limp beat of her tail. Why did dogs and cats place themselves where they would be most likely to be trodden on?

Jarvis stepped round Prune and ascended the mahogany staircase. He carried the resonant bronze pasha's tray with hieroglyphics. He might even find a stray coffee cup to put on it. The tray, far and beyond a duster, was a badge of office which made him indisputably a butler. Not a bad defensive weapon either. In this place you never knew.

No one seemed to be about. Five coppers had been doing nothing in a conservatory area with trailing greenery and robust cacti into which had been imported a computer and a coffee-machine. But where, apart from Prune, were the family? They were not at the pool. Being at the pool prior to the funeral might have been deemed inappropriate. Benny was rumoured to be in the city and Romaine might be galloping on Glad Rags. Gloria and Rudy were not in evidence but it was a big house.

The grandfather clock on the landing greeted Jarvis with random chimes. He walked past the Sinbad the Sailor vase, cornered left into a corridor with family bedrooms, and head-on into Benny

123

Benjamin. The pasha's tray bonged on Benny's knee. A lingering note in the base register merged with the tinnier chimes from the landing.

'Begging your pardon, sir,' Jarvis apologised. 'May we welcome you home? We trust your sojourn in the city may be classified a success?'

'I'm not sure I understand what you're talking about.'

'We have little doubt that the purpose of your excursion to New York fully justified that sense of bereftness which spread in your wake like a miasma following— '

'Jeffreys, what're you doing up here?'

'The windows, sir. It has been proposed I survey the situation overall.' Someone could have proposed it. 'Doris is gathering strength.'

'Who?'

'Hurricane Doris is understood to be bowling in our direction.'

'Jesus, is that a fact? Where is it now?'

'Latitude thirty, sir.'

'Where's that?'

Jarvis tucked the tray under his arm. How the hell did he know where? He had made it up.

'Off the cape,' he said. There had to be more than one cape. 'A very approximate latitude, meridian-wise.' On the Ptolemaic projection. He hoped Benny was not a geographer. 'But adjacent.' Why didn't he shut up? 'With winds gusting.'

'Gusting? A hurricane, gusting?'

'Gusting like the baying hounds of hell, devouring all in its path, smashing forests to tinderwood and townships to smithereens, sir.'

'I thought it was out to sea.'

'The weather bureau is fallible, sir.'

'The windows, Jeffreys. Hop to it. We may have to batten down.'

'Aye-aye, sir.'

Peckover readied himself to return Admiral Benjamin's salute, if there were to be one. Both this bloke and Rudy were given to nautical expressions. Perhaps they sailed together, fled their wives' bosoms for respite on the bosom of the deep. Their wives would be unlikely to stand in their way.

124

Time for Benny to be splicing the mainbrace, if he hadn't already started. Instead of saluting, Benny punched the air, a jab to an imaginary midriff, which seemed to be another habit of his. He walked round the corner of the corridor and across the landing. Listening to the footsteps descend the stairs, Peckover too jabbed to the midriff. 'Belay,' he murmured. He opened the door into the bedroom where, beneath folded shirts, he had found a gun.

No harm in getting rid of the gun. No great good either, very likely. A gun hadn't killed either Lou or Millicent but they were dead just the same.

Guns went off and a murderer was abroad. Burying this one on the dunes would be a gesture for peace and life. Five minutes, all it would take. Not a policemanly deed but these were exceptional circumstances, and he wasn't a policeman, he was a butler. He would set it all down in his report.

If half a dozen other guns were secreted about Ahoy, too bad.

He left the bedroom door open. Beyond the bed the door to the bathroom was mercifully closed. Here in the bedroom was disorder enough without having to see into the bathroom. Not ransacked, but the bed unmade, and on the carpet, shoes and pants and strewn sections of newspaper. A bedroom accustomed to a maid but at present without one.

He propped the pasha's tray against the end of the bed. On a bedside table lay *Invest and Grow: A Guide to Tax Shelters*. Rudy and Romaine's room, he was reasonably sure. He knew it when he slid open one end of the fitted cupboard and identified Rudy's peach tie and the collarless, custard-coloured jacket which had been bilious when he'd seen it on Rudy. Now that he had seen what some summer sports got themselves up in on the boulevards of Dunehampton the jacket seemed conservative. He felt beneath the stack of folded shirts. No gun.

He lifted out the shirts, probed between them, and replaced them. He groped among socks and underwear and patted the pockets of hanging suits.

Rudy had put the gun elsewhere. Or he was carrying it with him. Why would he do that?

Unless someone had borrowed it.

If that were the case there were several candidates. It didn't have to be Romaine. The absentees, Thwaite and Joop, one or

125

the other? Could be the police. Sergeant De Voto might have it and forgotten to have told him. Feet hadn't told him much.

Peckover decided to stop bothering about the gun and consider the bathroom. From behind the bathroom door issued an unnerving silence. He had no great faith in a sixth sense but he was fairly certain that someone was in there. Unless his imagination was overheated due to unaccustomed sun and under-nourishment from loss of appetite.

He stood with his back to the closet, watching the bathroom door and listening. He heard crickets in the trees outside and the growling ocean.

He should probably quietly close the closet door, collect his tray, and depart. Alternatively, he could do his job, which was to investigate.

What if he breezed in, if the door were not locked, and behold, Romaine starkers and towelling herself like a spindly Degas?

The carpeted floor creaked as he walked to the bathroom. He watched the handle, put his ear to the door. Jarvis the snoop. What did he think he might hear? Romaine drying her hands on a towel? Rudy shaving, scraping at bristle?

He recalled that this bathroom resembled the Taj Mahal, unless that had been one of the other bathrooms. He opened the door.

Correct, the Taj Mahal. Golden, sunken Jacuzzi, gold taps, ample gold in the arabesques and spurting fountain motifs on the walls and shower stall, rugs on the marble floor, a towel sloppily dropped. The nizam might have something to say about the towel. Lop off a hand or two.

No attendants of the bathchamber though, no houris. Nobody. Peckover walked in as if he were the proprietor. He did not hurl himself full length, or slam back the door into anyone who might be behind it, as someone was. He was reflecting that he ought to be taking more care – he didn't even have his pasha's tray – when somebody clubbed him from behind.

126

TWELVE

Behind Peckover's eyes blossomed his own personal fireworks display. You really see stars, it was not a fiction, he thought as he accelerated forward, downward, and his head banged on a plush rug.

⠒ He judged he might be on the brink of the tub but could not be sure, there being Roman candles fountaining in his eyes. His skull hammered.

Twice in two days, quite massively mugged. Was this a record? Any moment now the coup de grâce? He levered himself to his knees, waited for the fog to clear, and when it didn't he stood anyway. He'd had company but naturally now there was none. On an askew rug near the door lay a blunt instrument, a wooden back-scrubber with a two-foot handle which had not been there when he came in. He turned the Jacuzzi taps on, sloshed water around, and swabbed with tissues from a Kleenex box. At a sink he rinsed his mouth, chewed toothpaste, and rinsed again.

A face-cloth was wrapped round the scrubber's handle. So much for prints. The business end was bristles embedded in a circle of probably teak. Whatever the wood, it was an inch thick. He picked up the scrubber. *Pure Natural Bristle. Made in West Germany.* He might have known it. They made their scrubbers solidly, the Germans. Honed at Krupp's. He brought it into the bedroom and sat on the unmade bed.

He seemed to be able to see all right. The thudding in his head was mainly from a burgeoning lump somewhere above the right ear. A friend for the dunes lump on the top of his head. They could tell each other knock-knock jokes. He chose not to explore the lump. Let sleeping lumps lie.

This bathroom mugger was someone he knew or there was

no sense to it. Someone who preferred not to be discovered in the bathroom. That ruled out Rudy and Romaine. It was their bathroom.

Benny, exclude him, he'd gone downstairs.

Why be nervous of being spotted by a butler? A butler could be told, 'Hi, Jarvis, Romaine's sun oil, she said it was here somewhere.' A butler could be told, 'Go stuff thyself.'

Someone who knew he was not Jarvis and was up to no good, like trespassing. Lifting Rudy's gun from under the shirts. Such a one might be nervous enough to swing a back-scrubber.

The Sergeant and Davy Pugh knew he was not Jarvis. Chief Rosko knew but he was away looking after the Vice-President. Unless he had taken a few hours off. By now the FBI might know.

Footsteps were approaching along the corridor. Peckover pulled a fold of summery counterpane over the scrubber and stood up. He adjusted his black tie. He smoothed his hair, avoiding lumps. Jarvis on parade.

Rudy arrived in the doorway, stopped there, and said, none too genially, 'You.' He looked surprised but he could have been faking it. Scratching his crotch, indignant rather than ruffled, he came towards Peckover. He lacked the feigned innocence of one who had just cracked his butler over the head with a back-scrubber.

'All right, is it, if I ask what the hell you're doing here?'

'The windows, sir.'

'What about them?'

'It has been mooted they be precautionarily scrutinised against the onslaught of Hurricane Doris.'

'Who mooted that?'

'We believe there is a consensus.'

'We believe you're a liar.'

Strong stuff. Jarvis, monumentally dignified, drew himself up to his full six feet two inches. Rudy was right but he'd have liked to have thumped him just the same.

Rudy nodded towards the propped pasha's tray. 'That what you scrutinise windows with?'

'We appreciate sir's little jest.'

'You ever been in a hurricane?'

'Britain has of late suffered, as a result, meteorologists inform us, of what is termed the greenhouse effect, or global warming,

128

a hitherto unknown pounding from storms approximating to hurricane force.'

'Great. So you'll know that with a hurricane you don't need a tray, and windows don't get scrutinised, they get taped.' He had advanced to within two feet of his butler. Any closer and he would be eyeballing like an army drill instructor. 'Masking tape diagonally from corner to corner, criss-cross, right? We've got a caretaker does that. Tim Thwaite.'

'We understand Mr Thwaite is not available.'

'He's skipped town?'

'Sir?'

'You heard me.'

'The police are presumed to have the matter in hand.'

'I'm not asking the police, I'm asking you. There's a difference, is there?'

'We fail to catch your drift, sir.'

'You're full of gas and crud.'

In the butler's opinion it was Rudy, now heading for the closet, who was full of something. The son-in-law of two murdered Langleys had on a baggy, grass-green suit, the pants ending at the knees, the jacket a muddle of pleats, dangling belt-ends, buckles, and pouch pockets. He might have been heading off on safari. If he were about to change into something else, so much the better.

Rudy closed the closet door. 'You're spying,' he said. 'What're you looking for?'

'Should sir be dissatisfied with our services, we would be obliged for the matter to be aired with Modom Gloria, whose adjudication as senior family member, titular head of the household, and joint heretrix to— '

'What the hell's heretrix? She's going to be excommunicated?'

'Heretrix as in canon law for she who inherits.' Peckover did not think he had made up heretrix – there was executrix, matrix, Styx, coccyx – but he might have done. He hadn't expected Rudy to question it. 'Should sir have any complaint regarding we, Jarvis, who for thirteen years served— '

'Fourteen you said before.'

' —his earlship the Lord of Sowerby— '

'His Lordship the Earl of Sowerby. Get it right.'

' —devotedly, if we may continue, and with every satisfaction,

129

his Lordship being a gentleman, and Master of the Sowerby Foxhounds, which is not to say that persons aspiring to such a station may not be discovered in America, though we do confess that in our experience, albeit brief, the extraordinary American notion that all men are created equal has served most disastrously to eradicate from this side of the pond that particular breed, the gentleman, a term denoting chivalrous instinct and sensibility, as distinct from clods, much as you eradicated the buffalo which were wont to roam the grassy plains— '

'Christ sake, Peckover, cut it out.'

Gawd, I will, I do. Exhausted, Peckover closed his eyes for a long moment. Rudy went to the door to the corridor and shut it.

'Open it, what's the matter with you,' Peckover said, his cover slipping momentarily. 'The quality and the staff don't meet in the master's bedroom with the door shut.'

Mr Butterwick had had his students perform both master and servant in unscripted playlets. He'd have failed Rudy in each role. The bloke hadn't a clue.

Rudy opened the door. He flopped into an armchair and said, 'I can't take much more of this.'

'The humidity?'

'Very funny.'

'We try to be of service, sir.'

'Cruddy Brit horning in. By jove, jolly-jolly, honk-honk, we'll show you Yankee chaps a thing or two, clear up this nonsense in a jiffy, what? You're in over your head, Peckover. What's wrong with your ear?'

Peckover touched his ear. It was sticky. His fingertips, when he looked at them, were red.

'Someone was in your bathroom. I got in his way.'

'Who?'

Peckover sighed and shook his head.

'Jesus, it gets worse,' Rudy said, and slumped lower in his chair. 'It's the guy on the dunes again and if we believe that we believe anything. I guess I have to believe the dunes.' He stuck a hand in his pants pocket and scratched. 'Now the bathroom. You didn't see.'

'Not you by any chance?'

Rudy ran his finger round his neck, collecting sweat. 'What I'd like is to get on a plane and go. Anywhere.'

'Brazil?'

'Why Brazil?'

Peckover believed Brazil and the United States might not have an extradition treaty. Britain and Brazil didn't. A handy spot for desperadoes. He hadn't made up his mind whether Rudy qualified as a desperado. He had an air of desperation. Not having to be Jarvis and the pineapple of politeness was a relief.

He said, 'You know, Brazil. Rumbas, beaches.'

'Beaches suck.'

Observed more closely, Peckover thought Rudy looked seedy as well as pudgy and desperate. His suntan seemed to have yellowed. He was no longer the handshaking hearty who had welcomed him aboard at that first dinner. Did he miss Millicent? Had his wife and her wanderings become too much for him? Perhaps he simply disliked Brits. Understandable, plenty to dislike, the Brit traveller abroad for one, whether visiting copper or football fan in woolly scarf and rosette smashing windows on the Continent, tearing down a stadium or two.

'What did I do wrong?' Peckover said.

'Do what wrong?'

'Jarvis.'

'Jarvis is great. An Oscar for Jarvis. Over the top but that's how we like our butlers.'

'How long 'ave you known?'

'Before you did. I'm your reference.'

'You?'

'That cop, Rosko, wanted a Scotland Yard whizz over. We don't particularly know each other but we've met at fund-raisers, social stuff. He said I could invent a Wall Street pal who'd stayed at Sowerby Towers or wherever and the butler was a gem and going spare. Millicent bought it. If you're happy at Ahoy you can thank my salesmanship.'

'It's heaven. Thank you.'

They eyed each other across a carpet littered with shoes and sections of newspaper.

Peckover said, 'Didn't occur to you and Rosko it might be for

131

the greater good if I'd known you knew and we had a go at working together?'

'You and me? You mean I'm not your top suspect? Bust, el foldo, but with a wife who'll be flush once Mom and Pop join the great majority, as they have. Sure it occurred to us. Rosko said I should use my judgment.' Rudy tipped back his head and inhaled with a watery sound. 'Seemed it would be easier on both of us if we weren't watching each other all the time for signals. You'd be slopping soup on me.'

'Where's the gun?'

'This one?' Rudy took a pistol from a grass-green jacket pocket.

'Loaded?'

'No.'

'So what's it for?'

Rudy giggled. 'To trap detectives from Scotland Yard. If it's been moved, breathed on, I know.'

'That's all it's for?'

'Hell, Peckover, it's called self-defence.'

'Against who?'

'That would be an advance, knowing that.'

'You've got ideas.'

'I've got nothing.' He put the gun back in his pocket. 'You're the detective.'

'I was beginning to wonder. Detecting is asking questions. Only question I get to ask is, "Would sir take the red or the white, if sir can tell the difference?"' He sat on the bed. 'Is it Thwaite your wife's carrying on with?'

Rudy's fingers mopped inside his collar. ' "Carrying on" is cute. Has an Old World ring.'

'Is it Thwaite?'

'I guess so. We don't talk about it. What's it matter who? He wouldn't be the first.'

'But you don't care.'

'I didn't say I didn't care.'

'But you're not going to divorce her.'

'Very insightful. Want to hear why not?'

'I know why not. Why doesn't she divorce you?'

'Same. We're children of our grabby times. She tries to divorce me, I'd contest it and it'd cost her half her millions because I'm

132

lily-white and she's got the scarlet A on her forehead. We're simple folk. All I want is her money, half would be fine, nothing excessive. All Romaine wants is her money, a horse, the hot saddle rocking between her legs, and Thwaite or anyone exotic. Can you believe she thinks that nerd exotic? Correction, he's no nerd, he only looks like one. He's a gangster dressed up as an owl.'

'I wouldn't say no to a drink.'

'Ask Benny. He's got no shame, he'd drink with the butler.'

'Water.'

'Forget Benny.'

'Benny's going to be nicely off, same as you, long as 'e stays married and assuming Gloria's generous. Correct?'

'Only thing I know, whoever it is you're chasing, he's smarter than you and all the local bluesuits together. Scotland Yard is hauled in and what've you learned?'

'There's been progress.'

'Such as?'

Such as the Pearl Harbor paper was in custody, awaiting the experts.

Rudy was saying, 'For your information, Benny doesn't know what time of day it is.'

'Benny likes us to think 'e doesn't know what time of day it is.' Peckover recollected having made the point before somewhere. He still didn't quite believe it. 'Benny's tipple is soda water, tonic. 'Ow about that?'

'So collect his glasses, save the dregs, send them to Scotland Yard.'

'Why not to Chief Rosko? You don't trust 'im?'

'Jesus, I was being sarcastic.'

'Why did Benny go to the city?'

'Did he? Maybe he went to the opera. Maybe he went up the Statue of Liberty. Ask him.'

'I've tried. It isn't easy. I'm Jarvis, remember?'

In the bathroom Peckover drank three tumblers of water. Rudy and Benny might be covering for each other. Rudy had everything to gain by seeing Lou and Millicent buried. The benefit to Benny was less obvious but there was a matter of a thousand dollars he'd passed to Thwaite. Hush money? A bribe? A reward?

He swabbed blood from the ear area. He would trust Rudy

about as far as the door. Lily-white in matters of the flesh he might be, but a bloke whose only grief was for his empty wallet, who hung in with Romaine because of her money, you wouldn't rush to have him as company for an evening's pubbing. He might have a point about Thwaite though. A gangster dressed up as an owl. What was Thwaite up to, charging off to New York and not yet back, leaving behind the Pearl Harbor paper, and a thousand dollars from Benny, an unfed Puddy Tat, and his bike in a gravel pit? On the other hand, he didn't have a gun, far as was known. Rudy had the gun. Rudy might be more upset by cuckoldom than he let on. So was Thwaite the gangster, or Rudy?

Rudy had closed the door to the passage, shed the grass-green suit, and put on a satiny robe such as Noël Coward used to enjoy being photographed in. All he needed was a jade cigarette-holder and a leaner physique.

Rudy said, 'I'm going into the Jacuzzi. If you were real staff, you'd start it up, quit lurching about.'

Was Rudy gay? From outside sounded the grinding of a mowing machine. Peckover opened and left open the door to the passage. On the landing the clock chimed its song. 'Oh where and oh where is your Hielan' laddie gone?' Half an hour he'd been up here taking hurricane precautions. Time for whoever had clubbed him – Thwaite, Romaine, Gloria, Vito, Rosko, Daffyd Pugh from the valleys, Joop from tulip-land, Ms Prettyman the Seer, a rented mugger with notches on his arm – ample time to have skedaddled and now be taking his own bath prior to a social Saturday evening.

Peckover said, 'Does Gloria play around?'

'Gloria plays with paint. You seen her paintings?'

'No.'

'Not true. You've seen everything on offer at Ahoy.'

Prune appeared in the doorway with her tongue hanging out. She watched Rudy at the closet hanging up his suit, and Peckover by a window, looking out, hands in his jacket pockets, regarding a youth atop a raucous tractor-mower cutting the grass. Standards had gone to pot. Lou had never allowed such brutish machinery on the lawns. This throbbing beast would not have been out of place in Red Square on May Day. The bare-chested vagabond at the controls hadn't even attached the box. That would have

134

meant extra work emptying it. Grass-clippings sprayed in a green, allergy-inducing mist.

'Buzz off,' Rudy told Prune.

Prune trotted into the bedroom and lay down on the *New York Times* business section.

Peckover turned from the window. 'Lou's Pearl Harbor document, you know, Roosevelt's "A day that will live in infamy". We've got it.'

' "A date which will live in infamy." You're always getting things wrong, Peckover. What're you going to do with it, frame it?'

'Authenticate it.'

'I'll authenticate it for you. It's authentic as a three-dollar bill. Only place for it would be a police museum, in the vaults with the junk.'

'You sound positive.'

'No one's seen it except Thwaite. Now you if you say you've found it. No one had heard of it until the lawyers announced the codicil. Thwaite's forged documents before, you know that – don't you? Are you a cop making out you're a butler or a butler pretending to be a cop?'

'Why don't we wait for the analysis? Because Lou didn't talk about it, didn't wave it about, that's no proof he didn't have it in his safe for fifty years. I'd been him, I wouldn't have talked about it either, not with you lot. I can just see 'im at dinner, 'ead of the table, announcing "I have a first draft of Mr Roosevelt's speech showing incontrovertibly he connived at the Japanese attack on Pearl Harbor," and what do you lot say? "What speech would that be, Lou?" "Meant to tell you, Lou, the lawns never looked better." "They're re-running the Mets on cable at ten, Lou." '

Rudy took the gun from the pocket of his hanging jacket. 'Shallow as that, are we?'

'And sycophantic. It's all right, it's the way people are when real money's around, family included. Family, staff, caretakers – few are immune.'

'Most of us are immune from killing.'

'But not all.'

Rudy clicked open the cylinder, peered into its empty chambers, and swung it shut. He said, 'Lou and Millicent are dead and there's a cook and a caretaker out there nobody knows where, and if it wasn't them it's someone else. I don't envy you, not if you get close. Great, you're from Scotland Yard where it's all fancy deduction and if things get rough a clip on the jaw. Have you got a gun?'

'Got everything I need.'

'You don't have a gun. It's unbelievable. Nothing from Rosko?'

'I can look after myself.'

'How's the head?' Rudy put the gun beneath the pile of shirts. 'Home again after your fooling with it. If I'd been sure it was you I'd have left it there. I still don't know you know it's there, so if you kill someone with it you found it all by your genius self, as the fact is you did. It's nothing to do with me.'

'Except you bleedin' leave it lying around. What if there were children here?'

'Listen, Peckover, we've had two murders. I don't want to turn into a gibbering blob worrying about a third. You haven't a glimmer about the trouble you're in if you make so much as an inch of real progress.'

'How would you know that?'

'How would anyone know? Lou and Millie are dead, that's how. You get close, you'll need more than a gun. You'll need – Jesus, I don't know. The luck of the Irish. Are you Irish?'

'Some of my best friends are.'

'Tell them to say their Hail Marys. There's enough worms and grief at Ahoy without a phoney butler joining the new dead up in the sky, because next time you're hit on the head it's going to be with an axe.' Rudy was on the move, picking up shoes. 'I'm guessing an axe, there's one in the basement and another in the garden shed so it could be an axe. Could be with a roll of cable the TV mechanics left, or routinely, the American way, with a thirty-eight. The good news is you'll probably never know what.'

'Cocoa?'

'You're so flip. Cocoa. You get yourself killed, fine with me, you were warned, but you drag down your assistant, get him killed, that's not so good.'

Rudy gathered up shoes and sections of newspaper. The carpet was clear except for Prune. She lay watchful and sociable, swatting the carpet idly with her tail.

'What assistant?' Peckover said.

136

'Your assistant, flying in this afternoon. If he's as delicate a flower as you, another innocent out of cloud-cuckoo-land, and as accident-prone, much help he'll be. Bringing boxing-gloves, is he?'

'What're you talking about?'

'The new cook replacing Joop. How d'you like that? The ass-end of summer and we bring in a cook. He called from aboard Air India.'

'You didn't tell me.'

'I'm telling you. I told him you'd take the train to the city and meet him at Penn Station. You can fill him in on the way back. You've got four hours. How did you swing it anyway?'

'Damned if I know. Talked to Rosko, talked to the Yard, mentioned it to Benny. Benny may have been impressed. Is Benny a snob? This cook did the crumpets for the Duchess of Mincingham. Do we know 'is name?'

'Gordon someone?'

'Don't know any Gordons. Don't think I do. Is 'e a Scot?' Gawd 'elp us, all that was needed. Constable Gordon McHairy from auld Inveraray swirling his sporran and dishing up haggis and clapshot with drappit eggs and rumbledethumps. 'You spoke to 'im?'

'The phone rings, might have been Thwaite in the slammer wanting us to stand bail, how'm I to know? I'm in the wrong place at the wrong time. Loo? Blew? This one spoke worse 'n Thwaite or you, both of you, like his mouth's full of balloons. If butlers don't fill the boss's tub these days, at least get rid of that tray, and while you're about it, the dog.'

Rudy, barefoot and scratching his crotch, headed for the bathroom. Peckover observed ankles without teethmarks. Bony, hairless ankles supporting skinny legs which supported, invisibly under the satiny robe, pudginess.

Jarvis said, 'Soap and water, sir, and a smear of anti-fungal cream rubbed well in. You'll be right as rain.'

'Get lost.'

THIRTEEN

The windows of the train could have used a wash. In the aisle was a puddle which might have been condensation or it might have been anything. No air-conditioning. On the other hand he had a seat to himself, newspapers, a timetable, and his notebook in which to pen an ode should the muse strike. The train halted at Dunehampton College, took aboard a party of ragamuffin students, and pulled away. The glamour of an American train, Peckover decided, was its height off the track. You couldn't just step aboard, you had to climb, as school ma'ams in crinolines and gamblers in stovepipe hats climbed in western films. And of course, the whistle, something between a moan and a yell, the same bluesy, wrenching wail that chain-gangs used to sing about. Somewhere he had read or heard that the whistle didn't have to be mournful, it was up to the driver. Might be a brace of toot-toots informing Ella May that he'd be home in twenty minutes so would she put the coffee on.

Peckover looked at his watch. His assistant, the cook, had already landed, if the Air India flight was on time. But he'd be an hour or more queueing with his alien passport, then collecting his baggage, then customs. He'd be in trouble if he'd brought kitchen ingredients – a side of Scotch beef, a hundredweight of parsnips. Then finding a bus to Manhattan, then getting to Pennsylvania Station. The tricky bit could be recognising each other at whatever platform the train left for Dunehampton. The cook might recognise Our 'Enry but Our 'Enry didn't know any policemen cooks, not that he was aware of. He'd have to watch out for someone jetlagged carrying a canteen of kitchen knives and a spice-rack.

'Speonk!' called out a guard, awaking Peckover from a doze.

Peckover would not have known exactly what the guard had called out had he not found the word in the timetable. Speonk. It was a place. It sounded like a board game. First player to line up three speonks shouts 'Speonk!' and collects the kitty.

At Jamaica everyone debouched, crossed the platform, and pressed into a crowded, streamlined train that looked as if it could travel underground if it had to, which the train from Dunehampton never could have done. Jamaica, Long Island. Peckover lighted on two spare seats in a row of three. He ignored the girl-child in the window-seat, her fist crashing about in a bag of crunchy crispies, sat, placed his newspapers and hat on the aisle seat, and resumed his timetable study. Didn't look far from here to Penn. The train was hardly on its way, people were still looking for seats, when from the rear of the coach came a commotion.

'They drugged me!' a woman was shouting. 'They stole my bags and threw me on a train! I've been kidnapped! I'm not paying for any return ticket so don't even ask!'

Peckover turned to look. Other people were looking. Lolita in the window-seat, scattering chips, kneeled in her seat to look. Some passengers steadfastly refrained from looking. The source of the rumpus was advancing along the aisle, a begrimed witch with Medusa hair somewhere between the ages of twenty and seventy. A conductor in spruce blue tracked behind her urging her to please sit and calm it, lady.

Peckover faced front. If she were to become too unruly he might have felt obliged to intervene. In London. Not here, though. Not Jarvis.

'The mayor's my oldest friend! He'll have something to say!'

She sounded very fierce and close. Peckover glanced up – a mistake. Their eyes met. She wore a long, sleeveless, Old Testament sort of garment, terminal with mange. She lowered her eyes to the aisle seat, lifted them and fluttered her eyelids at Peckover.

Peckover put his newspapers and hat on his lap. He needn't have, he could have bared his teeth at her. Wotthehell. The girl-child leaned and stared, shedding salty crumbs on his sleeve. Trapped between Scylla the Slattern and chip-eating Charybdis. The conductor had evaporated cleverly away.

The beldam made herself comfortable. She smoothed her prophet's robe over her legs with hands which looked to have

139

just completed a day's gardening. At least she had stopped shouting. She moved her head close to Peckover's.

'They chloroformed me in the night and put me on a train.'

She didn't smell of chloroform. More of fish heads.

'They stole my manteau.'

'Your what?'

'Everything. My peignoir. The capuchin with the label – Lord and Taylor. They know quality, don't tell me they don't.' She put her hand to her bodice and rubbed a sample of Book of Jeremiah sackcloth between finger and thumb, demonstrating the quality. 'Maori. They shrink it with geyser water. You can't get it anywhere, not since the war.'

He would not be drawn into asking which war. She would only tell him.

She leaned closer and announced with pride, 'I'm a bag lady. I know what you're going to ask. If you're a bag lady, where are your bags? What's your name?'

'Percy.'

'Are you British?'

'Canadian.'

Peckover had never seen Canada, and perish the thought, he had nothing against Canadians, but he believed obscurely that his answer might be a conversation-stopper. It was too, for a while. After a station named Kew Gardens she started again.

'Got to get back to my affairs,' she muttered.

Business affairs? Love affairs? Peckover offered a nod.

'Get my affairs in order. Start over. Like after the crash of '29. A good crash sorts the sheep from the goats. Hey, Percy' – An idea had come to her, brightening her eyes, animating her voice, and causing anxious frown-lines to appear above the bridge of Peckover's nose – 'we'll go to my place! We'll talk about Canada!'

'Thanks, tempting, but I'm meeting someone.'

'Where?'

'Penn.'

'Penn Palace?'

'The station.'

'What I said!' She whooped, an unnecessary sound which startled neighbouring passengers. 'My place – Penn Palace!' She uttered further rapturous whoops. 'The Eden Suite! By the rest-rooms!'

She was shrill again, a happy hag. She would give him the tour. No one knew Penn as she did. She would show him the best trash cans for bran muffins and Danishes, the hidey-hole on the lower level where the cops met with their Bud, the phone booth where Willie-Boy Blake stabbed the tourist couple from Stockholm. First she would show him her own Eden Suite. She emitted another whoop. People looked then looked away. Peckover squirmed in his seat, striving for invisibility. Lolita lolled open-mouthed and ashen from three-quarters of a pound of crispy crunchies.

At Penn, the bag lady without bags fastened her coal miner's fingers on Peckover's arm and said, 'Stick with me, Percy.'

The tide of humanity off the Jamaica train surged along the platform, up stone steps, and into halls and corridors fed by swirling tributaries of rival trippers and commuters from other exits and entrances. Travellers, backpacks, briefcases, suitcases on wheels, dogs on leashes, amplified, unintelligible train announcements, a Sister of Mercy with a smile and a collecting box, panhandlers, candy stalls, bagel counters, pizza ovens, get your heels mended, get your photographs developed, buy your lottery tickets. 'Eden suite, here we come!' warbled the merry termagant. Peckover noticed a sign pointing to Long Island Rail Road Departures but Bag Lady was towing him in the opposite direction.

He would allow her a couple of minutes to show him her Eden Suite. She deserved at least that. And Peckover was too tired to argue. He doubted she received much attention. If she hadn't latched on to him, she would have latched on to someone else, or tried to, and most likely been rewarded with an obscenity.

She hauled him out of the throbbing concourse into a dim, unpeopled corridor with two empty, closet-sized alcoves, and ahead, floor-to-ceiling steel gates. The gates were padlocked. Beyond them stretched more blank corridor. Whooping, the bag lady started towards the alcove to the left of the gates.

'My Eden Suite!' she trilled.

She stopped dead and stared.

In the alcove sat a lone intruder, a trespasser, a sleeping somebody, one of the homeless, a derelict swaddled from head

141

to toe in rags, and encompassed by swollen shopping bags.

'It's me,' said the bag lady.

Her fingers dug so deeply into Peckover's arm that he gasped. He had to take hold of the fingers and pry them free. Her other hand was a fist against her mouth.

'Me! My caftan! My Inverness cape! My boots! My bags!'

Peckover advanced on the pile of clothing. He shook its shoulder and said, "Ello?'

If this were a caftan from Byzantium, or an Inverness cape from the Isle of Eigg, it had travelled badly. On the other hand, to have put it, them, any of these enveloping vestments, into a washing machine, would have been to risk their disintegration. No part of the uninvited guest was visible under the wrappings. He might have been a subscriber to a mystical Eastern cult.

Possession being nine points of the law, whether of the Eden Suite or this evil clothing, Peckover felt a pang of sympathy for the dispossessed bag lady. He plucked aside a contagious swatch of cape. This disturbed other layers, causing them to slither downward: encrusted woollens, cottons, what appeared to be a segment of tarpaulin with buttons.

The corpse's eyeballs looked about to pop out. The cord round his neck had cut so deeply into the flesh that it could not be seen. The cord's bloody ends dangled.

'Oh, my God.' The bag lady, for once, spoke in a whisper. Peckover said nothing, but stood staring at the very dead caretaker from Ahoy.

Peckover draped the cape back over Thwaite's head, returning to him the semblance of a zealot in a trance, or of any of the defeated who simply wish to close out the world.

'Go bring the first cop you can find,' he told the bag lady. 'That way. I'll go this.'

He propelled her into the mob in the concourse. She went obediently, flapping her bare arms. Peckover judged that, on balance, she would be better finding a copper than left with Thwaite, retrieving her bags and rags, and wrecking evidence, if any.

Peckover sidled through the throng. So where were they, coppers, when you wanted them?

Personally, he didn't want them. He'd only be with them until doomsday explaining who he was, who Thwaite was, and that being led to Thwaite by a bag lady was one of those impossibilities which do happen, but wouldn't have happened if he'd bared his teeth at her on the train, as anyone with his wits about him would have done.

At the third attempt he found a functioning telephone and dialled nine-one-one. He announced that a stiff was in the passage by the rest-rooms near the Long Island Rail Road bit of Penn Station, just across from a doughnut shop, and hung up before the switchboard woman could start her interrogation and shunt him around. He had never before used the word stiff but devined that she at the switchboard might grasp stiff though at sea with everything else. Not, he thought, sifting through dimes and quarters, and searching his notebook for a Dunehampton number, that he'd reason to suppose she would be less efficient than the switchboard bunch back home at the Factory. Sergeant De Voto was out but he reached Davy Pugh. He was at Penn, Peckover said, and so was Thwaite, dead, garotted by the look of it, and pass this on to the Sergeant, please.

He could be in trouble for leaving the scene of a crime. Not that anything would have been accomplished by his staying there, and not that anyone would know if the Sergeant and Davy Pugh didn't care and shut up about it. The cops here would be looking for Percy, a Canadian, but not very hard. He could, of course, return to the scene with his assistant, when and if he found him, which in this swarming multitude didn't seem too likely. He thought he probably wouldn't return.

Peckover backed out of the booth perspiring and not at all clear what was going on, where he was, or who, and when and how it would all end. He unfolded his train timetable.

'Guv!'

Peckover looked round. Steering towards him through the hordes came a flexible beanpole carrying a First World War kitbag and a ghetto-blaster and wearing sunglasses high on his forehead, a blithe white smile, and an even whiter mackintosh which reached to his ankles and at night would be visible for three miles. Was the apparition expecting rain? For whom had this whitest, longest raincoat ever, with aggressive belt and epaulettes, been fashioned? One of Napoleon's field-surgeons? It was, Peckover had little

143

doubt, fifth-hand from either Brixton Market or Camden Lock. The arrival looked like an aviator, Wright Brothers vintage, or might have done but for the floppy tweed hat worn backwards atop a tall, cylindrical hair-do. Part aviator, part trout fisherman.

'Blimey, the lad 'imself,' murmured Peckover.

Twenty-four, Londoner, scholarship boy, dutiful son of West Indian immigrants, hair shorn this season from nape of neck to top of skull, whence it soared like a column of the Acropolis before being sliced off flat – only yesterday an urchin on Brixton Road had accosted him, wanting to know, 'What music does your hair represent?' – Detective Constable Jason Twitty hardly knew what had hit him and thrilled to every moment of it.

Never before had he set foot in America. He felt like Columbus. Hail, Columbia! Mine eyes have seen the glory! She'll be coming round the mountain! He was going to become tremblingly horny for long-legged American girls, he knew it. At Kennedy Airport he had looked about him for muddled lasses seething to feel free.

As one of four hundred and fifty black coppers out of the twenty-eight thousand whites of London's Metropolitan Police, Twitty was bottom of the heap for trips to foreign parts, which even for the most senior officers arrived with the frequency of Halley's Comet. The super with the hot-house moustache who had summoned him from a drugs surveillance on Lavender Hill had told him he could thank Chief Inspector Peckover, or blame him if there was to be suffering.

'He says you can cook,' Chief Superintendent Veal had said.

'Henry said that?'

'Mr Peckover to you, saucy sod. Well, can you?'

'You mean like with ingredients and a pan and heat?'

'Don't charm me, you unspeakable bag of sheep-droppings. Are you a chef?'

'Sir, like you never imagined!'

'What I feared. Got your passport?'

'Sir!'

'What's that mean?'

'Don't actually have it on me, sir! Don't lug it around the stews of south London! Among my personal treasures, sir!'

144

'In your Chubb safe with the family heirlooms?'
'You've got it sir!'
'Your plane leaves in three hours. Miss it, you'll be hung from the rafters. Here's the file. The envelope is dollars, every penny to be accounted for. That means receipts, all right? You're not swanning off across the Atlantic to shop for clothes, understood?'
'Wouldn't dream of it. Very conservative, the Americans, sartorially.'
'They are?'
'My proclivity for excellence, wardrobe-wise, sir' – he had been wearing his drugsbuster's black leathers with silver studs and the cream, high-heeled boots – 'has clearly gone before.'
'Gone before what, you jackanape?'
'Gone— '
'Shut up. Heathrow. Meaning – say it – not where?'
'Not Gatwick, sir.'
'Pick up your ticket at the Air India desk. Terminal three.'
'Sir?'
'What?'
'Permission to switch to British Airways. Or Air France, Lufthansa, TWA— '
'What's the matter? What's wrong with Air India? Very smooth airline. They'll lull you with sitars. You a racist, Twitty? My God, you've joined the National Front?'
'The curry, sir. Delicate stomach. Delhi-belly.'
'Get out of here. Wait – stop.'
'Sir!'
'Keep an eye on him.'
'Him?'
'Him.'
'Our 'Enry.'
'Cheeky bugger. How many times have you worked with him?'
'Two times, sir.'
'He mentioned you. Said he could use some back-up and you were a cook.'
'Book, he must have said book, he'll be doing a book of poetry and he sees me as sort of his muse. You know, a blackie, the contrast, light and shade, a literary metaphor for the conflict between— '

145

'Go! Out!'

'Sir!'

Boarding had been through first class, occupied by Indian princes in business suits and silk-swathed maharanees who wore a jewel in their nostril and had a red bullet-hole between the eyes. His seat was half a mile away among the untouchables, who included a young, exhausted group of unshaven Aussies and their bleary Sheilas who hadn't slept for days. A motherly hostess in a sari had handed out packets of betel nuts, tiny slivers of God knew what with the texture of chippings from a slate quarry and a mild, not wholly disagreeable taste of mildew. He had sucked one experimentally, though not for long because wasn't betel what turned your mouth blood-red, as if your wisdom teeth had just been extracted? Dinner had been a choice between curried chicken and uncurried fish. The forward sections of the plane saw a Hollywood movie he wouldn't have said no to, but here among the outcasts the film was Indian. Its entire action took place in a fog-filled room into and out of which excitable families kept parading, waving their arms and shouting like demonstrators. The film must have cost all of two hundred rupees to make. The black customs officer at Kennedy Airport had eyed him and his white raincoat, and said, 'What statement you making there, brother? Vanilla fudge, way to go?'

Out of the building and into the air. Oh, man, was it warm!

An airport bus and a taxi later, alighting at Pennsylvania Station, he had paid the taximan with a flourish of dollars. He knew them by heart. There had been nothing much else to do on Air India, not when you found you couldn't watch the film. The in-flight magazine and *Vogue* had taken two minutes, his mind had been too manic for *Emma* – he should have brought something more pertinent, like *Life and Times of Al Capone* – and the Langley file, carefully shielded from a Bengali in a nightgown to his left, and a slumbering Aussie in sensible shorts and bush hat to his right, was a couple of sheets of meaningless family background and a photo of snowy-haired Lou Langley scowling at the helm of a grass mower, hands on its handles and chest puffed with the resolution of someone about to take off for Mars. So, the one dollar was Washington, a five was Lincoln, a ten Hamilton, a twenty Jackson, and so on. He wished he had paid more attention in history classes at Harrow, not that his class had been burdened with much American history beyond a tea party and a gold rush. A fifty was Grant and a century Benjamin Franklin. Or vice-versa. He hadn't been given many of those.

Now, steaming with sweat, hefting kitbag and dormant ghetto-blaster, inhaling popcorn and pizza smells, and following signs pointing to the Long Island Rail Road, Constable Twitty shouldered through the mob.

Goodness gracious, and there in his hat with his nose in a timetable was the guv!

'Guv!' Twitty shouldered diagonally, dumped his kitbag and ghetto-blaster at Peckover's feet, and extended his hand. 'We can't go on meeting like this.'

'I'm not Guv, clodpole. I'm Jarvis, or I will be if ever we get to Ahoy.' Peckover gave the hand a single shake. 'Pick that stuff up. Next train's in six minutes.'

FOURTEEN

Peckover said, 'First, you got a pink card?'

'Weapons training? No.'

'Good. So we don't get involved in that. Mine's expired. No pink card, no shooting.'

'Bad as that, is it? You make it sound hairy.'

'No, no.' Peckover waved a dismissive hand. Mustn't unsettle the lad. He'd hardly arrived. Hadn't even seen Ahoy yet, inspected the kitchen. Other hand, no sense him imagining he was on holiday. 'But here be dragons, lad. I'll give you a précis.'

The train sped eastward. No caterer with a trolley of beer and sandwiches passed along the aisle, and the pair from Scotland Yard understood from the strolling conductor that none would.

Peckover summarised. Lou Langley dead, Millicent dead, Thwaite dead. He showed Twitty the sizeable lump above his ear and described two personal muggings. He described Rudy's gun and its location, slandered Crescent Rump, guessed at fornication between Romaine and Thwaite, now ended for ever, if it had existed, and hazarded at motive and opportunity for Joop, Rudy, possibly Benny, and Thwaite. Thwaite had seemed to have had reasonable motives for doing away with Lou, and perhaps Millicent, but he hadn't put the bag lady on a train and dressed in her rags. Well, he might have. But he hadn't throttled himself.

'What we 'ave is a psycho at large, unless he's thoroughly ordinary. A killer anyway, and the closer we get to 'im – I'm not saying we're in a hundred miles – the dicier, right? In lieu of pink cards and artillery we may have simply to run like the clappers, comes the crunch. You're taking steroids, I hope, like the Olympics lot?'

'Doesn't sound much to laugh at.'

148

'Don't be solemn. It's only three murders.' Peckover refrained from adding, 'so far'. 'Lou Langley, felled while mowing his verge, may or may not have come into possession of a paper revealing that President Roosevelt knew in advance of the Japanese attack on Pearl 'Arbor, and in the long-term interests of his country, as he saw it, he did nothing to prevent it. We have that paper. Question is, is it the real thing or a forgery? Sergeant De Voto's supposed to be looking after that. Feet of the Photo, he's on our side, I think. So, the late Thwaite, scholar and fellow-countryman, forged once – he may 'ave – and could have done so again. Now he's gone we're that much further from finding out. With me so far?'

'Not especially.'

'Why'd you bring that filthy great radio?' Peckover scowled at the ghetto-blaster on the floor between Twitty's feet. 'You're not in Brixton now. This is Demuresville-by-the-Sea we're going to. Boss-lady, Gloria, she has refinement, she tells us what time dinner is and how many you'll be cooking for, so decorum at all times, please, meaning no thrashing, stereophonic caterwauling. Her sister's Romaine and you stay clear, get it? She doesn't say much but she's hot-blooded, so we gather. All we need is mis-cegenation-across-the-sea. What I'm saying, you're not banging about the place playing your 'eavy metal rock and frightening the dog.'

'It's short-wave for the cricket.'

'I might've known.'

'Final Test, Guv – England could win!' Twitty, aflutter, jabbed his guv'nor's arm. 'We made five hundred and six in the first innings, then skittled them out for three-twenty-one!'

'Skittled who out?'

'West Indies.'

'Whose side are you?'

'How do you mean?'

'Well, look at you.'

'I'm English.'

'What about your progenitors, your cultural inheritance?'

'What about yours? You've got Danes back there, Saxons, Jutes— '

'Jutes?'

149

' —Frenchmen from Normandy— '

'Watch it!'

'England's got this spotty berk from Lancashire, nineteen, bloody marvel. He made a hundred and nineteen— '

'Spare me.'

'I've been trying to. There's something you should know.'

'I'm not listening.'

'I don't cook.'

'You bleedin' do, mate. Any luck you'll 'ave tonight off because it'll be nine before we're back and they'll have given up and gone to their tennis club's grill room. But you can start thinking about breakfast.'

'Miriam cooks.'

'Miriam isn't 'ere. 'Ow do you know she cooks?'

'You told me last time out. She feeds the Royal Archaeological Society every day. She brings half of it home because the quail eggs in chestnut purée are too exotic for your workaday archaeologist with his bucket and spade.'

'What's in your devious mind? Headphones and the satellite hotline? Want her to talk you through boiling an egg?'

'Not me, you. You can cook, must do, married to Miriam. Must have rubbed off, some of it. Why not a switcheroo? You cook, I'll butle.'

'Don't make me laugh. I can cook, certainly, up to a point.' Overcome by modesty, Peckover smirked and shuffled his feet. 'This is absurd. What makes you think you can butle anyway?'

'What makes you think, with respect, you can?'

'Impudence! The Reginald Butterwick Academy of Domestic Service is what. What's your qualification? Weekends with their Royal 'Ighnesses at Windsor Castle?'

'No.'

'Ever seen a butler in action?'

'Yes.'

'You 'ave? Where?'

'Holidays at schoolmates' where there were butlers, like a month at Snotty Carmichael's. His parents have a castle near Inverness.'

'They wear Inverness capes?'

'What are they?'

'Never mind. What was it like?'

'Freezing.'

'Gawd, Christmas in the Highlands.'

'It was August. On the twelfth everyone shot grouse. The butler drove a Land Rover filled with smoked salmon and decanters of Bonnie Och-Aye Double Malt. Smarmy, that one, racist of course, but they're a mixed lot. One in Cheshire called me Master Jason. He had to go jogging every day with his lordship, a sprig of about forty. The butler was eighty. He carried a brandy flask like a Saint Bernard but I never found out which of them it was for. He'll be dead by now, fetched up in the ferns by the roadside with his jogging-pumps pointing at the sky.'

'What I'm saying, butling can kill you. You be a cook, cock. I'll 'elp as far as I can. I assume you brought some cookbooks.'

'Two. Bought them at Heathrow.'

'Good lad. What are they?'

'One's a big bugger, cost a bomb. Don't worry, I've got the receipt. Julia somebody and a bunch of women – Froggies, I think, some of them. *Mastering*— '

'Throw it away.'

'Hell, I only bought it this morning! What's wrong with it?'

'Nothing, it's seminal, if you don't mind spending twelve hours making tripes à la mode de Caen, and if you don't, I do. You're not 'ere to sweat over a hot stove, lad, whatever the Langleys might think. You're 'ere to astonish me with your boarding-school education, your insights born of innocence, and to leap through the window screaming "Geronimo!" if things deteriorate, as they are doing. What's the other?'

'*Budget Bangers and Mash*. Something of that sort. Who cares?'

'Stop sulking.'

'It's a paperback. Kind of how to survive in a bedsit with one gas ring.'

'Absolutely the job. English cooking?'

'Haven't opened it.'

'Toad-in-the-hole? Spotted dick? Marvellous! Not healthy cooking is it, these bangers recipes? Bowels and fibre and cholesterol? Gloria might be in favour but none of 'em are fanatics.'

'Wasting their time if they are. We're all going to be expunged by Doris, aren't we?'

151

'Doris? The 'urricane?'

'They keep talking about it on short-wave. Radio Baffin Bay, judging by the static.'

'Can't worry about 'urricanes. Where is it now?'

'Bowling up the east coast. Couple of days away.'

''Urricanes, monsoons, typhoons, they're oriental weather, I don't believe in 'em. This is the western hemisphere, temperate and civilised.' Peckover sank low in his seat, put his knees up against the seat in front, and placed his hat over his face. 'That's weather I'm talking about, lad, not people. Wake me at Dune'ampton.'

If the guv'nor's Cadillac at the rail station impressed Twitty, as it did – 'Oh!' he crooned, snuggling, and 'Ah!' stroking its plush – Ahoy caused his jaw to sag. In angler's hat and aviator's coat, toting his baggage, in the spell betwixt dusk and dark, he tagged alongside Peckover, past steps leading to a columned portal and panelled door which would be the front entrance – it wouldn't be the cook's and butler's entrance – past shingled buttresses, extensions, outcroppings, then leftward round the side of the house, gawping at boundless lawns seeping away into darkness, a rose garden, yew trees, a glass porch, an illuminated pool with a cabin, and beyond the pool a smudge of bosky coppice, charming as a Watteau painting, if he had been in the mood for charm, which he was not, suddenly once again apprehensive because he was not, now that he was finally here, Constable Twitty. He was a cook.

Eggs and bacon were all he had ever cooked. No one had ever complained about them. Still, he had never cooked them for anyone except himself and girlfriends, and usually the girlfriends had ended up doing it. Here he might have to tart the dish up, throw in a tomato and a tin of baked beans.

He was being led interminably round the oceanside shack to what he supposed would be the staff and tradesmen's entrance. Even in the land of the free, servants would have their place, which would not be breezing in through the columned portico. He could hear and smell the ocean but he was not thrilled. Anxiety reigned. Breakfast!

He should not have looked up. High above, precarious, at an

angle on a rooftop, and doing nothing for Ahoy's symmetry, sat a monstrous satellite dish. Would it bring him loud and clear the cricket on the BBC World Service?

Up steps, along board walkways, between iron furniture on a deck, and towards a screen door. As the butler and cook neared the door, it opened, and through it came Benny Benjamin, glass in hand.

'Ah, Jarvis,' he said. 'Grim tidings.'

'Indeed, sir,' said Jarvis.

'Thwaite. You heard? At least it didn't happen here. This our new cook?'

'This is he, sir.'

'Welcome aboard, sailor. Apologies for the rough seas. It's one hand for yourself and one for the ship. What's your culinary speciality?'

'Yes, well,' Twitty began, and was saved by Benny interrupting with 'All engines ahead, steady as you go,' and waving him and Jarvis vaguely through the door, having forgotten the question.

Ping-pong table, washing machine, much space. Peckover opened a door and said, 'This is you. Park your stuff.'

'Oh, my ears and whiskers! Where's the basket of fruit?'

Twitty removed his aviator's coat to reveal pinstripe wedding trousers and a cossack blouse with a high collar such as is worn by Red Army dancers and some dentists.

''Urry it up. 'Ere's where I am.'

Into basement space again, through an open door, the light on, and into the butler's room. Twitty observed Japanese decor. Was that Miriam, framed on the dressing-table? In an armchair sat a copper with a moustache and a clipboard, writing.

'Make yourself at 'ome,' Peckover told the policeman. 'Constable Twitty, meet Sergeant De Voto, and vice-versa. Where is everyone?'

'Thwaite's apartment.' The Sergeant put his pencil in his pocket. 'Family's upstairs. Benny you just saw. Start from where you picked up your bag lady.'

'She picked me up. On the train from Jamaica. I don't even know 'er name.'

'Jasmine Ellen Sprague, homeless and harmless.' The Sergeant looked down at his clipboard. 'Forty-one, divorced, former dancer with the New York City Ballet, no fixed address.'

'You know more than I do.'

Peckover took off his jacket and recounted the encounter with the pile of raiments that was Thwaite at Ms Sprague's Eden Suite, Penn Palace.

The Sergeant said, 'There's a Dr Stone in Middlehampton, a handwriting savant, he's taking a look at the Pearl Harbor paper. Monday, I've got a second opinion coming up from the Library of Congress, a documents analyst.'

'Guv – er, Mr Jarvis?'

In the doorway a lustrous redhead had caught the cook's eye and was trying to catch the butler's. Twitty had not previously been treated to the slow-motion gait which now bore the guv'nor towards her. He supposed this to be the definitive butler's walk, commanding attention, and given just that little extra ounce of flatulent grandiosity, quelling all who might be tempted to snigger.

'Modom?'

'Jarvis, it's all so ghastly.'

'Grievous, modom.'

'What is going on?' Now her eyes were on the Sergeant, who was on his feet, preparing for departure. 'Have you any idea?'

'We have not been apprised. May we introduce the new cook?'

Jarvis crooked a finger in the cook's direction. The cook, approaching, thought the redhead wore a wary look, as if about to flinch, as would he if he were family, as he suspected she was – Gloria, could it be? – and her home invaded by local fuzz and staff from across the sea. The guv was hilariously hoity-toity, his head tilted back and his nose in the air. Sergeant De Voto exited with a murmured, 'Pardon me.'

Jarvis, eyeing the ceiling, addressed the cook. 'Modom in her graciousness has made herself available to discuss menus.'

Twitty bowed.

'A nice English breakfast,' the lady said. 'Say nine o'clock, would that suit, Mr – ah – ?'

'Kofia, Sandy Kofia. Folks from Ceylon, originally. That's Sri Lanka nowadays. Rather a trouble spot. Immigrants to Jamaica.

Not your Jamaica. Island in the sun, you know?' Twitty paused in case she wanted to take notes. 'Ma'am.'

'Most interesting. Lunch we'll keep simple, Sandy. Just sandwiches, perhaps a Caesar's salad, and fruit. Dinner, we'd like you to surprise us. You may need to go to the store. Jarvis probably knows the stores by now, he seems to find his way about. Wouldn't you agree, Jarvis?'

'Modom?'

'The china's in the rosewood cabinet. Ask Jarvis. I'm afraid this can't be quite what you're accustomed to, Sandy, the circumstances, everything . . . '

Instructions had become apologies. The apologies trailed away. She's putting on a show, Twitty judged, but she's forlorn, and why wouldn't she be? Smashing and forlorn like whatsername, the film star, the one everyone raves about. Marilyn Monroe.

'We rather leave it to you, Sandy. Let's not have frozen food.'

She glided away between laundry appliances, an indoor barbecue, the table-tennis table.

'Get in there,' Peckover told Twitty, and closed the door. 'Who's Sandy Kofia? What the hell sort of name is that? Thought you were Gordon someone.'

'S. Kofia – Escoffier. More class than Gordon Blew, as a name, wouldn't you say?'

'Reckon you should know about class. School you went to, castles in the 'Ighlands. So you've seen me in action, Jarvis the performing seal, what d'you think?'

'Honest, Guv, amazing.'

'Really?'

'Brilliant. You should be in Shakespeare. Only one thing.'

'Yer? Careful.'

'What's this "modom"?'

'What about it?'

'You keep saying "modom". The word's "madam". "Ma'am" is even better. You say "ma'am" to the Queen.'

'Butterwick says "modom". Blimey, he should know, he charges enough. Anyway, too late to change, it's become an 'abit, so I'm stuck with it, and so's Gloria. I'll show you the kitchen. I need a pot of tea. Then bed.'

'Bit early, isn't it?'

'Grab your sleep while you can, lad. Things have a way of 'appening here at three in the morning.'

Nothing happened at three or at any other hour of the night, not as far as Peckover was aware. Nothing much happened the next day either, apart from mosquitoes and greenly thickening mildew. Not anyway until evening.

Which is not to say that butler and cook were not kept on the go. Breakfast. Lunch. Snacks and potations for friends of the Langleys who called with flowers and commiserations. Iced tea on the terrace.

The family attended morning service at St Peter's Church and returned with the Reverend and Mrs Roberts as unexpected lunch guests, thereby causing a minor panic in the galley. More egg sandwiches were slapped together, their crusts sliced off delicately, and for the most part left uneaten. Gloria informed the staff that it might be an excellent idea to have coffee and snacks on hand at all times for the investigating officers. Peckover considered the idea one of the three or four most appalling he had ever heard. Was Gloria merely being gracious or did she believe that the more Sergeant De Voto and his troops were fed and watered, the swifter their brains would whirl, and the sooner they would solve all, make the necessary arrests, and fold their tents and steal away?

Twitty thought that the guv'nor in his yellow and white butler's gear and black tie looked like a ballroom dance band leader but he didn't say so out loud. He sat in matching, floral shorts and tank-top on Joop's bar stool studying the bangers-and-mash paperback. The recipes appeared to be British with an occasional infusion of foreignness, such as possibly Balkan. He rather liked the sound of lamb's head and barley with brain sauce.

Sergeant De Voto kept Peckover and Twitty more or less in touch. The preliminary findings faxed from the NYPD medical examiner reported that Timothy Thwaite had died from strangulation by a twenty-seven-inch length of rubber-sheathed electrical extension cord between the hours of three and seven p.m., Friday.

The documents king from Washington, DC, would be a T. Ashton Watts, up to his eyeballs in degrees and awards, and expected Monday. The Sergeant's view was that the qualifications

156

were soul-stirring but no one he had ever known who put an initial in front of his first name was to be trusted.

Nothing on a missing cocoa cup and can of Hershey's, two days ago, or was it three? To the Sergeant, the cocoa, and Millicent, and the butler getting himself assaulted on the dunes, seemed as far back in history as the Yankees winning.

The Sergeant sat in front of a video screen in Ahoy's ice-blue cop-populated, conservatory area with the hibiscus and avocado trees pushed aside and the filing trays brought stage centre. He tapped buttons, watched, and waited.

EX DR STONE, MIDDLEHAMPTON. 2.30 P.M. SUNDAY.
ROOSEVELT DOCUMENT ANALYSIS NEGATIVE.

Great, that was something. Only question, what in hell did 'negative' mean? A forgery? Not a forgery? Too soon to say? No opinion?

What did the experts know? For all his blue-chip reputation, and fee to match, Dr Stone could be wrong, whatever his opinion, as T. Ashton Watts might be wrong. The consultants with the track record and power breakfasts who had guaranteed the Howard Hughes manuscript genuine, they'd been wrong, and the Brit professor at Oxford University who'd claimed the phoney Hitler diaries the real thing.

Tap. Tap tap. These were the machines could give you leprosy.

The bag lady hadn't murdered Thwaite. Someone had drugged her and kept her blankets and bags and got her out of the way by dumping her on a train. Probably made a show of her being a falling-down drunk. The someone who killed Thwaite dressed him up as the bag lady, a fixture, part of the Penn architecture, because he wanted time to be out of the way too, the more time the better, maybe to get back to Dunehampton and build an alibi.

Someone who was waiting for Thwaite at Penn. Or on the same train. Someone Thwaite probably knew or why would he accompany the someone into an empty side-turn away from the crowds? Natural to step into a side-turn to conduct business, like a handover of blackmail money.

Benny. Thwaite was blackmailing him, or taking bribes, was

157

Peckover's theory. He'd already got a thousand bucks out of him. So, Benny the perpetrator, case sewn up, promotion to captain for Mrs De Voto's bright-eyed boy.

Too bad Benny hadn't been in the city on Friday. He'd been here. Yesterday, Saturday, he was supposed to have been in the city. Had anyone checked?

BENJAMIN GAYLORD BENJAMIN. BORN 1942 PHILADELPHIA. EDUC OAKWOOD, PENN, BROWN UNIV. RI. SERVICE US NAVY 1964–

Tap. Cancel, green-out. He'd seen all this junk. Benny had money, he wasn't sleeping around, far as was known, and he couldn't have killed Thwaite. If he'd killed Lou and Millicent his reasons were clear as mud.

The Dutchman, he could have been in the city and waiting for Thwaite.

All the Sergeant knew was that tomorrow on Channel Eleven the Yankees were playing the Red Sox and he was going to catch the game whether it meant vanishing without a word or standing on a table and announcing, 'Take over, you guys, I'm watching the game.' The Vice-President was flying back to Washington at ten so the Chief would be back being low-key and taking over, and high time.

Taking over and taking a bunch of abuse from the politicians and the press if a breakthrough wasn't made soon, and taking the glory if it was. Hail to the Chief, and good luck.

Tap tap tap tap.

JOOP DEN BEETS. REQUEST MAY 14. INTERPOL ATTENTION G. ROSKO, CHIEF OF POLICE, DUNEHAMPTON, NEW YORK. SUBJECT BORN 1957 HAARLEM, NETH. OCCUPATION SHIP'S STEWARD, COOK. DIVORCED. NO PERMANENT ADDRESS. SUMMARY OF CONVICTIONS ISSUED MAY 12. MIN JUSTICE DEPT CRIMINAL AFFAIRS & PARDONS, NATIONAL POLICE RECORD 41008 UTRECHT CEDEX 01. 1971–73 OFFENCES AS MINOR, BREAKING & ENTERING (32), BURGLARY (17), 2 YEARS REFORM SCHOOL, APELDOORN. 1976 CAR THEFT, CARRYING CONCEALED WEAPON, 6 MONTHS, VOORNE. 1978 BURGLARY WITH AGGRAVATED ASSAULT, 18 MONTHS, VOORNE. 1981

CREDIT CARD FRAUD, ASSAULT ON POLICE OFFICER,
2 YEARS, WILLEMSDORP, 1984–88. BURGLARY, ILLEGAL
POSSESSION FIREARM, GRIEVOUS BODILY HARM, 4 YEARS,
VOORNE (EXTRAD MARTINIQUE, WI).

The Sergeant frowned at the screen. Had he tapped the wrong code, tuned in on a program no one had tuned in on before? Where had they all been? On vacation? Asleep?

From breaking and entering to grievous bodily harm and on to terminal bodily harm of, say, just by way of example, Lou and Millicent Langley, would be no big deal, not the way this bozo had been shaping.

But that wasn't it. More to the point, this background on Joop had been requested by the Chief back in early May when Lou Langley had been mowing his lawns like a bandit.

FIFTEEN

Twitty chopped the cucumber slowly. He was uncertain what he would be doing with the cucumber, but it was here, and it had to be chopped because you never saw anyone eat a cucumber whole, like a banana.

He chopped slowly not because he was tired. He merely didn't know how to chop quickly, like he'd seen a TV chef chop in a blur of steel. These kitchen knives could cost a bloke a finger. He was near to swooning just imagining it. If he'd been a murderer in search of a murder weapon he'd not have messed about with extension wire, he'd have come to the kitchen. A flick from one of these beauties and your victim's head would be bouncing on the floor. *Vive la Révolution!*

Twitty had decided he did not much enjoy being a chef. He particularly did not enjoy dressing like a chef. Over his shorts and tank top he had donned the stained, blue-and-white-striped butcher's apron he had found on a peg behind the door. Individuality shone through only in the dancing-master's pumps on his feet, white patent leather with silver buckles from Lambeth Walk, the shop by Lambeth North tube with the tutus and tambourines and cast-off Salvation Army jackets. What he would have liked was a chef's toque, the starched headpiece with a hundred pleats, he had read somewhere, one pleat for each different way you could use an egg. Toques had to be a French invention. Who else would want to use eggs a hundred different ways? What was wrong with frying them?

He wondered if he should have peeled the cucumber. The skin was tough and waxy where it was green, and elsewhere mottled with squishy brown patches, but the skin was all that kept the

160

inside from melting over the chopping board in a milky ooze of pips. This was a cucumber of yesteryear. He could slather it with something. Did they have mayonnaise?

Not a great deal of anything in the cupboards except cans, but cans were good, and anyway Gloria had said he was to surprise them. He would empty the two cans of El Paso chili into the casserole, add the Campbell's mushroom soup for moisture, slosh it around, and stick it in the oven. He might crumble some cheese over it if he could find any. With spuds. And cucumber salad. There wouldn't be much cucumber salad but they might not want much once they'd tasted it. And unless they ate with their eyes shut, they might not want to taste it. He could eke out the chili with a couple of onions. Plenty of onions here. And ketchup. And oh, as I live and breathe, here was curry powder! And Spanish brandy! This chili would put hair on their chests.

No garlic. Odd, that. Educated family like this, you'd have thought they'd have so much garlic hanging from the ceiling you'd be banging your head on it. Not that he kept up with food and health matters, you'd need a staff of chemists and secretaries, but the last he'd seen, garlic was the world's sole remaining foodstuff which not only didn't actually kill you but was good for you, or it was if you had rheumatism.

Peckover came in in his dance band conductor's uniform, twitched his nostrils, and said, 'What's the smell?'

'What smell?'

'Something burning?'

'Give me a chance, I haven't started yet.'

Peckover peered aghast over Twitty's shoulder at a gangrenous hillock of green circlets and milky sludge on a chopping board. 'You're not giving them that?'

'I'm not. You are. It's the cook wot keeps in the kitchen, it's the waiter wot gets the blame. Might not look so bad once I find something to cover it up.'

'Pooh! It's you!'

'What is?'

'You smell like roasting cheese. What is it?'

'Tomcat. Sexy, eh? Heathrow duty-free. She said it was a new line. Actually, it's got some French name like Boeuf Brut. You

can borrow it, but be sparing, it cost more than the air fare. There
was a tubby fellow looking for you. Rudy Pardo. The one you say
has a gun.'
   'He wasn't holding it?'
   'Didn't look capable of holding anything. Holding on, you ask
me. Shaky, distracted.'
   'What did he want?'
   'You.'
   'He's not the only one. I was waylaid by Feet. He's being
helpful because he wants help, as don't we all. Joop's got a long
record.'
   'Could get longer if he's not found soon.' Rummaging, Twitty
found a can of cherries. 'Fab! Do they realise how lucky they
are?'
   'His record includes beating up coppers.'
   'Sounds like your phantom of the dunes. Guv, you're blocking
my only path to the tin-opener.'
   Peckover, sidestepping, took from a pocket of his butler's jacket
a sheaf of print-outs from the Sergeant. He said, 'Hottest from on
high is the verdict of our graphologist, Dr Stone.'
   'If you mash up butter and flour and throw cherries on it, do
you get cherry crumble? My mum makes crumbles.'
   'This Stone says the yellow legal pad paper is correct for
Roosevelt, and the fountain pen, and the ink, Waterman's,
but not the calligraphy. The calligraphy's too correct.' Peckover
held the print-out not quite at arm's length. Idiotic to keep
resisting glasses, really was. Everyone over forty wore glasses.
'Roosevelt's writing was quick and slanty with Greek "e"s, like a
three backwards, except he'd also do an ordinary closed-up "e",
all of which demonstrates, our Dr Stone assures us, qualities of
orderliness, caution, energy, and 'igh ideals, at which point 'e loses
me because he's going beyond his brief, into fortune-telling.'
   'Have you seen the salt?'
   'The penmanship on the Pearl 'Arbor paper is too quick and
slanting, like a caricature, and not one closed-up "e". A forgery,
the man says. Too like the real thing to be the real thing. Like
a bad tracing. One fake Day of Infamy speech, courtesy of the
late Tim Thwaite. What do we deduce from that?'
   'If the family killed Thwaite to try and keep Ahoy to themselves,

they jumped the gun. They should have waited for Stone's testimony in court.'

'Killing Thwaite might 'ave nothing to do with the will. 'Ow about a good old-fashioned *crime passionel*, Thwaite as Romaine's lover? Enter some hot-blooded defender of her honour bearing extension cord.'

'Not Joop then. The Dutch aren't hot-blooded. They haven't time. They're too busy keeping the sea off the tulips.'

'The family don't come across as furnaces raging out of control either. Not the men anyway.'

'They might after eating chili à la Twitty,' Twitty said, lining up Tabasco sauce alongside curry powder and red pepper flakes.

The swing door opened to admit first Prune, labouring forward very close to the floor, then the coppery tresses and uncertain smile of Gloria, who held a bottle of champagne. While Prune lay prone on the tiles, slapping them with her tail, Gloria hovered in the doorway, outnumbered by staff, voluptuously unattainable. She wore drooping gold earrings which probably had once belonged to Catherine the Great, and a silk, Nile-green trouser suit of the sort that millionaire couturiers present to the First Lady in the hope that she will wear it on national television with the label showing.

She said, 'Good evening,' and wrinkled her nose. 'Is there a peculiar smell?'

'Tomcat,' Peckover said.

Prune lifted her head.

'Excuse me?' said Gloria.

'French, modom.' What are you complaining about, you're not even in the kitchen, Peckover wanted to tell her. Snuggle up to the lad and get a real whiff. 'A new line in men's toiletries, as modelled by the cook.'

'Really. Everything all right, Sandy?'

Twitty stared uncomprehendingly. Was she addressing him?

'Smashing, ma'am. Apart from a possible salt shortage.'

'We try to hold back on salt,' Gloria said. 'Would you mind giving Prune her dinner? There's Wagg in the bottom cupboard. Jarvis, perhaps you'd put this in the freezer for ten minutes.' She had to take a step into the kitchen to hand over the champagne. 'We'll have it in the green drawing-room.'

'A celebration, modom?'

163

'Romaine won her medium pony conformation hunter class. She has a chance for the Grand Prix.'

'That is most excellent news.'

'We're due for some, wouldn't you say?'

'Extra oats for Glad Rags?'

Gloria regarded the butler warily, unsure whether he was entering playfully into the spirit of celebration or being sarcastic. The butler was not sure either. As she backed out, Rudy arrived. Holding the door for her, he enquired into the kitchen. 'Do we have peanuts?'

He allowed the door to close behind Gloria.

'We need to talk,' he told Peckover.

'Talk then. You met Detective Constable Twitty?'

'I can't talk here. After dinner.' Shaving, Rudy had nicked, of all places, his ear. He looked shifty, blubbery, and unwell. He wore the same peach tie and burgundy jacket that he seemed to wear every evening, as if making changes were beyond him. 'Late, say midnight. If anyone's still up you can be neatening, but there won't be. On the west deck.'

'Which deck's that?'

'Where we have breakfast.'

'I could lay the table, get a start on things.'

'Very funny.'

'Say it now, what you have to say.'

'You're the one's going to be taking time, asking questions.'

'We might drop by.'

Rudy, scratching between his legs, eyed Twitty. 'He doesn't have to.'

'This is the cook, mate,' Peckover said. 'You want peanuts, be nice to 'im.'

Twitty emptied menacing chili into a casserole. ' "God sends meat, the Devil sends cooks," ' he announced. 'Who said that? Somebody said it.'

Rudy swore pointlessly on the subject of peanuts and shambled from the kitchen. Peckover read the label on the champagne. *Flying Goose. Demi-Sec. La Fantaisie Vineyards, Quaha, NY.* He put it in the freezer, slaughtered a mosquito with a clap of his hands, and collected cutlery. Twitty found Wagg: Vitamin-Enriched Gourmet Dog Food. He was delighted. Anything Prune left could

164

enrich the chili, if she didn't slobber into it too much.

He said, 'You trust that geezer?'

'Like I trust an English summer,' Peckover said.

Benny Benjamin breezed in carrying an ice-bucket and calling out, 'Ice, shipmates!'

Twitty muttered, 'It's Paddington Station here,' and bestowed on Benny a smile of rapturous welcome.

'Sun's over the yardarm,' Benny warbled. 'We're losing time.'

Prune gulped Wagg. Peckover stepped over her on his way to the freezer with the ice-bucket.

He said, 'We are merry this evening, sir.'

'We are? Dammit, Jackson, you're right, we are.' He peered over Twitty's shoulder into the casserole. The cook, with a wooden spoon, was sloshing the contents to a mucous colour and consistency. 'Queer-looking stuff,' Benny opined, unasked. 'Bit pungent, wouldn't you say? What's the silage smell? For Prune, is it?'

'Remains to be seen, sir.'

'Romaine,' hazarded Peckover.

'Romaine what?' Benny said.

'The cause for cheerfulness, sir. Her triumph on Glad Rags.'

'Isn't that something?'

'And now for the Grand Prix.'

'That so?'

'Weather permitting.'

'Expecting squalls, are we? Any update on Doris?'

'Never mind Doris. What about Tim Thwaite? He a cause for cheerfulness too?'

Twitty, his back to the guv'nor and Benny, stopped sloshing. Prune licked her dish clean, continuing to lick when nothing remained.

Benny, frowning, said, 'What's that mean?'

'I don't notice any of you prostrating yourselves with grief over your caretaker being murdered.'

Twitty sloshed fast. Prune waddled to the door and sat.

Benny said, 'Exactly what are you saying?'

'Thwaite's dead and the champagne is chilling nicely.'

'You're out of line, Jarvis.'

'Death and champers, but no connection?'

165

'Out of line, Jarvis, and out of here pronto, any more of this.'

'You've got the name right – twice. Must be losing your concentration.' Peckover tugged on the ice-tray's lever. The ice creaked. 'The police are asking what you were doing in the city.'

'I haven't been in the city in weeks. Look, who are you?'

'Jarvis, sir, with your best interests at heart. I have my ear to the ground. The police are asking questions. They will want to know where you were.'

'Sailing.'

'Can anyone corroborate that?'

'Ought to, there were five of us. If they want to know, why don't they ask?'

'They may also want to know about the thousand dollars you gave Thwaite shortly before he was murdered.'

Twitty turned on the oven at five hundred.

Benny said, 'What thousand? This is garbage.'

'Quite so, sir.' Peckover clattered ice into ice-bucket. 'But forewarned is forearmed. They would appear to have it in their heads that Thwaite was blackmailing you.'

'Their heads,' Benny exploded, 'are cloth!' He snatched the ice-bucket.

'That you were a party to Mr Thwaite's forging of the Pearl Harbor draft, whereupon he put the screws on.'

'I've never seen the Pearl Harbor draft! Never heard of it until Lou died! It's insane!'

Peckover agreed. He plugged on. 'A dissenting opinion, sir, would seem to be that the thousand was not blackmail but a bribe.'

Bull's-eye. If not a bull's-eye, an inner. Benny's mouth flapped soundlessly.

Twitty let Prune out through the swing door.

'Bilgewater,' Benny croaked, and plunged his hand into the ice-bucket, as Mucius Scaevola had plunged his hand into the burning brazier in 499 BC.

'A bribe,' Peckover prompted, 'on account of an affair of the heart.'

'Is that so? Whose heart?'

Whose indeed? In for a penny.

'Romaine.' Peckover said.

Benny crunched ice in his fist. 'Thwaite told you.'

166

'He was drinking hard— '

'Thwaite, drinking?'

'Gin. In vino veritas. He showed me the cash in the book he'd written.'

'Traitor pusbag.' A lump of ice whizzed from Benny's fist and skidded across the tiles. 'He said he wasn't sleeping with Romaine and didn't want the money. But he was. I did it for Romaine. Goddam, I did it for all of us.'

'Why?'

'I'm soft. Bastard Brit homebreaker Thwaite. Why can't Romaine stick to horses?'

'Or to Rudy.'

'Yuck, Rudy. So it's a crime giving somebody money?'

'If your money's spurned, your alternative could be more extreme, sir.'

Twitty, mashing potatoes, glanced round at the guv'nor and Benny standing nose to nose. He had seen somewhere a wooden mallet which was a meat stomper. That's what had been written on it, Meat Stomper, so you would know. Just waving it might be enough if Benny became obstreperous.

Benny said, 'Say it, Jarvis. This dissenting opinion would like to believe I killed Thwaite?'

'Truly most unfortunate, sir.'

Cursing far more colourfully than Rudy had, Benny Benjamin barged with the ice-bucket through the swing door and out of the kitchen. Peckover reclaimed cutlery. Having pulverised the potatoes and added curry powder, Twitty rinsed grapes under the tap.

'*Chili véronique*?' Peckover said.

'Who?'

'With grapes. Twenty minutes if we're going to be on time, lad. There's bread and peas and stuff in the freezer. You could heat 'em up. Look on it all as a challenge.'

'You're the challenge, Guv. You've upset Mr Benjamin. Just when they're trying to celebrate.'

'It's us should be celebrating. Admitted the bribe, didn't 'e? One small step for truth and light.' He watched Twitty improve the mashed potato with pepper. 'Steady with the seasoning, lad. This isn't Madras.'

Twitty gave the pepper pot a final vigorous shake. The lid fell off

167

into the mashed potato and with it an avalanche of ground black pepper, thereby creating three-alarm mash, or mash vindaloo. He sneezingly spooned out the lid and as much pepper as could be removed without reducing the amount of remaining mash to a single portion for an invalid.

'Gawd,' murmured Peckover.

He brought cutlery, crockery, place mats and napkins to the oak refectory table beneath the chandelier. Would the Reginald Butterwick Academy of Domestic Service have seated the family at the table's four compass points or bunched them together at one end? He opted for the compass points. Let them celebrate at long distance. If they had anything of note to say they'd have to shout and he'd hear it in the kitchen. If they wanted to bunch up, they could bunch themselves.

In the kitchen he swaddled champagne in a cleanish towel and set it on the pasha's tray with four glasses, and in the absence of smoked salmon a bowl of pretzels. Softly, liltingly, basso profundo, he sang, 'What shall we do with a drunken sailor?'

Twitty, wearing an oven glove with the slogan, Thin Cooks Can't Be Trusted, checked the casserole in the oven, and yelped. He nursed a scorched forearm where it had touched a five-hundred-degree oven rack. Charred hair warred with Tomcat.

'Put it under the cold tap,' Peckover urged. 'Cut a potato in half. Miriam's remedy. The starch helps. Wait – a mash vindaloo poultice, the very thing.'

Chin in, shoulders back, bearing the tray, Jarvis advanced on the swing door. 'Put 'im in the scuppers with an 'osepipe on 'im,' the butler sang.

Passing the refectory table, he cast a maître d's eye on his four covers at north, south, east, and west. Looked all right. They'd be needing a jug of water. Better open a bottle or two of the Cantenac Brown. What kind of a celebration was one bottle of champagne no one had heard of?

No more than he had guessed three evenings ago that the lamb, cold cuts, and flan with Gauloise ash were to have been Millicent Langley's last meal, did it now enter his head that never again, after tonight, would all four of them – Gloria and Benny, Rudy and Romaine – sit down together. But now it was time to serve the fruits of Twitty's labours.

168

SIXTEEN

They looked on in silence as Jarvis popped the champagne cork and poured with slow, consummate professionalism, uncertain only where his left hand ought to be, whether behind his back, where the Duke of Edinburgh would have had his, or holding his lapel like Mr Gladstone.

Romaine wore pearls, a black top, and a skirt to her tanned ankles. The left ankle sported a bruise which Peckover supposed to be from stirrup chafe, or an untoward jolt over the water-jump. Strumpet, he thought, presenting the tray to Romaine's versatile horseperson's, whoresperson's hand. You have brought down on the House of Langley, contributed anyway, the wrath of the gods and much aggro.

He announced, 'If it please, modom, the staff are delighted to offer their congratulations on your victory in the medium deformation hunter category.'

'Conformation.'

'Precisely.'

'Thank you, Jarvis.'

In the kitchen the cook had found a pound of dried apricots and was heating them in milk in a frying pan as a side dish which might become the main dish should chili Twitty go unappreciated. Sergeant De Voto, arrived by the servants' stairs, was eating the last of the pretzels. Compliments of the cook, he stood guard over a glass of Spanish brandy. A roll of fresh computer print-outs protruded from a pants pocket. When Peckover came in, the Sergeant took them out and leafed through.

'That unfinished letter you saw, the one a guest wrote to – here it is – Barb and Emil. "Romaine . . . we think she has a man." The guest was Sylvia Ellis, Palm Beach, and Barb's her sister.

169

Palm Beach has talked to Sylvia Ellis and she doesn't know who Romaine's man is or was. In her list of who it wasn't, Thwaite comes top.'

'Hope she 'as a good reason.'

'Instinct. Palm Beach found her convincing. She's known Romaine since college and she met Thwaite a couple of times.' He licked pretzel crumbs from his moustache. 'If it was Thwaite it wasn't in his apartment, any fornicating. Unlikely they'd choose a local motel because they could walk into someone who knew them, like one of Thwaite's students with a vacuum earning tuition money.'

'Why not 'is apartment? Scarlet carpet, all those mirrors. Very arousing.'

'The cat. Romaine's allergic. Her eyes run and she breaks out in a rash. Thwaite would have spent the night bringing antiseptic.'

''Old on. Jason, lad, I hear a rumble of distant bellies. Everything ready?'

'No.'

'Fine. Move it. Get it out on the serving table.' Peckover poured himself a glass of water and drank it down. He told the Sergeant, 'Benny's thousand to Thwaite was a bribe to keep him away from Romaine.'

'Benny said that?'

'It was elicited. I'm inclined to believe 'im. Snag is' – Peckover's eyes swivelled in search of the brandy but failed to locate it. He didn't really want any anyway – 'I wouldn't be surprised if whassername in Palm Beach isn't right too. Other words, Benny has it half right. Romaine's playing around but it wasn't with Thwaite.'

Twitty said, 'Why don't we ask her?'

Silence.

'Oh, boy, mind like a laser,' said the Sergeant.

'The cook has a point,' Peckover said, assembling serving spoons.

'Davy Pugh already asked her and she blew up,' the Sergeant said. 'We guessed she would. Much the same as asking your Queen, I don't know, anything personal, like how much her earrings cost.'

'Romaine denied having a bloke?'

170

'Romaine blew up. Denying didn't come into it. Davy says he could have lost his eyes.'

'She blows up in court, the judge'll strap her down,' said the cook, peering into the oven at frothing chili. What was the fizzy lather on top? 'We have here, from an astonishing new talent, a seamless dish which may be eaten on different levels. Nominated a Dish-of-the-Month-Club Alternate Selection.'

'What're you burbling about?'

'Is truth chili, master. Make he who eat babble truth. Or just babble. Need moment more for full burnt flavour.'

Twitty loped from the kitchen and into the dining-room with the first tray of found food: chopped onion garnished with yellowing parsley, hard bread in a basket, Joop's ageing currant bread on a gold-rimmed Limoges plate, a bunch of grapes with bare, ruin'd stalks where late the fruit-flies sang, a dish of warmed-up chick peas, apricots Armenia, and Cucumber Delight fortified with nutmeg, cinnamon, cloves, a bay leaf, and pinches of sundry, co-agulated, larvae-moving substances from jars lined up in the spice rack like a guard of honour summoned to the wake of their former commanding officer, Brigadier Percy Griddle-ffetlock, Battle of Omdurman, 1898.

'O cinnamon, where you gonna run to?' Twitty sang as he loped, sweating salty rivulets. The guv was in a singing mood, why not his aide-de-camp?

'It's me going to have to tackle Romaine next,' the Sergeant growled. He smiled angelically. 'Unless you'd like to, Henry?'

'I'm spoken for. I 'ave a date with Rudy. Midnight on the breakfast deck.'

'Keep your head down and don't lend him money. Like to hear about Joop? Joop's back in town.'

'Who said he left?'

'He probably didn't. He's hiding out on the beach, playing beach bums, blending. His problem is he's had too much sun, he's suffering.'

'So bring 'im in.'

'Sure, easy. Have you seen the beaches? There's a million people out there.'

'Who's he hiding from – you?'

'Right, if he killed Millicent.'

171

'If he killed Millicent he'd hide further away than the beaches.'

'Maybe, maybe not. If he didn't kill her, he'd still hide. Why wouldn't he, with his record? He's okay at Ahoy up to the moment Millicent is murdered, then his only impulse is to be out of here fast.'

'How do we know all this?'

'Four o'clock this afternoon he was nursing his sunburn in Harrigan's.'

'A hut on the beach where the afflicted can buy calomine lotion.'

'A grogshop behind the theatre. Quaint, smoky, safe, it's not Boston, you're not leaned on if you forget to put a dollar in the Our Lady of The Sorrows box.'

'Proceeds to bazookas for the cause? Don't tell me we've got an Irish dimension.' Peckover looked behind him as if for sudden death in an IRA beret. He saw only Twitty fanning the casserole but he continued to look, as if for his hat, the exit to the airport, and the first flight back to London, home, bed, and a blanket over his head. The IRA could put an end to you, by accident if not by calculation. For all he knew they might have a representative or two on Long Island. 'Sorry. Harrigan's. Mijnheer Joop.'

'Drinking. He got obnoxious with the barman, Pat. He smashed a glass. When Pat called the police, he left. We'll find him.'

'We're sure it was Joop?'

'Pat knows him.'

'That Palm Beach woman, she have Joop on her list of Romaine's possible bedmates?'

'She doesn't have a list and she's probably never heard of Joop.'

Twitty said, 'She was a guest here, ate his food, didn't she?' He poked with a spoon at chili Twitty, pretending to test it for doneness.

'Question is,' Peckover said, 'is anyone going to eat yours? At least give 'em the chance. Get it out there.'

Oven-gloved Twitty bore the casserole into the dining-room. 'Gwine where those chili winds don't blow,' he bluesily moaned. It was music night at Ahoy. Twitty's ever-expanding record collection of largely rock, soul, heavy metal, punk, funk, and clunk, included a maverick handful of Bessie Smith and Blind Lemon Jefferson.

Sergeant De Voto looked at his watch and said, 'Time to call the Chief.' He drank down the brandy, shuddered, and exited by the servants' stairs.

Jarvis checked his tie, shot his cuffs, draped his sommelier's napkin over his forearm, and slow-marched towards the green drawing-room. He stood in the doorway, waiting to catch Gloria's eye, motionless, yet almost visibly quivering with grandiosity. Surprised by sun, each of his pinkly English pores leaked stifling exudations of the majesty, contempt, and oiliness, of butlerdom.

'Dinnah is sarved, modom.'

After dinner, Gloria opened the door into the kitchen. The staff were drinking tea.

'Sandy, Jarvis, that was so nice. Thank you. So spicy, and sweet, and, well, so very good. We look forward to you both being with us in the city. Let's talk about it tomorrow.'

Also after dinner, the person who intended to kill Rudy Pardo telephoned him to say they must meet and talk. Rudy said no, maybe tomorrow, and hung up.

Rudy needed to talk to Peckover. How much to tell him he didn't know but there might be hope with Peckover. Did he mean hope or solace? Some solace. The guy wasn't a priest, he was a cop.

Talk to the Sergeant, any of the local bunch, the FBI, they'd have handcuffs on him before he could blink and it would all be over.

It was all over anyway. His mind wasn't right. Last couple of days, he had wanted it to be over. Curled up for ever in nothingness. What could anyone do? Peckover would listen. He might have ideas, and he probably wouldn't have handcuffs.

A plea bargain looked like the only hope. Rudy was not sure he even cared.

He sat in a canvas chair, in shadow, on the glass-walled west deck, his hand in his burgundy jacket pocket, holding the gun.

He remembered his mother buying him shoes at Alexander's and being sharp with the sales girl. They had moved on from

173

shoes to scratchy shirts and an over-large suit he would grow into. He saw her puzzling with eraser-tipped pencil over the Sunday crossword, darning socks, bundled up in fur and wool as she shovelled snow from the driveway.

Rudy's killer hung about outside in the dark, circling, waiting, watching lights in Ahoy go on and off, and, by this hour, mainly off.

Butler and cook cleared up and switched on the dishwasher. There were no leftovers. The family had polished off the lot.

'You'll be for it, lad.'

'What've I done?'

'Made Romaine go off 'er diet is what. Two soddin' plates of chick peas, you should 'ave seen her. Fat chance she'll have now in the Grand Prix.'

They split to the oases of their separate rooms. Peckover locked his door, checked the windows, showered, and weighed himself. 'One hundred and eighty-two pounds,' intoned the scales. 'You have lost four pounds. Have a nice day.' He lay on his bed and shut his eyes. He would have telephoned Miriam but in London the hour was three thirty in the morning.

Twitty, too, showered. He splashed liberal Tomcat on his person, hoped Gloria or Romaine might tap lightly on the door and enter wearing something diaphanous – if they weren't racially prejudiced, he certainly wasn't – then sat at the table in his baggy new surfer's swimming trunks which he hoped he'd have an opportunity to use, though not tonight. The trunks were patterned with a Hawaiian pineapple motif and reached to below the knee.

He hoisted the aerial of his ghetto-blaster, switched on, and hunched and twiddled like a radio ham in search of a Mayday emergency, or at very least a voice from a million miles away calling, 'G'day, cobber. Bondi Beach here. Fair dinkum. Waltzing Matilda.' What he wanted was cricket, which he wouldn't receive live at this hour, but there might be *Sports Report* with the scores. The BBC World Service, when he tracked it down, came through adequately audibly but less so than the mullah who, a hairbreadth below, was summoning the faithful somewhere in Pakistan, and, a hairbreadth below the mullah, a stereophonic marimba band

174

of gongs, gourds and xylophones from a Botswana game reserve. He recovered the BBC, listened to the end of *The Farming World*, and then to *New Ideas*, in which amateur inventors told how their invention would change the course of history. A bright spark with a Devon accent had invented a lightweight collapsible chair, simplicity itself, which you could carry in your lunch bag or hang from your belt. After *New Ideas* a voice informed him that the BBC World Service was closing now on this wave band. Twitty seethingly and in vain twiddled for an alternative frequency.

Five minutes before midnight, Peckover knocked on Twitty's door and opened it.

'Put on a shirt, mate. You look like a sunbather. We'll take the scenic outside route. I'm not going through the 'ouse and bumping into Benny and stepping on Prune.'

'You know the way?'

'Can't say I do. West deck, it's glass. If we know where the sea is we ought to be able to work out which way is west.'

Ahoy's environs lacked floodlighting. They stood amid iron deck furniture, peering into the night. In the darkness ahead were formless dunes. They could hear the thump of breaking waves.

'This way then,' Peckover said.

They descended steps. A stiff breeze was blowing. Peckover wore the sensible shoes, grey flannels, and business shirt he had left London in. He went first. Underfoot was sand and tufty grass which eventually became a brick path, then a lawn. Lawn was to be preferred over dunes but not by that much. They could step in a claw-tooth mole trap, be savaged by rose bushes. When he stopped to see if he had the least idea where they might be, Twitty bumped into him from behind.

Buttresses, a veranda without glass, the dim, distant white of the pool house, a glint of swimming pool. Here was south. He forged on, shadowed by Twitty, his eyes now adequately accustomed to the dark. He found a path leading to the right, westward, round the side of the house. Blurred shapes of cars loomed in the driveway's parking space. Towering, gloomy rhododendron bushes looked like the Victorian mausoleums of Calvinist businessmen and empire-builders in a Scottish graveyard.

They walked along the unlit west side of Ahoy towards an outline of steps leading up to a glass-walled deck. A sawing of cicadas filled the night. The air was damp, hot and in motion, the wind plucking at their hair, tugging Peckover's shirt, and causing Twitty's Hawaiian bathers to billow and flap. They halted at the foot of the steps.

'Here's where they 'ave their scrambled eggs.' Peckover spoke in a whisper, looking up at the glass and seeing only murk on the other side. 'There's a phone that looks like a rabbit. P'raps there's Rudy. You want to go first?'

'Me?'

'Only joking. Testing your mettle. Hope it's perkier than mine. You ever have presentiments?' Peckover put a foot on the bottom step and pressed down cautiously. 'Just stay close.'

He mounted the steps, Twitty one step behind. Opening the door an inch, two inches, he winced at the stridulous symphony of grating, rasping and twanging from anti-bug mesh and steel springs. He opened the door wide and stepped inside, Twitty at his back like the rear end of a pantomime horse. The door swung shut with a clang behind them.

Directly across the deck were the sliding glass doors through which he had wheeled in the breakfast trolley. To the left was a wicker table with the rabbit telephone and magazines. To the right, more tables, chairs, the trolley with laundered napkins, and Rudy in a heap on the floor. His head had been crushed. His hand held a familiar gun which Peckover presumed had not been fired. If it had been someone would have heard and presumably done something. In any case, on a table had thoughtfully been left a rock the size of a canteloupe melon and smothered with blood, skin and hair. The lake of blood on the deck smelled sugar-sweet and seemed to Peckover to be still creepingly spreading, if you watched it hard enough.

Twitty clapped his hand to his mouth.

'Outside, old son,' Peckover said, steering him to the door, opening it, nudging him through.

He picked up the telephone by its ears. Not only did the appliance look like a rabbit, it was of the breed which had musical push-buttons on which you could play 'Oh, I do like to be beside the seaside', if that's what you felt like doing. Peckover didn't.

SEVENTEEN

Ahoy's foundations cracked and shifted under the weight of cops summoned from their beds. Their racketing presence would later be looked back on by Peckover, a trifle mystically, as a warm-up for the yet greater onslaught to come.

Radios tuned to WCBS, WINS, and to the local Rogue Harbour station, kept everyone abreast. Whether indifferent to such worldly matters, or unaware of what was happening, the Dunehampton College station ploughed on with music by Bach and Hindemith.

'The storm's centre is expected to reach eastern Long Island between nine thirty and ten this morning,' cried the demented Rogue Harbour newscaster, thrilling to each five-minute update. He urged the populace to tape windows, bolt furniture securely, clear loose objects from shelves, unplug electrical appliances, and be sure to have available a portable radio, flashlight, candles, and supplies of food and drinking water. 'Fill the bathtub. Remember, we'll need all the water we can get for washing and for flushing the toilet. With a critter like this one there's no knowing how long some areas may be without power. Veronica?'

'Thank you, Hank. Just in, we have four fatalities in Riverville, New Jersey. A car carrying four teenagers was washed off the Wockensee Bridge into floodwater bringing the number of known deaths to seventeen directly attributable to this definitely the most violent hurricane to hit the tri-state area since the big one of 1938 so we're looking at something a whole barrelful more savage than '86 when the moon and tides were on our side which isn't the case this time so it looks like we're in for a real battering unless the direction changes but we'll keep you posted on that one. Hank?'

Hank read a cursory item on a murder in Dunehampton: Rudy Pardo, son-in-law of recently slain Millicent Langley, and three months earlier of Lou Langley, founder and former president of Langley Incorporated, the nation's second largest manufacturer of paper containers. Then came a commercial for the great American road belonging to Buick. Then back to Hank and Veronica repeating that all residents of ocean-front property plus the entire estate section south of the highway should be prepared to evacuate their homes if there were no velocity dissipation or directional change as every present indication and the weather bureau deemed unlikely so please stay tuned for up-to-the-minute news. Emergency relief centres with child and pet facilities had been set up at the firehouse at Route 27 and Mellick Avenue and at the high school on Hampton Way.

All police leave was cancelled. The west deck, where milled technicians, was cordoned off. Dr Webb, medical examiner and musician, offered his opinion that life at Ahoy was little different from a Verdi opera.

Sergeant De Voto snarled, 'If that documents nut in Washington isn't already on his way he's not going to get here. There'll be no more flights into New York.'

'He's at La Guardia waiting for a limo,' said Agent Carson Eisner. 'Should be here for breakfast.'

'Thanks for the information.'

Television crews taped the house from cellars to roof space with blithe indifference to the cost of their employers' film. A lighting technician pocketed a jade paperweight as a memento. News reporters borrowed books. *Invest and Grow: A Guide to Tax Shelters* disappeared into the handbag of the girl from the *Middlehampton Sun*, not that she would ever have cause to open it. Filched for professional purposes were family photographs. Framed snapshots vanished from mantels and the tops of bureaus, after which routine procedure the reporters were reduced virtually to interviewing each other, police and staff being cagey almost to the point of silence, and the family, such as remained of it, being held incommunicado. Grim, unapproachable Sergeant De Voto sequestered Gloria, Romaine and Benny in a third-floor rumpus-room which had its own bathroom and kitchenette, though the bathroom had no towels and the kitchenette only a container of

178

Morton salt. A temporary measure for their own safety, he assured them, and they were too dazed to protest. Davy Pugh at his side, he questioned them on their doings and whereabouts after dinner. None had been to the west deck. If they had they'd hardly have admitted it. Coffee and victuals would be brought on request, the Sergeant said. Who would prepare and bring coffee and victuals he neither knew nor cared. The new cook, he supposed. It wouldn't be Vito De Voto. Outside the door, as sentry, he posted Officer Ozzie Tripp, who otherwise would be off in search of the booze cabinet and getting himself into trouble.

Embarrassed and sullen as for the most part they were, with good reason, the police were cagey not only with the media but with each other. Lou Langley, Millicent Langley, Timothy Thwaite, Rudy Pardo. Unsolved and hardly to be boasted about. The two or three police who chattered in the hope of seeing themselves on TV, regardless of the wrath that would be visited on them from above, were the least informed and most inventive. A patrolman who had put in for a transfer to Brooklyn identified Timothy Thwaite as the lover of a famous bag lady and assured the thrust microphones and scurrying ballpoints that Rudy Pardo had been impaled on garden shears and might not have bled to death had he left them in his chest instead of pulling them out. The media, insufferable but not stupid, gleefully filmed and noted these nuggets anyway.

Least joy of all to the media, their profoundest disappointment, were the publicity-shy staff, a cook and a butler. Other than a glimpsed, distant sighting or two, they were not to be found, almost as if they were being deliberately evasive. Media frustration was great because, in the first place, staff were notoriously disloyal the moment a cheque was wafted under their nostrils, and secondly, this staff was rumoured to be British, therefore snooty, comical, and fair game.

'Rudy's gun is a Smith and Wesson out of the ark and hasn't been fired in a dog's age, or cleaned,' the Sergeant told the staff. 'Eisner's checking it out. He claims he knows guns. Knows everything. Thinks he does.'

They stood by a picture window with damask curtains in an empty sitting-room – De Voto, Pugh, Peckover, Twitty – and looked out at activity on the front driveway. An ambulance

179

received Rudy's body in a bag. Cops climbed in after it. The ambulance drove along the gravel, through the gates, and away. A single, impertinent cheep from a bird broke the silence. Peckover wondered if he detected a hint of pallor in the sky. He hoped so. He'd had enough of this night.

He said, 'Eisner has no opinion on why Rudy had the gun?'

The Sergeant shrugged. 'So's he could defend himself. But he wasn't given the chance.'

'He was expecting me, far as I'm aware. I get twitchy thinking about it.'

Twitty said, 'He wanted to talk to you, not shoot you.'

'How do we know what he wanted?'

'Permission to be creative, Guv?'

'No. Go on then, get it over.'

'The Langley file Mr Veal gave me is pathetic. All right, it's out of date, and what's more, I know I've not been here long— '

'Get on with it.'

Twitty had changed into white cricket flannels, tennis shoes, and a ruffled, Byronic, bleached-yellow blouse with singe marks from over-zealous ironing and cuffs that flopped over his hands. He inhaled and closed his eyes. An image of inhaling, trembling Ms Prettyman summoning Kufu floated in Peckover's memory.

'Rudy was a bad lot driven to malefaction by finding himself a pauper among a load of bloated moneybags,' Twitty said fast. 'To hurry along his wife's inheritance he pays someone to get rid of Lou Langley. Joop, f'rinstance. Pays good money. Rudy knew Lou's grass-mowing habits— '

'Didn't 'ave any money, though,' Peckover objected.

'Shut up, give him a chance,' said the Sergeant.

'You shut up,' Peckover said. 'Fair question, innit? Rudy's paying to be rid of Lou, what's 'e paying with?'

'A promissory note,' Twitty said. 'An IOU. Details. Going to have money once Lou's gone, isn't he?'

'No, he isn't. Romaine gets it.'

'Romaine has lovers,' continued Twitty. 'Rudy's price for putting up with her wanderings is a cheque, a donation to himself, a biggie. What I'm saying, Rudy's bad but not beyond redemption, like no conscience at all, so when it all gets out of hand – Millicent, Tim Thwaite – he goes to pieces. He may

180

have engineered those murders, but he may not have, I've not got that far yet. Whatever, suddenly it's as grisly as *Macbeth*, bodies piling up, and Rudy's at the end of his rope. He needs to talk to someone about his chances of wriggling out, someone he can sit down with— '

'You're talking about a lawyer not a bleedin' copper.'

'I'm not. What would he pay a lawyer with?'

'You just said. One of his IOUs.'

'The lawyers come later. Right now Rudy wants to know his chances and believe it or not you strike him as the sympathetic sort.'

'Your creating is a wonder and a marvel.'

'Point is, the gun wasn't for you, or for Joop— '

'Joop or whoever.'

' —or whoever, who got to him before we did. The gun was for himself. He's ready for the worst. You hear Rudy's confession, as much of it as he's telling, but instead of talking about loopholes and plea bargaining and six months instead of life and turning Queen's evidence, or whatever they do here, you blow your whistle and charge. In that case he puts the gun in his mouth, and boom, off to the Happy Valley.'

Twitty stared through the window. He seemed to have finished. Cameramen were loading equipment into the back of a station wagon. Ahoy's outside was in uproar from a myriad of birds cheeping and chirruping their dawn chorus.

Peckover swallowed a yawn. He was not indifferent, just weary. 'Leaves more questions unanswered than it answers.'

'I buy it, some of it,' the Sergeant said. 'I talked with Romaine, asked her about the boyfriend.'

'She blow up? Don't tell me she named names.'

'She denies it. No boyfriend.'

'She's lying to you or she was lying to her mother,' Peckover said. 'When I brought that cocoa she was making excuses to Millicent. She told her she'd not be seeing the bloke when she was back in the city.'

'One question that bugs me, why was Joop's record available to the Chief back in May but not to us?' said the Sergeant.

'*Achtung*, company,' said Davy Pugh.

A tribe of scribes and cameras was advancing through the

181

sitting-room. With casual briskness the policemen exited in the opposite direction, stepped up their pace through a sun parlour, and dispersed in the hall.

Peckover escaped to his room to think, and Twitty to seize BBC cricket, with luck. Then he would investigate outside and clean up his unfortunate accident before anyone stepped in it.

Ahoy continued to creak with comings, goings, and radios bleating the latest on Hurricane Doris, unerringly on course for eastern Long Island.

A limousine decanted T. Ashton Watts, curator, documents department, Library of Congress. Agent Eisner asked him if he was crazy. Hadn't he heard of Doris? Didn't he realise everyone was about to clear out?

' . . . scheduled to hit closer to eight thirty advancing the weather bureau's estimate to ten for its arrival in southern Connecticut by which time we'll be making a start writing the insurance claims especially on ocean-front properties where some owners may be looking at driftwood or not even that, just an empty space like gaps in a five-year-old's teeth. Hank?'

'Thank you, Veronica. Sea-rescue spotter planes have called off the search for . . . '

Too much for Prune, the excitement. She relieved herself on the sitting-room's Afghan rug, waddled fast from the scene, and lay down in a corner, flapping her tail, watchful for retribution.

In Beachport, a vice-presidential aide had presented Chief Rosko with bleary thanks for his services and given him the green light to elbow the leave-taking from JFK and hustle back to Dunehampton. Rosko arrived at Ahoy at about the time a fiery nail-clipping of sun would normally have been poking itself above the satellite dish on the roof's east ridge. This morning there were only granite skies and wind. His first act was to have Gloria and Benny Benjamin and Romaine Pardo taken to the station house for questioning.

Sergeant De Voto said, 'Hope you know what you're doing, Chief.'

'So do I,' Rosko said. 'Call it PR in the widest sense. We're going to be publicly seen to be doing what we ought to be doing, namely, the pursuit of justice, no favourites, each and all equal under and subject to the law. We'll be gentle with them. Couple

182

of hours, they can come back here, if they're foolish enough. What chance do you give this place?'

'It's back from the ocean. It's survived a hundred years.'

They sat among the computers and files of the ice-blue conservatory, now the makeshift murder-room. The Chief looked beyond the pushed-back palms and hibiscus.

'You haven't taped the windows.'

'Haven't taped my own windows,' said the Sergeant. 'I'm trying to cope with four murders. Chief, I take it we'll be gentle as in complimentary champagne. These people have friends who have friends.'

'You're talking friends? You forget where I've just been.' Rosko grinned. His right foot jiggled on his left knee. 'Eighteen holes yesterday with Mr Vice-President himself and entourage. Plus he won, three and two.'

'The local channel showed ten seconds of it but they didn't show you. Just him.'

'Would I steal his limelight? It's who you know, Vito, and I'm now a buddy of the Veep. Only waves coming this way are from out there. Doris. We're going to have to get out. Where's our butler?'

'Sleeping, if he has any sense.'

'The cook – Twitty?'

'Same, I guess.'

'What kind of a guy is he?'

'He has a theory of Rudy as instigator. Rudy started the ball rolling by putting out a contract on Lou so's to get his hands on his money.'

'What do you think?'

'I think it's too bad Rudy isn't going to be able to tell us. I think we have to find Joop.'

'We'll find Joop.'

'What I'm saying, find him before he winds up like Rudy and Tim Thwaite and the old couple.'

'Sounds like you have a theory too.'

'What's theory? I'm a redneck cop. What I have is this fanciful thing that soon as there's someone might be able to tell us something, soon as we start looking for him, he gets dead. Joop is now suspect *numero uno* and I worry about him. If we'd got

183

that computer report on him back in May we might have been quicker off the mark.'

'It was never in the computer in May. First I knew was yesterday. What's in the computer is a virus and we start with the computer company.' Rosko stood up and scratched a mosquito bite on his ear. 'See our stuff's shunted back to the station house before it's washed away to Nantucket. Do I say hi to the overseas help or let them sleep?'

'Let 'em sleep.'

'Short on stamina, the Yard. Think they've been in a hurricane before?'

'They'll love it.'

'Yeah?'

'They've come waltzing into carnage they don't have a clue about, and we don't either, and they know it. Peckover's been mugged twice. Doris'll be a respite. Like the commercial break when you've given your life to the Yankees and they're being beaten stupid by a team of one-eyed Reillys from some place you never heard of.'

'My dad was a Dodgers fan. He cried when they went to LA.'

'You told me.'

The direct line from the station house was ringing. The Sergeant answered it.

'Good,' he said, and after listening some more repeated, 'Good.' Nodding, listening, he said, 'Good,' and put down the phone.

'Salary increase, across the board, it's been approved,' Rosko said.

'We've got Joop.'

EIGHTEEN

Chief Rosko put his head into the butler's room and said, hi, how's it going, but he couldn't talk now. He and Vito were away to the police station to gaze on Joop. Sorry he couldn't invite the Yard but the Yard was still staff, far as the family knew, and they'd be back soon, Romaine and the Benjamins, and maybe in need of succour and home comforts while gathering their valuables, before abandoning Ahoy to Doris. Not that Henry would be missing anything. Gazing on Joop wasn't an attractive prospect but gazing was the most anyone could do for the present. Joop was legless and speechless. Three cops it had taken to lift him off the floor at Harrigan's and out to the car.

Peckover was tying his tie. He said, 'Doesn't sound like someone who's just converted Rudy's head into mulch.'

'Else that's exactly what it sounds like,' Rosko said.

'Do me a favour, all right? Check 'is ankles for teeth marks.'

'No problem.'

They raised a hand at each other, like string puppets, signifying farewell. Peckover put on his butler's jacket. When God, bone tired, switched off the lights of the universe and everyone went whirling into the void for ever, there'd be those whose last words would be, 'No problem.'

He knocked on Twitty's door and opened it. Twitty was not present but his ghetto-blaster was emitting a continuous buzz on the short-wave. Peckover switched it off.

For lack of a hurricane costume, Twitty had put on his Hawaiian bathers and the cossack shirt with the high collar and pearl buttons. Had Superintendent Veal told him Long Island was prone to hurricanes he'd have packed one of those amazing yellow sou'westers and matching tarpaulin jacket and pants, like

185

herring fishermen wore, or he might have if he'd had time to go shopping. He had filled a pail of water in his kitchen – he thought of the kitchen as his – and toted it outside and round the house, skirting mammoth shrubs and a pond with lilies – he supposed they were lilies, but no botanist, Constable Twitty. He refrained from dashing for fear of spilling the water, and stepped daintily, like a cygnet in *Swan Lake*. Walking through the house would have taken a fraction of the time this trek was taking but in the house were coppers and enquiring journalists, unless they had all gone home.

The wind howled like a dog. Twitty rounded a plot of shuddering rose trees, then more bushes, perhaps hydrangeas, their defunct balloons of petals pale and stooping in the gale. At least it was day, he could see. He searched the grass by the steps up to the west deck, and turned and circled, seeking the scene of his transgression. He halted by a blotch in the greensward. Lou's greensward. Lou would have had a seizure. The blotch wasn't much, a discolouring, a minor defilement. All the same. Sanitary Twitty hoisted the pail, aimed, and sluiced the contents over his blotch of post-Rudy vomit. A London drizzle would have taken care of it, in time, never mind a hurricane. But he had been disgusting and he had done what he had to do to get rid of it.

The glassed-in deck looked empty. A few hours ago it had been all bustle and scientists. He climbed the steps with his pail, trooped through Ahoy, meeting nobody, and found Peckover in the kitchen making tea.

'Guv, could be nothing, but come and see, if you've time.'

'I've time. Nothing 'appening here. Rosko and Feet are viewing Joop in the clink. Lord knows what the family's doing. Thought I might do a spot of gardening. Prune the coreopsis.'

'You could start by picking up some litter. I'll show you.'

Heads bent into the wind, Twitty and Peckover tracked across the lawn at Ahoy's west side. In the parking area a police car disgorged Benny, Gloria, Romaine, a uniformed copper as attendant, and a long-haired gent Peckover couldn't at first place, distant and blurred as they all were, shimmering in wind, dark, and the first fat splatters of rain. Ah, right, the bloke was the family cleric, the Reverend someone. Roberts.

For the offspring of Lou and Millicent and the remaining spouse,

186

now was a time for clergymen. Millicent's funeral tomorrow. Rudy's thereafter.

What about Thwaite's funeral after the post-mortem? Did anyone have it in hand? Thwaite would be able to pay for it, he had the bribe from Benny if nothing else. His estate might yet be worth Ahoy. Could a corpse inherit a house?

''Ope this won't take long, lad.' Peckover, trudging, had to raise his voice to be heard above the wind. 'I'm on duty, and in case it slipped your mind, so are you. They're back and they could be clamouring for your kedgeree as only you can make it.'

'Does Joop smoke?'

'Smokes Gauloises. Smells like burning wool.'

'Cigarettes?'

'Not bleedin' french fries, mate.' He had to shout. The wind bayed, the shrubs performed eurhythmics. 'French, though, Joop's fix. Why?'

Twitty searched the ground by the yew tree, one of a clump of three, sombre, swaying columns eight feet high and dense to within inches of the ground. Twenty yards further on was the glassed-in deck. The conical top of the yew leaned with the wind.

Twitty pointed with his foot and said, 'There, litter.'

In the grass were spent matches. Perhaps a dozen. The yew would have hidden a smoker standing here from anyone looking out from the deck.

'Could've been 'ere weeks,' Peckover said.

'I don't think so.'

Peckover, squatting and scrutinising, said, 'I don't either.' He planted his fingers like prongs in the grass to avoid being toppled by the wind. 'What makes you think they 'aven't? Been no rain, not till now. They're timber, right? They're not cardboard book matches, going to disintegrate overnight. No good to birds unless it's nest-building time, which it isn't. Might've been here since Columbus.'

'When was the lawn last cut?'

'Good lad.'

'Ta, Guv.'

'You saw it being cut?'

'Yesterday when you were off with the Sergeant somewhere. This brawny yob with the pectorals was up on a great mastodon

187

of a mower sending the grass showering up in the air – and presumably down again.'

Freshly dead, half-inch grass clippings lay on the growing grass. On both lay the strewn matches, some flat, others tilted, but not one with a grass clipping on it. The wind was ferocious but didn't seem to bother or shift the cut, trodden grass, or the matches. Perhaps here by the yew was sheltered, surmised Peckover. Perhaps if and when the wind were to uproot the yew, the matches and grass clippings would be whisked away too. Meanwhile the assumption had to be that a litter-bug had dropped matches here at some time since the last mowing, yesterday. Peckover unplugged his fingers from the lawn and stood up.

'Doesn't 'ave to be a smoker. Aren't any left in America, are there? They're all skulking in doorways and caves. Could be an arsonist.'

'Could have fallen out of a helicopter.'

'I'm mulling, lad, don't get sarcastic. Think he succeeded in lighting a fag?'

'Might have. Only takes the first sulphurous flare and a mouthful of sulphur to light up. Could have lit a dozen cigarettes with these matches. Does Joop use matches or a lighter?'

'Not the point, is it, old son?'

'No,' agreed Twitty.

They looked at each other in the wrenching wind. The point was, here was a harvest of matches but no butts.

Twitty said, 'Was it windy yesterday?'

'Breezy. Pretty blowy by midnight.' Peckover shouted louder through the spattering rain. 'Candles would have guttered.'

'You've been waiting all your life to say guttered and now you've done it,' shouted Twitty.

Adrift in the New World, on a Long Island lawn, in an incipient storm which might shortly bring a tidal wave across the lawn and flatten Ahoy, the London policemen stood with feet squarely planted and observed the matches. Postdating yesterday's mowing, each match wore its blackened head, not one having burned longer than an instant. If the fellow had been tidy enough to put his cigarette butts in his pocket, why hadn't he done the same with his perishing matches?

Twitty shouted, 'So who smokes a pipe?'

'Or cigars?'

'Sod cigars. Show me cigar butts. Show me ash. A pipe, Guv.'

Troubled Peckover accepted that one flare of a match, before the wind extinguished it, wouldn't light a pipe. In his Technicolor imagination he saw outdoors pipe-smokers on yachts and soccer terraces cupping their hands to strike matches and discarding, where they stood, dozens, scores of them, wind-demolished. A pipe-smoker had stood patiently here, might have, peeking round the yew for activity on the deck, such as the presence of Rudy, and trying to get his pipe going in a breeze that marked the beginning of Doris.

The police car which had brought back Benny, Gloria, and Romaine, had left. Now another arrived. From it stepped Sergeant De Voto and Chief Rosko wearing raincoats.

'Speak of the devil,' Peckover said.

'Which one?'

'You've met the Sergeant. You're like old friends. You've seen 'im smoke?'

'No.'

'What about Mr Rosko's 'abits?'

'How would I know?'

'Well then. C'mon, lad, back to the hub, the nerve-centre, the Piccadilly Circus of Ahoy, where all paths converge and the world and his wife must sooner or later meet.'

'My kitchen.'

'Hole in one, Constable.'

'Everybody out!' Sergeant De Voto called, clapping his hands, striding into the conservatory where stood the potted palms and police computer. 'Or are you aiming to swim?'

Present were only Davy Pugh and Agent Eisner, packing files. The rest of the murder squad and the last of the media had left.

The Sergeant said, 'Where's our precious documents scholar from Washington?'

'No sweat,' said Eisner. 'I sent him to the Colony House.'

'Great. Could be the last we'll see of him. The Colony House happens to be a registered historic inn, 1798.'

'What's your beef? The Library of Congress will pick up the bill.'

'For the funeral? I'm not talking bed and breakfast. Dunehampton gets a zephyr, the Colony's roof goes and another wall falls down. The Colony's got personal injury suits against it.'

Rain beat on the untaped windows.

Gloria came down the staircase wearing a black mackintosh with its collar turned up, a redheaded Marlene Dietrich, circa 1940. She hailed Chief Rosko.

'Have you seen Jarvis? Or the cook?'

'No, ma'am.'

'Please tell them they should come to us, my cousin, William Archer, on Mawaga Drive. Assuming they have nowhere else. Will any of your officers be remaining here?'

'Not if they can help it.'

'Perhaps you could ask Jarvis to lock up.'

'I'll give him the message.'

Down the stairs in a cloak came Romaine, dark of countenance, deprived of further medal possibilities, at least for today. There would be no Grand Prix in a hurricane. She strode past Gene Rosko without a word, as if Hurricane Doris were his fault.

On the Rogue Harbour radio station Hank and Veronica announced cancellations. Cancelled were a travelling rodeo in the Elks parking lot, which came as a benison to the rodeo, eleven of their fourteen cowboys being in plaster or on crutches; the Big Apple Circus with a troupe of Chinese acrobats, nine of whom would later abscond and apply for asylum; an antiques fair; a celebrity wine-tasting at the Parfait Vineyard; swimming championships at the Surf Club; tennis finals at the Grass Club; a parade by the Middlehampton Fire Department in which grown men, heavily moustached and muscled, tossed lollipops to children, buckets of water over each other, and fired a cannon which sent household pets bolting over the horizon; a poetry reading by Phyllis Forst, 'Dunehampton's Emily Dickinson'; and numberless private parties and backyard barbecues with smoke, carbon-crusted chicken pieces, corn, and wine chilled to arctic frigidity.

190

'Cancel the day!' cried Veronica, giving up. 'The day is cancelled!'

Hank announced, 'The eye of Doris will reach us very shortly. Be sensible. Stay indoors. To date this hurricane has caused seventeen known fatalities.'

Benny Benjamin, wearing a sea-captain's cap, came down the stairs soberly, carrying Prune.

'Abandon ship,' he said without conviction. The hall was empty. He kissed the sleek top of Prune's head.

Sergeant De Voto pushed through the swing door into the kitchen and found the butler and cook buttering currant bread.

He said, 'If that's for the family, they're leaving.'

'It's for us,' Peckover said. 'The Last Supper. Only it's breakfast. Where's the Chief?'

'I thought he'd be here.'

'I expect 'e will be. You and 'im and Jason can have a nice chat. I'm off to Thwaite's place, see if I can round up Puddy Tat.'

'It's taken care of. She's at the station house.'

'She'll be company for Joop.'

'I'm transferring Joop to the county jail.'

'More secure?'

'You could say that.'

'Is the county jail in the Chief's jurisdiction?'

'No.'

'He's happy, you moving Joop?'

'He doesn't know.'

'He's going to.'

'Not from either of you, not yet, okay?'

'You've got something we don't know about, like something concrete?'

'Nope. You?'

'We've got matches. I wouldn't call them evidence and after Doris I'd not bet on us having matches. They'll be on their way to the Azores. Vito, you've got to have something better than matches to shift Joop off the Chief's turf.'

'I've got zip. He knew nothing of Joop's police record in the computer until yesterday, he says. Matches where?'

'Near the west deck.'

'Eat,' Twitty said, proffering currant bread.

'I couldn't keep it down,' the Sergeant said. 'Look, I called the Chief at seven last night and mentioned you and Rudy had a rendezvous, midnight on the west desk. Along with a bunch of other stuff. I checked in again at ten. The message he'd left at the hotel was he was at a farewell-to-the-Veep party. He might have gone to the party and he might not. He might have gone and left early. He could have been here at midnight. He could have made it on the expressway to Penn in time to dope the bag lady and meet Thwaite's train, and for all we know he was at Ahoy the night Millicent was killed.'

'It had occurred to me. It's the most depressing thought I've had all year.'

'I never said any of this.'

'I never heard it.'

Outside the sky was dark, the wind blasted, the rain bucketed. Twitty, watching through the window, saw six yards of leafy maple bough plummet in a swirl of twigs and lesser branches. He did not hear its thump on the ground, such was the clamour of the gale.

The Sergeant said, 'Turning out to be quite a day and it's hardly begun. Doris. The Yankees game a washout. Now I've shunted Joop off, over the Chief's head. This could be the first day of my last days as a cop. What the hell. You get stale. Too bad about the pension. Wonder what they pay security staff at Yankee Stadium.'

The door swung open and Chief Rosko came in.

He said, 'Butler and cook are invited to join the family, some place on Mawaga Drive. In the phone book under Archer. I'd call them before the power goes, Henry. Brother, it's brutal out there.'

'Spot of rain won't hurt us, Gene,' said Peckover. ''Ope it won't because I've got to show you something before it's washed away.'

'Show me what?'

'Another nail in Joop's coffin. Only take a minute. Let me get my coat. The west deck's closest, it'll save us going round the 'ouse, so see you there.'

Before Chief Rosko could protest or tell him to get knotted, Peckover departed down the servants' stairs. He was not at all sure what he was doing. Perhaps hurricanes affected mental stability.

192

In Twitty's room he rummaged in the wastepaper-basket. Apart from an empty Air India ticket folder with stapled baggage-claim stub, and a sachet of betel nuts, the remnants were Joop's. Slim pickings but they might have been worse.

He plucked from the basket a scrunched, blue Gauloises packet, went into the bathroom, and doused the packet under the tap.

He almost forgot his coat. Coming from his butler's room, hat on head, buttoning his raincoat, he bumped into Twitty. He raised his hat to him.

'Don't ask, lad. Not one word. We're embarking on a secret and mystifying operation, codename Cock-up.'

'You need me?'

'Why? Where were you going?'

'Nowhere.'

'Course I need you. What d'you think you're 'ere for? No point us both getting wet, though. Come to the west deck and stand by.'

'I'll get my coat all the same.'

Bet you will, Peckover thought, heading for the staff stairs. Eye-catching garment like your coat, I'm surprised you ever take it off.

On the west deck the Chief said, 'I'd forget the hat, Henry, unless you never want to see it again.'

'We Brits never lose our hats.'

Just our marbles. Let Operation Cock-up commence.

NINETEEN

Detective Chief Inspector Peckover, a.k.a. Jarvis, butler to the Langley family at their summer cottage, Ahoy, Dunehampton, clamped a hand over his hat. When he unlatched the stressed and shuddering door, it tore out of his hand and slammed against the wall. Wind and rain roared in, blowing chairs over and sweeping magazines and the rabbit telephone from the table.

Holding the rail with one hand, his hat with the other, Peckover went down the steps into Hurricane Doris. The Chief dragged the door shut then trod behind. On the other side of the door's mesh screen arrived Twitty in his white aviator's coat. He placed his face against the mesh and his palms on either side of his face as if this were what was required to prevent the door from being blown in. Behind Twitty appeared Sergeant De Voto. They peered through the mesh at their intrepid colleagues.

The Sergeant said, 'They're going to be carried away like Dorothy and Toto in *The Wizard of Oz*.'

'That was a tornado.'

'What do you know about it?'

Off balance on the bottom step, Peckover grabbed both rails. His hat ripped from his head, bumpily climbed the shingled wall, and disappeared above the roof.

'Over the rainbow,' said Twitty.

Heads down, Peckover and Chief Rosko set off across the lawn. Within moments they were drenched. Phooey to raincoats, thought Peckover. They would have been better off wearing no clothes at all.

'Hope this is going to be good!' the Chief shouted.

I hope so too, Peckover mutely agreed.

He aimed past the yews, past resisting rose trees, and past the frothing pool, its contents heaving and slopped over the tiled rim as if, in its depths, some giant blender were at work, set at Whip. Onward into the blast he strained, the Chief a pace behind. At the edge of the copse he paused, looked to left and right, then entered into the thicket. Not a great deal was to be seen, only scrubby, dense trees and darkness, but anyone would have known where he was from the crunching and snapping of branches underfoot.

'Joop was here!' Peckover shouted. 'So what was 'e doing if he wasn't watching the house? C'mon!'

'Chrissake, not in there, you crazy?'

'Right, this way!' bawled Peckover, who in hurricane conditions heard poorly.

He barged big-shouldered into the trees. Rosko bent to tuck his trousers bottoms into his socks.

'Found it!' Somewhere in the copse, not far in, Peckover's cry of discovery was accompanied by sounds of rending branches. 'Gene? Where are you? 'Urry it up! Let's 'ave some corroboration here!'

Rosko high-stepped into the trees. Peckover grabbed his sleeve and pointed to a scrunched Gauloises packet among the sodden twigs and leafmould. Close by, a branch cracked and fell with a rush and a thud.

Peckover yelled, 'Can we assume Joop? Or is it going to be the door-to-door round-up of Gauloises smokers?'

'Get outa here!'

Chief Rosko was already on his way out, glowering, shaking himself, flicking away unconfirmed ticks, bugs, nits, chiggers and weevils from his ears and neck.

'Gene, take it, it's yours! Exhibit number six or seven! We don't 'ave too many!'

Peckover caught up. The Chief took the Gauloises packet and stuffed it into his raincoat pocket.

'Come and dry off!' Peckover shouted. 'Got to tell you about the Pearl 'Arbor paper!'

Peckover surged ahead, happy to be away from collapsing trees, and aiming away from the west deck. They blundered through the wind to the south side of Ahoy and its rim of sandstorming dunes. A rim was all that was left.

'Holy Mary,' said the Chief. 'We can't say we weren't warned.'

Where sandy dunes tufted with scrub, reeds, spartina grass, and wild beach plums had offered scratchy annoyance to walkers, and haven for careful lovers, the ocean boiled, flinging its spume high, cracking like gunfire, revelling in conquest. The steps up to the deck and basement area were remarkably unconquered and intact, so far.

They struggled across the deck to the basement door. Doris had pretty well cleared the deck of its furniture, catapulting tables and chairs into a tangle of ironmongery in a far corner. Peckover and Rosko achieved the sanctuary of the ping-pong table and washing machine area, heaved the door shut, and gasped. Not far distant sounded a crash of glass from an imploding, untaped window.

''Struth,' breathed Peckover.

'So what about the Infamy document?'

'The what?'

'The Pearl Harbor speech?'

'A new bloke's 'ere to look at it.' Peckover, taking off his coat, arrived in his room. 'An Ashton Watts from the Library of Congress.'

'I know that.'

'Eugh!' yelped Peckover.

He was staring at the underside of his wrist, by the watchstrap. He pinched the skir between thumb and forefinger.

'Gawd! This one of 'em?'

'Where?'

'Oh, my Gawd!'

They shared an instant gazing at the black speck on the tip of Peckover's forefinger before he flung out his arm, spastically fluttered his hand, flicked his fingers, flicked them again, then wiped them on his pants and went on wiping. After regarding again the now speckless finger he turned his attention to slapping and brushing his pants.

The Chief swore and stepped away.

'At least we know what to do,' Peckover said, throwing off his jacket. 'Dunno about you, mate, but for me it's shower, inspect yourself, and wake up the bleedin' doctor.' He kicked of his shoes. 'You'd 'ave thought an 'urricane would've sent the bleeders back into their 'oles.' He took off his trousers. 'Aseptic meningitis, right? Bell's bleedin' Palsy.' He ripped off his shirt and the Marks & Spencer underpants with the map of the London Underground which Sam and Mary had given him for Christmas. 'All we need, soddin' Lyme disease. Blimey, you should know. Your wife should.'

Peckover, naked and anxious, watched the Chief for confirmation. The Chief surpassed him in agitation, brushing his neck and face with his hands. His eyes went from Peckover to the floor and walls where a speck of a flicked tick might have landed. He stepped to the wall mirror.

He said, 'You prick, you should have kept it.' He peered in the mirror, angling his head and lifting his earlobes. 'Should have used tweezers. The doctor needs to see it.'

'Bit late, innit.' Peckover was on his way to the bathroom. 'You can be after me. I might be a while. Wait – have Twitty's. This way.'

Peckover jogged nudely from his room and into Twitty's. In the cook's bathroom he removed the key from the lock and palmed it. The Chief loomed over his shoulder, flicking at his head and flapping his wrists and ankles.

'Clean towels,' Peckover said. 'Cleanish. Up to you. I'll be 'alf an hour. Less if the power goes. That 'appens, you'll find me outside taking nature's sluice. I mean, that could do it. Purification by Doris.'

Rejecting, before it began to divert him, the image of two big policemen in the buff jigging in a hurricane, he left the Chief and the room. Under his butler's shower he soaped himself fast, rinsed and spluttered, stepped from the shower, and looked into the room.

Nobody.

He turned off the shower, cursorily dried himself, and put on most of his butler's raiment. No point in the tie. Six minutes after leaving the Chief he was back in Twitty's room. From behind the bathroom door sounded pelting water.

No Chief's raincoat, clothes, or gun. He had undressed in the bathroom.

Peckover stood outside the bathroom listening for the diminution of racket that would signal the switching off of the shower. He had to listen carefully because there would be no sudden hush. Shower and hurricane merged in a common, watery roar.

197

He stepped to the closet, slid the door open, and peeped in. He plucked up the bed's counterpane and bent down and looked. If the Chief was a villain he was not to be trusted. By definition. Ergo, you couldn't be too careful.

Where was the lad and where the Sergeant?

Peckover put his ear to the bathroom door and listened to the pelting of the shower.

If there were ticks, wouldn't the Chief have found them by now? Placed them with tweezers in a tick-tube and corked and labelled it? The bloke was paranoid about the buggers. Should he breeze in and offer to inspect the tricky spot between the shoulder blades?

Joop in a Ford truck had run Lou down, a contract paid for by bankrupt Rudy to hurry up his wife's cut of the inheritance. Did that make sense? Was that what Rudy had had in mind to confess on the breakfast deck?

Confess in exchange for what? Absolution? Mercy from the court for blowing the whistle. It had all become too much for Rudy. After Lou, Millicent. After Millicent, Thwaite. Blowing what whistle?

Rudy had wanted his father-in-law dead, but not to do the job himself, and he wasn't acquainted with hitmen. Who knows most about crime, after criminals, often more than criminals? Coppers. One copper Rudy knew was his wife's lover, Gene Rosko. Rosko qualified as, in Millicent's words, not one of us. Any copper would.

Rosko wasn't going to do the job himself either. Why not? Perhaps back in long-ago May he was squeamish, hadn't yet discovered that murder was easy. With his copper's nose for an ex-con he thought he might have the answer in Joop. He might have met Joop in Harrigan's or he might never have met him, he might have merely heard Romaine mention him, the Dutch cook who had jumped ship and wasn't strictly legal. He puts in a request to Interpol, back comes Joop's long-playing record, and he has the answer. He should have obliterated the record instead of leaving it in storage but he's a cop, not a hacker.

Peckover listened to the shower. Hooks for clothes were behind the door but would Rosko's gun be hanging there? Might, if it were in an ankle holster. Might be on the toilet tank or in the sink. Rosko would certainly carry a gun.

He murdered Millicent because she'd found out he was having it off with Romaine and threatened to disinherit her. Romaine hadn't waited until morning to telephone and tell him so. Rosko the fortune hunter – unless he loved her, which he might – probably promised Romaine they'd marry after each had got a divorce. May have meant it, his missus being this changed creature with Lyme disease.

He murdered Thwaite because the myopic prof had the bad luck to see him through his pebble-lenses on the dunes the night Millicent was murdered and the butler attacked. Thwaite couldn't go to the Dunehampton police because if you couldn't trust the Chief, who could you trust? He scarpers off on the train to talk to the police in New York and get protection. Rosko reaches Penn first, telly extension cord in his pocket. To buy himself time and an alibi he hides Thwaite's body by kitting him out as the bag lady.

He murdered Rudy because Rudy had become unreliable. Rudy was unhappy about Millicent being killed. Then Thwaite. He must have brooded about his own prospects. He decides to talk to Scotland Yard, the forces of light, but again Rosko is there first.

Next on the list would be unreliable Joop. Credit to the Sergeant for shunting Joop out of Dunehampton. Here, Rosko ruled. He'd have found a way. Joop hanged in his cell, a suicide, or shot while escaping.

After Joop, anyone else who guessed the truth. Like Sergeant De Voto.

Like Our 'Enry, doing his job.

If it was the truth, or close, his reconstruction. If it was, Rosko was the beauty he had tangled with on the dunes and who'd knocked him senseless in Rudy's bathroom.

There was a way of finding out and it would take only a moment.

Peckover leaned against Twitty's bathroom door and heard the shower. How long did a tickophobe need to wash non-existent ticks off his body? Rosko had been in the shower fifteen minutes. If in the shower was where he was.

Outside lashed Doris, its din mounting, diminishing, and rising again. Twitty's room was as dark as if the curtains had been drawn. Peckover switched on the light and looked about him. The lad travelled unaccoutred apart from his mad threads and the joke radio.

He selected a table lamp with a marble stem and pleated shade, unplugged it, and removed the shade. Round the bulb was a wire scaffold. Outside the bathroom door, gripping the lamp, Peckover listened to the shower.

Where were the back-up troops? Planning the lunch menu? Operation Cock-up was on course, living up to its name.

The shower stopped.

Peckover believed it had stopped. He strained to hear. Doris raged, Ahoy shivered and creaked.

He raised the lamp above his head and opened the door.

Rosko had one foot out of the shower, one foot in. He was bending for a towel on the floor beside the bath mat. The ankle of the foot out of the shower, on the bath mat, sported an irregular oval outline an inch and a half across. There must have been bleeding because the oval had reached a scabby stage. Rosko looked up. For longer than necessary, it seemed to Peckover, perhaps three or four seconds, he and Rosko stared at each other.

'That a tick bite?' Peckover said. 'Big bleeders, aren't they?'

'You set me up. You set me up and I walked into it.'

'Back 'ome we'd say fit you up.'

'Henry, you're not going to see home again.'

The bathroom was filled with light and steam. The walls dribbled. And Peckover had his answer. Rosko's shoes lay crookedly by the toilet, his raincoat was heaped in a corner, other clothes hung over a towel rail. The gun was where?

'Only one question,' Peckover said. 'Jasmine Ellen Sprague, the bag lady, she said you chloroformed her.'

'Chloroform? That's neat. Green Chartreuse, Henry. Ladies love it. It's a secret formula of French monks, what the label says. Over a hundred proof, stronger than malt whiskies. There's a Bacardi rum that's a hundred and fifty-one proof but why would I want to kill her? That answer your question?'

'She can identify you.'

'Ah, the beard.'

'Right.'

'Sorry, Henry. No beard. Scarf, shades, look for them off the expressway, exit thirty, somewhere there. We were singing "Little Brown Jug", after five minutes. Fifteen minutes, she'd drunk half the bottle and was unconscious. Don't bet on the bag lady, Henry.'

The Chief was still staring, bending, as if awaiting the starter's pistol for an Olympic sprint. Lamp raised and aimed, Peckover stepped into the bathroom and looked behind the door.

Nothing. Not even a hook. He sensed rather than saw Rosko lurch at him from the starting-block. He swung the lamp, trying not to swing exactly gently, but not with the ferocity with which the Chief and his stone had split Rudy's skull.

He was allowed no time to dwell on the consequences of killing Rosko with a single marble swipe, though he was to consider them later: the suspension from duty, the enquiry, Miriam's dismay, Sam and Mary's assumption he could now spend his life, in retirement, playing pirates and performing conjuring tricks, the whole hassle and publicity and headlines in the tabloids, dateline Dunehampton: London Bobby Cleaves Top Cop's Cranium. In the instant he swung he was concerned with stopping the fellow, discouraging him, and with absolutely not spattering his brains over the bathroom walls.

Rosko's foot skidded in bathroom wet. He fell forwards, downwards, and received the blow on his shoulder. The lamp's wire scaffold buckled and the bulb exploded, sending forth a myriad slivers of glass.

Rosko lay in a sprawl on the floor and nursed his shoulder. Above him stood Peckover holding the lamp and breathing hard. He reached to the towel rail and one-handedly clenched and squeezed garments for a gun.

The gun had to be somewhere. He threw the clothes at Rosko. 'Get dressed.'

'You win, Henry, but you lose.'

'That's too profound for me.' Peckover hooked his foot round shoes and kicked them towards Rosko. 'Ask the warden if you and the rest of the lifers can 'old philosophy classes.'

Rosko found a shirt sleeve. When he inserted his arm he winced from the blow on his shoulder.

Peckover said, 'It would never 'ave worked. Know why?'

'What wouldn't have worked?'

'You're not one of them.'

'What're you talking about.'

'Romaine. Rudy came to you, you recruited Joop. Goodbye, Lou. And you arrogantly assumed that The English Butler, being so unused to Dunehampton's ways, would be nicely out of his depth. Right?'

Rosko, sitting, buttoned his shirt.

'Millicent, Thwaite, and Rudy, on the other 'and, they're all your own – how would you put it? – your own 'ands-on achievement. Right? Millicent's cup and the cocoa that went astray was you muddying the water and wasting everybody's time.'

'All supposition. You're going to have to whistle for evidence and you know it.'

'We'll start by photographing that poorly ankle. Then you'll sing to us. You and Joop, a duet, *tremoloso con agitazione*, with a pretty little solo from Romaine.'

'Dream on. You're a disappointment, Henry. You're a sad advertisement for Scotland Yard.'

He started to stand to pull on his trousers. Peckover lowered the marble to ten inches above Rosko's head.

He said, 'You can do that sitting.'

Rosko, sitting, put on his trousers. He zipped them. He put on his shoes. Then the lights went out.

In homage to Doris, lights went out all over eastern Long Island. In Ahoy they went out wherever they had been left on, their extinction accompanied by silence from two left-on radios. Rudely quenched was Hank and Veronica's update on the weather – nothing less than this power failure would have rendered the indomitable pair mute – and on the college station, Don Giovanni and Zerlina singing 'Là ci darem la mano'. A listener identifying herself as Crescent Rump, gallery owner, telephoned the college station to say she was cancelling her membership because not only did its personnel not so much as mention the hurricane at a time when the island was hurtling to an Armageddon of flood and fire, but for reasons best known to itself it insisted on playing mopey Mozart love muck when the least it could do would be to play the *Götterdämmerung*. Power in some areas would not return for three

202

days. No drinking water, no bath water, no flushing of lavatories, no television. Chocolate Chip, Rum Raisin, Cherry Garcia, Mint Oreo, Mocha Double Chunk, and Heavenly Hash would turn to glop in freezers. Standby steaks and legs of lamb would grow soft and furry.

Telephones continued to function except where uprooted trees flattened the wires, but getting through was troublesome because panic and complaints jammed the lines.

The dark in the windowless bathroom was not total but it was a surprise. Rosko, who may have been expecting it, was marginally quicker off the mark than Peckover, throwing himself sideways as the stem of the marble descended. He landed on his raincoat. The marble struck the tiled floor, jarring Peckover's wrist.

'Freeze or I'll kill you!' Rosko screamed.

In the new dark, Peckover was unable to see quite what the situation was or that fumbling Rosko did not yet have his gun. Rosko's manic confidence was enough to make him hesitate. The Chief was slithering across the tiles, tearing at his raincoat, and now climbing to his feet.

'Drop that lamp!' Rosko shouted.

Peckover thought he would hang on to the lamp. He swung it at dodging, ducking Rosko, catching him on the hip, then hopped sideways as Rosko raised a gun. The gun flashed and banged. Peckover threw the marble, hitting the Chief in the chest. He wondered if he had been shot. He felt nothing, but the pain would take a moment to arrive. As he dashed out of the door the gun fired again.

Through Twitty's room and into the basement area. The servants' stairs, beyond the ping-pong table and washing machines, were too far. He raced for the door to the deck.

He who fights and runs away, lives to fight another day. Rosko had missed twice. He was perhaps groggy from whops from the marble. He might not miss again. Peckover opened the door on to the deck.

The doorhandle wrenched from his hand, the door flung wide, the hurricane howled in. Behind him sounded shattering glass, crashings, and splintering wood. Ahead thundered the ocean. Along the deck, past his legs, bowled a chair. Peckover could see only sheeting rain. The din was such that he could not tell if specific detonations were from the last throes of the ping-pong table or Rosko and his gun.

He lowered his head and charged into the rain and across the deck to the steps to the dunes. He found the rail and clung to it as he started down. A wall of water hit him. He never saw it. He was no longer holding on to the rail or to anything. He was in the ocean.

Impossible to breathe. No ocean bed for his feet. The tormented ocean hugged then tossed him. He did not know whether he was going up or down, whether about to be flung against the house, or if already he were far out to sea. The bursting hurt was in his chest and head.

Not waving but drowning.

He was up, floundering, gulping air, seeing only exploding foam. The clamour was a monstrous, continuing salute from massed cannon as if for the Queen's birthday. A hill of water fell on him. He swallowed much of it. He was down again where there was no air, weightless in the bottomless ocean.

He wanted it to be over soon. Nothing he could do about it. I'm sorry, Miriam. Sam. Mary.

Rosko had won. Freeze or I'll kill you. Absurd, melodramatic. Why would anyone want to kill a butler? Rosko had killed the butler as surely as if he'd put out orders: kill the butler!

Sorry, Mr Butterwick.

He was up again, surfaced, and choking. There was air but he couldn't breathe.

'Guv!' he heard, or he heard something, through the tumult.

Sorry, lad.

He smiled an awash, looney smile, wondering if this might be the calm that was said to visit people before they went down for the third time, their whole life returning to them in a gift-wrapped package.

Henry Peckover, this was your life.

The smile stayed in place when the next briny wall slammed him down, down, and down.

Full fathom five.

Sea nymphs.

Ding-dong.

TWENTY

Detective Constable Twitty had left the Sergeant grubbing on hands and knees through the medium devastation of the breakfast deck. Sergeant De Voto was in quest, somewhere among the debris of deck furniture, of a rabbit telephone which ought to have been silent but was ringing.

Twitty was avid for his aviator's raincoat. If a hurricane wasn't the time for it, when was?

He had taken a wrong turning out of the conservatory-cum-murder-room and found himself in an obscure ante-room. He retraced his steps, opened a door which he believed would lead approximately to the kitchen and servants' stairs, and walked into a bar, possibly a wine cellar, except strictly it was not a cellar. Squadrons of bottles, here at attention, there prone. He would have given a quid for a pineapple juice. He shot a leg backwards to prevent the door snapping shut and incarcerating him somewhat as the wine freak in Poe's 'The Cask of Amontillado' had been incarcerated. He backed out, discovered the main hall, and from there it was plain sailing to a refectory table, thronged by thrones, above it a worryingly swaying chandelier. In the kitchen he poured a glass of milk. Superintendent Veal in his snug office, a frail summer drizzle outside in Victoria Street, had made no mention of hurricanes. Had he known all along but kept quiet about it? Twitty felt guiltily elated. You didn't get hurricanes in Brixton, except for the one which the weather forecaster celebrities who were paid more than airline pilots hadn't uttered a peep about because they didn't believe it. This Doris was as if gravity was about to be switched off and at any moment Ahoy would be plucked up, frolicked with, then dismembered and strewn to the four corners. This would be something to tell his children once he found a doting, big-hipped chickaloola to do him the honour. Or the right chickaloola found him. Why hadn't she already? He was employed, musical, horny, and where in the west was a ritzier dresser?

He took for ever groping down the pitchy servants' stairs. Cuddled against the bottom step lay a splintered green section of ping-pong table. The door to the deck was closed but rattling, lashed by Doris.

He looked first in the guv'nor's room, expecting to find him there with or without Chief Rosko. No guv.

'Do-de-o dah dah dah,' sang Twitty to himself, perturbed, flicking his fingers.

Henry had last been seen with Rosko and the growing consense was that Rosko was a villain. Still, Henry could take care of himself.

Outside boomed the hurricane. Twitty recalled a hurricane in the Caribbean some years ago – Hugo, was it? – and the newscaster chillingly announcing 'Not a building on Montserrat remains.'

In his cook's room he put on his raincoat. Anguished by new milk, recent water, and tea and juice, he sidestepped into the bathroom and peed. The bathroom seemed to him steamy, sweaty. Its gloom was barely penetrable, but he made out on the floor a rumpled towel and the base of a lamp with no bulb or shade. He flushed the toilet, the last flushing it would have until power returned or someone went into the ocean with a bucket. He ran from the bathroom, the bedroom and paused among demolished slabs of ping-pong table.

'Guv?'

The mesh screen of the door on to the deck had come partly adrift and flapped and banged. Twitty opened the door and left it open and swinging as he plunged into the storm. His unbuttoned raincoat spread like wings behind him. He didn't see Henry, but approaching came a drowned, moustached rat, waist-deep in foamy ocean, on the ocean side of the deck's rail.

Sergeant De Voto clung one-handed to the rail on his journey to the steps. Twitty, also holding one-handed to the rail, reached for the Sergeant's free hand, but couldn't find it, the hand being tucked away somewhere. He located instead an armpit, then a

206

waist, and hauled De Voto up the steps, across the deck, and into the basement.

'Where's Henry?' the Sergeant wanted to know.

'I'm looking.'

The Sergeant was regarding the hand which had been tucked under his arm, or in his pocket, somewhere wrapped away, and which was washed white by the ocean, though not all of it. The top joint of the little finger was missing. The new top to what remained of the finger, unwrapped and exposed, now bloomed with blood.

'My gun's out there.' He sounded aggrieved. 'Blown away.'

'By Doris?'

'By Rosko, you nut. He's going to kill us. He's got to. You've no gun, right?'

'No. Right. Rudy had one. You could— '

'It's at the station house. Find yourself a dark corner and stay there. Where's a phone?'

'My room, in there. Is Rosko outside or in the house?'

'Outside. Or he was.'

They looked uncertainly towards the servants' staircase, then at the clattering door to the deck.

'Shut that door for a start,' the Sergeant said. 'Will it lock?'

'What about Henry?'

'Try praying.'

Sergeant De Voto, nursing his hand, accelerated into Twitty's room. Doctors stitch fingers back on these days, Twitty reflected. First you had to have the finger.

He fumbled pointlessly with the lock. The mesh screen hung flapping from a single screw. Rain deluged in and upon Twitty.

Someone was in the ocean.

Twitty lurched on to the deck. He wrapped an arm round the post at the head of the steps. The someone had gone.

'Guv!' Twitty bawled, and Doris gulped the bawl.

Might not have been Henry. Might have been Rosko. Pale flotsam in a black breaker. He had seen someone. Not far out, twenty, thirty feet. Rope-throwing distance.

There he was, flung up in a spout of spume and froth. Twitty knew he would do nothing if he thought about it for even a moment. If he thought about it, he would look for rope and seek out the Sergeant. They would discuss it. Twitty went down the steps and into the ocean.

At Harrow he had been a decent swimmer, on the school team, winning against Eton, and losing a few times. This was not those swimming pools. The water engulfed him and dragged him under. It spewed him up. His pale companion in distress was not to be seen.

'Guv!'

A breaker slammed him.

He was helplessly somersaulting, though whether above or below the surface he couldn't be sure. Which was up, down, and which way lay Ahoy, he had no notion. An arm's length in front rose up the pale face of Henry, eyes and mouth open.

Twitty grabbed him with both hands. He tried to encircle him with his arms. So much for lifesaving techniques learned in the placid school pool: the backward haul, the forward breaststroke, if the victim co-operated, ducking him if he went berserk, the swimming a length underwater. They were underwater now but there was no question of swimming. The next moment they were tossed to the surface. Henry neither helped nor hindered. He was a sack of sand with useless limbs and a hinged, lolling head which could be the end of them both if it cracked against his own head. A wave swallowed them. They were jolted on to the sea floor, if that was what it was, scraped along it, then thrown up into the wind and rain. Twitty glimpsed above him the painted ledge and rail of the deck. As he reached for it he was sucked away. He clung to Peckover, one hand clamped on his arm, the other under his chin, doing its best to keep the unresponding head above the waves. The next surge tumbled him into something bone-crackingly solid which he succeeded in latching on to. He watched the next wave bearing down and gulped air before it struck. He wished the guv'nor might have done the same.

They were beside and partly under the steps up to the deck. Watching with salt-blinded eyes the charge and retreat of the sea, timing his efforts, hugging the rail, lugging his burden, Twitty manhandled Peckover up the steps. The ocean was neutral. It sucked you out and cast you back. It might not have cast him back, it had been under no obligation, but it had done so. Only by luck was he still standing. Sprawling, to be precise, on the deck, beside the guv'nor.

Not that he need overdo the luck when it came to enquiry-time. This had been the stupidest act of his life. But if any credit were to be handed out, he'd accept it.

From the look and weight of him, unlikely the guv'nor would be making the enquiries.

Weary Twitty refused to dwell on that. He dragged Peckover into the basement, lay him supine, knelt, put a thumb and forefinger in his mouth in search of his tongue, which was there, then an ear to his chest. Twitty was not sure he was getting all this in the correct sequence. He could not hear Henry's heart but with Doris's caterwauling he wouldn't have heard the Stones live on stage at their jolliest, nose-thumbing decibel level either. He pressed his mouth over Peckover's and blew four fast breaths. He was supposed to have done this already, in the sea, but what with one thing and another . . .

All he needed now would be for Rosko to walk in.

Mouth away. One, two, three, four, five. Mouth-to-mouth again and another blast of salty breath. He had hardly breath for himself, never mind Henry.

He was shaking, he discovered. Shock. He fingered Peckover's neck, trying to find the pulse in the carotid artery, and though he failed to find it, that didn't have to mean anything. In first-aid class he had sometimes failed to find a subject's carotid artery, but its owner had been alive none the less, resigned to the groping, and wearing an air of unquenchable disdain.

Twitty shut his eyes and resumed mouth-to-mouth. There had been cases where, after you did this for an hour or more, the patient revived. He didn't relish keeping at this for an hour, but he had the time, if Rosko stayed away.

The hurricane shrieked and thrashed. Spray came spattering through the door, further irrigating the London policemen on Ahoy's basement floor. A hand fastened on Twitty's neck.

'Aagh!' gasped Twitty, and opened his eyes.

'Gerronouta that!' said Peckover.

Peckover rolled retching on to his side, away from Twitty, who could not have said whether the guv'nor's distress was due to near

209

death by drowning or the kiss of life. He was not sure he cared. This was the thanks he got.

He said, 'You're for hospital, Guv.'

Peckover ceased choking for long enough to say, 'Belt up.'

'That was cardiac arrest.' Was it? Twitty thought it might have been. He wasn't a doctor. 'You're half dead. You've got to be watched for complications.'

'Poppycock.' Peckover struggled into a sitting position, panting, then foully belched. 'Pardon' he said. He put his hands to his head, testing to see if it was there. 'You forget where you are, mate. Go to 'ospital here? America? You'd 'ave to sell your house, put your wife on the streets. What 'appened?'

'You fell into the foaming brine.'

'Rosko. Where's Rosko?'

'Last heard of, looking for us.'

'Jesus! What're we sitting here for? And the Sergeant?'

'Lost some of his finger. And his gun. Rosko shot him.'

'Idiot.' Peckover reached out an arm. ''Elp me up.'

Twitty put his hands under Peckover's arms. He was unclear who the idiot was. 'Henry, I've been wanting to tell you something.' He helped Peckover to his feet. 'Are you listening?'

'Get on with it.'

'You can be an astronomic pain.'

'What?' Peckover was affronted. 'Me? What makes you say that?'

They found Sergeant De Voto watching through a broken window on the landing with the grandfather clock and Sinbad vase. He had swathed his finger in a washcloth found on his travels, either seeking Rosko or avoiding him. In through the window blew the hurricane. The Sergeant's back was to the wall and he watched with his head twisted sideways.

'Keep out of sight, the bastard's on the prowl,' he said, and pointed through the window. 'Tell you one thing, I'm not going near him without a gun.'

Twenty feet below, Chief Rosko was peering through a ground-floor window. Bent into the wind, holding his gun, he moved to the next window and looked in.

'Where's our back-up?' demanded the Sergeant. 'Davy Pugh's

210

supposed to be on his way, if a tree hasn't killed him. Everyone else is out on emergencies. What do they think this is, a barbecue party? I know where they are. They're down in cellars with their rosaries. They're eating doughnuts with refugees at the firehouse. You all right?'

Peckover was listing.

'No, he's not,' Twitty said, propping up Peckover with hands on his arm and shoulder. 'He went sea bathing and his heart stopped.'

'Balls,' said Peckover. 'Stop fondling me.'

'Gladly. Guv, before you fall down, why don't you find a nice bed and lie down. Go beddy-bye.'

'Only place I'm going, you delinquent whelp, is after Rosko.'

'Our hero. Going after him with what. Rhyming couplets?'

'Less of your lip. That bugger tried to do me in. And Vito. Don't want to alarm you, lad, but you're on the list too.'

The Sergeant said, 'Plus this bozo, whoever he is.'

Through the racket of the hurricane sounded a police car's siren along Tonic Lane.

'Great, just great,' said the Sergeant. 'Nothing like announcing yourself.'

The flashing light which accompanied the siren's wail sped along the far side of Ahoy's high hedge.

'Either the Chief throws down his gun and surrenders,' the Sergeant said, 'or he has to kill us all, clear out, and who's to say he was ever here? It's called slaughter of the material witnesses.'

'It's called a load of cobblers,' Twitty said. 'Kill us all?'

'You think he's not going to try?' The Sergeant stepped back from the window. 'Not a gun between us three hicks and he knows it. All that might stop him is whatever artillery this car's bringing. He knows that too. Please, you two stay here and keep bugging each other.'

The siren whined to silence in Ahoy's forecourt. The grandfather clock was chiming 'The Bluebells of Scotland'. Through the broken window, in the garden below, Rosko was not to be seen. The Sergeant ran across the landing, down the stairs, through the hall, out of the front door, and into the hurricane. Twitty followed, looking back over his shoulder at tardy Peckover and calling, 'You're not needed! You're a heart case!'

211

'You're a head case!' called Peckover.

Not one of his more glittering shafts but it would have to do. He was not feeling a hundred per cent.

On the driveway stood the police car with its headlights on and engine humming. Davy Pugh in black oilskins was making no headway with the radio, such was the static, but he persevered. Sergeant De Voto identified the car and groaned. This was Rumba, the banged-up reserve, overdue for auction, and stripped of its armoury unless Davy had had the foresight to re-equip it, and small chance of that. Known as Rumba, without affection, because of its slipping gears and tendency to jerk, jolt, and stall. Now was the first time in three months Rumba had been out of the garage.

The Sergeant tried to yank open the passenger door. Davy had it locked and was leaning across the seat to unlock it. His other hand lifted in greeting. A gun banged and the windshield shattered. In place of a windshield was nature's biggest cobweb.

A second bullet smashed the passenger window in front of the Sergeant's face.

This time there was no cobweb. Shards of glass flew into the car. The Sergeant saw Davy's reaching arm, wavy hair, and surprised eyes. He ducked, turned to run, and collided with Twitty.

'Go!' he yelled. 'Scatter! Go!'

The gun cracked and sent a third bullet neither he nor Twitty knew where.

Peckover would have scattered back into the house but he was too far from the door and the gale had slammed it shut. He saw Rosko walking along the drive with his head hunched forward, aiming his pistol, left hand gripping and steadying his wrist. Officer Pugh stamped on Rumba's accelerator. The car jolted towards the Chief, but wide, its driver steering by guesswork behind the cobwebbed windshield. Rumba picked up speed, swung right, as if having scented Rosko's position, and sideswiped a mighty sycamore. It flipped on to its side and skidded from gravel on to grass, churning up mud and creating a Passchendaele out of Lou's holy lawn before striking a second sycamore. There it stopped, no longer ripe for auction or anywhere except the knacker's.

Peckover fled from crazy Rosko on a zigzag course into the hundred-mile-an-hour wind. His legs seemed to be chained. He sprinted in slow motion across waterlogged lawn. The gun banged, shockingly close. He kept running, weaving, alert for harbour, wherever that might be, and for the delayed hurt which would tell him he had been shot. Where was the ocean? He did not want the ocean again. He heard a voice.

'Henry?'

In the rain-bucketing gloom he saw no one. He ran in a crouch on chained, bicycling legs.

'Guv!'

'Get out of it! Split!'

Two were an easier target than one. If Rosko missed the butler he might wing the cook. Twitty, an antelope, insisted on lolloping alongside. The jackanapes was shouting unintelligibly. Perhaps he had gone totally round the twist and was not shouting but singing, a rock song, something celebrating cosmic harmony and sexual intercourse. By an odd, almost mystical understanding which took them both by surprise, they swerved in unison behind a clump of buckling, resisting yews and stood there gasping. Peckover held on to a bough for anchorage. Twitty, antelope though he might be, was also in need of rest and recuperation.

They peered round their pitiful yew defences. Rosko too had halted, thirty paces away in the centre of the lawn. He was slowly twirling, an adagio dancer with a levelled gun, finding his bearings, and a target.

Rosko knew where they were. So, exactly, did the London pair. They stood on spent matches. The glassed-in breakfast deck, diagonally ahead, had lost its glass. The ocean and besieged steps up to the basement deck were behind them, round the corner of the house. Distantly was the dark of the wind-torn copse where a Gauloises packet had been discovered. Along the edge of the copse ran the Sergeant.

Feet planted apart, Rosko aimed at the Sergeant. Distracted perhaps by a rending sound from Tonic Lane, then a thud, as from a toppled tree, and too canny to waste bullets on so distant a moving target, Rosko did not fire.

Peckover wondered if Davy Pugh, last seen in a superannuated police car folded round a tree, was alive or dead.

Rosko's gun banged and a branch of shot yew tree struck

213

Twitty's hip. Peckover dropped to the ground, pulling Twitty with him.

Run, he should have ordered. He should not have needed to order anything. They should simply have run. But they had already run. Before running they had been in the ocean. He couldn't speak for the lad, but for himself Peckover believed he needed a holiday before he would ever run again. He peeped round the yew. Rosko was walking towards them, gun raised.

'Run!' Peckover bawled.

They ran. They had hardly started when they were aware of a peculiar confusion in the sky directly above, a further darkening of the morning. Was it morning still? Peckover looked up, and Twitty looked up, and across the lawn, at the edge of the copse, the Sergeant looked up. Davy Pugh, latecomer, arrived on the lawn with mouth and chin bleeding, hands bleeding, and his head of thick, sodden hair pricked with slivers of car window. He looked up.

Lawn centre, Rosko looked up, cursed, and ran.

Blowy Doris had blown Ahoy's satellite dish from its moorings. The dish gyrated upside-down above the lawn. Crosswinds so buffeted it that its precise line of descent was not to be predicted, but it whirled briskly and with not too many slips, skids and hesitations. Watching from the fringes of the lawn stood scattered Peckover, Twitty, the Sergeant, and Davy Pugh, and from the middle of the lawn, Chief Rosko, who ran and switched direction as the dish closed on him, almost as if it were manned and guided, which it was not. Then he stopped running.

Rosko stood with his head tilted back and arms stretched in front of him as if to ward off the dish, or perhaps catch it and throw it back on the roof, or shoot it. Afterwards, the debate would be whether he had stood there because he had decided that killing four policemen, on top of the other murders, was too much to ask of anyone, and the dish was a way out. The stalk speared him, and the spinning dish, weighing in at roughly the poundage of a small hippopotamus, fell on him and did the rest.

On the lawn's fringes no one moved. When finally they did, they converged on the dish at little more than walking pace, heads bowed into the storm, as if haste were not going to rescue the Chief, and in the improbable event that it might, prompt action

214

was the last thing they wanted. No one was confident that they would be able to lift the dish either. Forklift trucks might be needed. Perhaps a helicopter.

Twitty caught up with Peckover. He called out into the wind, 'I think it's abating!'

Peckover responded with a sidelong look of mixed sorrow and puzzlement. He stored away Twitty's opinion on the weather as not only the most irrelevant and inappropriate he had ever heard, but demonstrably not true.

One blessing: Lou Langley was not here to view these impudent alterations to his lawns. The satellite dish had sliced like a cookie-cutter into the earth. All that could be seen of Rosko was a hand, palm uppermost, a wrist, and a couple of inches of sleeved forearm, protruding from under the rim of the dish. The Sergeant squatted and sought the pulse.

After a while he stood up and shrugged.

Shouting to be heard, Davy Pugh said, 'At least he doesn't have to worry about Lyme disease any more!'

'Don't bet on it,' said the Sergeant. 'Where he's gone they deal out Lyme disease with the brimstone and sulphur.'

215

TWENTY-ONE

Doris moved on across Long Island Sound to Connecticut. In Dunehampton the wind dropped, the rain stopped, the sky cleared, and by late afternoon a ball of fuzzy, lemony sun burned in a blue empyrean. The air was crisp, winey, washed clean of bugs. Oinking chains of geese clanked overhead.

Tonic Lane was in one respect privileged. True, trees were down, houses were flooded, some had lost their roof, and two were mournful debris floating on the ocean. But Tonic Lane's summer dwellers being for the most part remarkable achievers, or scions of achievers, acquainted with people in high places, they were among the first to have power restored. Such anyway was how sour rumour interpreted the promptness. At Ahoy, lights and radios came on to greet the return of Gloria, Romaine, Benny, and Prune. The refrigerator resumed humming, not that it contained anything worth refrigerating.

Twitty washed his hands of mealtimes. For himself he had discovered a passable cache of apples and some softening cheese biscuits, which he believed Americans called crackers. He didn't know if he was still supposed to be a cook. No one had told him anything. If he was expected to cook, he would cook, if someone gave him something to cook, though he would much rather not.

While the guv'nor took four aspirin, then waded to his bed, and slept, Twitty sat knee-deep in floodwater with his ghetto-blaster, twiddling and seething as he sought the World Service. He felt only middling. He had showered and sprinkled himself with Tomcat. He wore a kind of Athenian tunic, what you would have worn when matching wits with Socrates in the market-place, beside the Venus de Milo, when she'd had her arms. He should have felt untormented, having policed satisfactorily and cooked fabulously,

216

but though he twiddled and twiddled with slow, agonising care – all he asked was the cricket – he kept getting what sounded like a high-stakes cock fight in Thailand.

At Ahoy arrived a beringed woman with cruel sunglasses, curved and lethal like Indian arrowheads. Crescent Rump was anxious to discover if Gloria's paintings had survived the hurricane. She intended to buy the lot. Her offer would be risibly stingy, but she would sigh and be prepared to increase it – what after all was friendship for? – by five per cent. Ms Rump believed the paintings would fetch a sack of money. What was required was promotion. She would use the slaughter that had taken place in Gloria's family, right here at Ahoy, to promote Gloria to celebrity status. With delicatesse, naturally. Nothing crude. Gloria would assume the name Gloria Ahoy and so sign all her work, which would be titillatingly titled, like *Carnage*, *Poseidon's Pyre*, and perhaps something which would re-echo an image of satellite dishes.

Dished, perhaps?

Awake, laved, and reasonably bushy-tailed, though uninterested in going for a swim, Peckover dialled London and reached the babysitter. He dialled the Royal Archaeological Society and caught Miriam in the kitchen. He told her he was in top shape, never better, all had gone swimmingly, and it was over. He'd be home in a couple of days after the post-mortems, so to speak, and paperwork. He would save being a tourist for another time, visiting places like New Orleans and Tombstone. Miriam said she was glad, and Mary was great, but Sam had been in trouble at school for fighting.

'That's bad,' said Peckover.

He saw his son a roughneck, growing up a street brawler, sent down for six months for hitting a taxi-driver with a brick.

'It was Sharon Mills, the school bully,' Miriam explained across the Atlantic. 'She's twice Sam's size. She started it. They pulled each other's hair.'

'I 'ope he made her bald,' Peckover said.

Miriam said she had to go. The timer had pinged. She was experimenting with a turkey-wattle garnish. It was decoration,

217

she hoped they wouldn't eat it. She was behind, loved him, had to hang up.

'Love you. Adore your behind,' Peckover said.

He didn't feel in the mood for Frank Veal. Later, after one or two of them ol' sourmash whiskies. Jack Somebody. Doc Snakebite.

He put on his butler's jacket but compromised by wearing Marks & Spencer tennis shorts and leaving off the tie. He was not sure whether he was Jarvis or Peckover. No one had told him. He ventured forth, marauding, because he should find Gloria and say something to her, if only 'All's well that ends well', though probably not that. The first person he saw, click-clacking down the main stairway with canvases in her arms, was his neighbour at the channelling, the one with the sinister sunglasses.

Peckover flattened himself against the wall, then scuttled from sight.

The strewn glass, the splintered deck furniture, the overturned police car, and the embedded satellite dish on the south lawn shocked Gloria and Romaine, and to a lesser extent, Benny.

Gloria telephoned the sisters Eve and Hannabelle O'Kaplan and negotiated, for cleaning up, a Croesus fee which left Eve and Hannabelle jigging and crowing and playing pat-a-cake. Gloria and Romaine consoled each other with reminders that the damage could have been worse. They had not yet learned that beneath the dish on the lawn was Dunehampton's Chief of Police.

No one was keen to impart the news, particularly to Romaine, who after losing both parents and her husband was now rudely deprived of her lover, undesirable though he had been. Peckover, who would have steeled himself, had slept and not yet seen them. Twitty considered that passing on such information was not the cook's job. Gloria and Romaine might have found out for themselves had they visited the dish, round which milled a score of police, awaiting the arrival of construction machinery, but they chose not to. Davy Pugh, reeking of disinfectant, chin and hands criss-crossed with Band-Aid, proposed that no one need tell them.

Sooner or later, he reasoned, news of the Chief would leak

through by a natural osmosis. If the news didn't leak through, the job of messenger was obviously the Sergeant's, who was having his finger attended to.

Sergeant De Voto was at the hospital in a state of bliss. He had found an ante-room with drawn shades and a TV on which the Mets were playing the Cardinals in St Louis. The Mets were losing. Lately the Sergeant had considered switching his allegiance from the Yanks to the Mets. Now he thought he would give the Yanks one more chance.

He would be able to see the entire game before his turn for a doctor came round. The emergency room was wall-to-wall hurricane victims.

A German exchange student at the college, Fritz Bayer, nineteen, ferociously physical, had mild penile warts from couplings with one or more of two dozen female students. The hurricane was not responsible for the warts. Fritz had had them for four months but had been too embarrassed to bring them to the hospital. He judged that today the medical staff would be under so much pressure from hurricane injuries that they would be frazzled and dispose of the warts without making American jokes of the kind known as one-liners.

Forty miles away, in the county jail, Joop den Beet asked for a lawyer. He announced that Chief Rosko was the guy the police wanted. He could spill beans would curl your hair, man. Did anyone have cigarettes? For cigarettes he would spill beans.

Gloria and Romaine learned of what was under the satellite dish from Benny, who heard it on the radio. They watched the lifting operation from a high window overlooking the lawn.

Peckover, Twitty, Davy Pugh, and the Sergeant, his finger voluminously bandaged, formed a quartet on the lawn a little apart from the action. An employee of the highways department was manoeuvring into position a crane's moving arm, cable, and hook. Twitty wore his Athenian tunic over long khaki shorts such as were formerly worn by Britain's colonial administrators. He would sooner not have been there but it was part of the job. Would, he wondered, Rosko be revealed with a flourish like an

219

uncovered roast duck on a platter, or lifted skewered and dangling as the dish was raised?

He reflected that in a Hitchcock film, which he would far rather have been watching than the here and now on the lawn, the dish would have been raised and Rosko would not have been there.

Agent Eisner joined the quartet with an air of urgency. He said, 'Watts, the guy from the Library Of Congress, he says the Pearl Harbor draft is the real thing. He's wetting himself. He wants to take it back to Washington for tests.'

'God bless the experts,' Peckover said. 'I 'ope you'll introduce him to our graphologist in Middlehampton, the one says it's like a bad tracing.'

'Who do we believe?'

'Spin a coin.'

Twitty said, 'Look, if it's a forgery, why couldn't Lou have forged it?'

'Don't muddy the waters, lad,' murmured Peckover.

More experts would move in on the Day of Infamy speech, Peckover guessed. Currently the score was a draw. Whether Roosevelt allowed Pearl Harbor to happen was unresolved and perhaps ever would remain so, amen.

Same as not a few points in the Langley file, though the outline was clear enough, in Peckover's view, and should become clearer when Joop gave his version, and Romaine, and the bag lady, who could always be given a sip of Green Chartreuse, or a tumbler of it, see if that revived her memory. Rudy, needing cash, dangles a cut of his wife's inheritance in front of Rosko. It's Rosko's if he can send Lou to his reward. Rudy hopes for a slice of Romaine's inheritance in return for to. rating her affair with Rosko. Rosko rents Joop and a Ford truck. When Millicent threatens to disinherit Romaine, the old lady has to go. Next, Thwaite, who sees on the beach more than he ought to have seen. After Thwaite, Rudy, because he's about to chat with the butler.

The crane lifted the dish effortlessly into the air, and Rosko with it, skewered beneath the dish's belly.

The time had come. They borrowed a modest selection from Twitty's discovery, the booze cupboard. They added glasses from the kitchen, gave not a thought to uncivilised ice, and stole down the servants' stairs and into Peckover's room. The floodwater had receded, leaving underfoot a squelchy carpet.

They toasted each other in Kentucky firewater. Twitty, having taken a cautious sip, coughed, then poured the remainder down the bathroom sink. He found the Amoretto di Amore palatable, however, and even more so the Fine Tawny Porto. The porto slid down as easily as pineapple juice. After further toasting – to the Yard, the Queen, the President of the USA, the Presidium of the USSR, Feet, Davy Pugh, the bag lady, the comity of nations, the England cricket team, Prune, Lassie, movies with Marlon Brando, Beethoven's Fifth Symphony – they refilled each other's glasses to the brim with gentlemanly courtesy.

When Gloria knocked on the door, such was the carolling that however loudly she knocked she never would be heard. She opened the door.

In the middle of the room her butler and cook were high-stepping towards and away from each other, backing and advancing, holding the hem of their shorts as if they were skirts. They were dancing what appeared to Gloria to be a corrupt cockney version of the French can-can, kicking their legs high, and singing with sonorous feeling.

> Knees up, Muvver Brown –

They pronounced it Brahn, rhyming roughly with darn.

> Knees up, Muvver Brown,
> Come along, dearie, let it go,
> Eeh-aye eeh-aye eeh-aye-oh –

Twitty was first to notice Gloria. His kicking and trilling trailed to a stop. Peckover noticed her, and the song and dance ceased. Mr Butterwick had given no instructions on a situation such as this.

Gloria said, 'Jarvis, is it true?'

'Modom?'

'You're a policeman? And Sandy? From Scotland Yard?'

'That is the case,' Peckover said, and he bowed his head.

'I'm stunned!'

'We may well imagine. A most human response. May we present our sincere regrets for any inconvenience.'

221

'But, Jarvis, does this mean you won't be staying with us? You'll be leaving?'

'We fear so.'

'This is so disappointing!'

'If modom would care to join us in our little routine.'

Peckover squared up to Twitty and looked him in the eyes. 'Take it from the birthday, lad, after the eeh-aye eeh-aye eeh-aye-oh. One, two.'

More or less in tune and in time, kicking their legs, holding their hems, linking arms and circling, Peckover and Twitty put on a command performance. After an uncertain start, the show gathered in raucousness.

It's yer bloomin' birthday,
We'll wake up all the town,
Knees up, knees up, don't get the breeze up,
Knees up, Muvver Bro-o-own!

But Gloria had already backed out, like a theatre critic with a deadline, and closed the door.